WHERE THE DARKNESS GOES

KIERSTEN MODGLIN

Cover Design by Kiersten Modglin
Copy Editing by Three Owls Editing
Proofreading by My Brother's Editor
Formatting & Graphic Design by Kiersten Modglin

First Print and Electronic Edition: 2024
kierstenmodglinauthor.com

*To the ones who bring the light on the darkest days
and the ones willing to sit with us in the shadows*

"In the midst of darkness, light persists."

MAHATMA GANDHI

CHAPTER ONE

TESSA

This has to be a bad omen.

As far as I can see, the storm has erased the world. Against the dark gray sky, ominous clouds loom. Thick raindrops smack into my windshield with a roar so deafening I can no longer hear the music playing from my car's speakers. The raging storm outside competes with the cyclone inside my core. The swell of dread grows in my stomach, gnawing at my organs with a foreboding sort of panic as real as the heartbeat in my chest, and on its own, it would be enough to make me consider turning around.

As if I wasn't already.

"Kick me when I'm down," I mutter.

Apparently taking it as a challenge, the universe offers a steel-toed boot to the kidneys in the form of a loud *THUNK* and an agonizing jolt of the car.

A pothole.

My stomach skydives. I curse to myself as I grip the steering wheel tighter with both hands, navigating the car to the flooding shoulder and into the nearby church parking lot as the wheel wobbles and clunks. The shaking is so treacherous, I can't pretend to hope I'd make it to Ernie's garage, the only mechanic shop in this sleepy town.

I drop my head forward, slowly and gently tapping it against the steering wheel in an effort to calm myself down and slow my breathing.

Get it together, Tessa. We will figure this out.

With newfound determination, I look out the windows, searching for the world I know is out there. I haven't seen another car in ages, which means no one will be by to help unless I call for it. It's Thursday, so no one will be at church, either.

Unless You feel like sending a miracle. I turn my eyes up to the sky, but it's useless.

Putting the car in park, I lean across the center console and dig my phone out of my purse, looking for my brother's name in my recent calls.

I can't remember what time he said he was leaving town, but hopefully I can catch him before he heads out.

There's no one else I can call for help anymore. The thought is more depressing than I'd expected. Will is all I have left.

I tap Will's name in my call log, disconnecting the Bluetooth and turning it up as loud as it goes before I press it to my ear, though the ring is still barely audible over the clamor of the storm.

Lightning cracks overhead, followed almost immediately by a clap of thunder that makes me jolt.

Pick up, Will. Please pick up.

As if denying my requests, the phone goes to voicemail just moments later. I groan, end the call, and try again.

Without any luck, and as tears begin to prick my eyes, I open my phone's browser and search for the number to Ernie's garage. It was one of the numbers Mom kept taped to the fridge all my life. There were quite a few there, and I could probably remember everyone on the list: our pediatrician, Dr. Jacobs; the church; the school; Ernie's garage; a handyman we used occasionally when things went wrong around the house; and Dr. Tubb, our dentist. I can see her scratchy handwriting so clearly in my mind—the list etched out on a yellowing scrap of notebook paper—but I definitely don't have any of the numbers memorized.

Across the top of my screen, the blue bar of my search moves slowly, stopping midway as if it's a toddler stomping its foot. Refusing to do what I've asked. The storm is making the internet slower than usual, which is truly saying something.

Damn it. I scroll through my contacts, racking my brain for anyone else I could call, but just as I'm about to give up, my screen goes dark with an incoming call. *It's Will.*

"Hey, thank god. Where are you?"

My brother's calm but wary voice comes through the line. No matter what is going on, he always sounds a bit too casual. The voice of someone who's never had anything bad happen to him. "Sorry. I'm fighting airport traffic right now. This storm has grounded everything."

"I know. I'm stuck in the middle of it right now. It's really coming down."

He sighs as I hear his blinker turn on. "Damn. I was hoping you'd make it to the house before it hit. Where are you?"

"Sitting in the church parking lot. I hit a pothole, and my tire's flat," I tell him, raising my voice as the sound of the rain gets louder outside. "Any chance you can come pick me up? The internet on my phone isn't working, or I'd call Ernie's."

There's a long pause, and I can practically see him running his hand through his perfectly coiffed blond hair. Undeniably at ease. His flight has been canceled, and he's dealing with it as if a road was closed and he'll just have to go around. As if it's a simple detour and not the plan-ruining update most people would make it out to be.

"Uh, I'm having to drive to Huntsville, so I can't backtrack, but I'll figure something out, okay?"

"No, it's fine. I can call Pastor Charles. I probably still have his number in my phone."

"He'll be getting ready for the funeral, so I wouldn't.

4

I have Ernie's number saved. I'll give them a call and see if someone can come get you. Just sit tight."

"Oh. Right." *The funeral.* The reason I'm here. "Thanks."

"No problem. Stay right there until someone comes for you, okay?"

I puff a breath of air through my lips, moving the hair from my face. "Not like I can go anywhere."

"Says the girl who made sneaking out look like an Olympic sport."

"Says the boy who taught me how."

He chuckles, and before I'm ready, he's gone. After placing my phone down, I grab my purse and haul it across the console and onto my lap, digging for one of the snacks I always keep on hand.

I'm not even hungry, I know. Just nervous. The idea of being back home, the idea of staying in my brother's house alone while he's gone, the idea of seeing my mom for the first time since right after her accident. Most importantly, the idea of going to the funeral—

I cut the thought off at the root. Right now, I don't have time to get upset. Too much is happening. Placing my purse back in the seat next to me, I turn the heat up and wait.

Through the thick, gray haze of the rain, I spot a truck slowing down at the entrance to the church parking lot, and my heart instantly hitches. It's been years since I saw Ernie himself, and I have no idea who currently works at his shop, but I'm sure I'm

5

about to see a familiar face. I just hope it's also a friendly one.

The truck makes a slow turn into the empty parking lot and pulls to a stop next to me. The headlights flash as the truck is shut off, and then I try with all my might to make out the figure walking toward me.

It's a man, I know almost instantly. Thin hips. Broad shoulders. But that's all I can decipher through the storm. When he reaches my door, I roll down my window cautiously, just in case this isn't actually who Will sent for me.

The inside of my door is drenched in seconds, but I barely have time to process that as I hear his voice.

"Heard you need a ride?"

My jaw snaps shut, and I stare at him as if this is a dream, as if I've completely lost my mind. He looks almost exactly the same—dark curls gathered around his head and those piercing brown eyes. His jaw is sharper, face thinner, and his usually clean chin and cheeks have a solid amount of facial hair across them.

I'm completely blank. Every thought, emotion, or action I'd prepared moments ago has been wiped from my mind in a split second.

"*Garrett?*"

"Good to see you, too," he says with a laugh. His voice is different from Will's. Every bit as calm maybe, but there's a weight of conflicting emotions in his timbre. An unspoken history yet to be defined.

6

"What are you doing here? Do you work for Ernie now?"

His eyes drift up as rain continues to pour down his face and into his eyes, and it's only then that I register I'm also being soaked by the storm. He squints one eye shut, raising his voice as a crack of thunder booms. "Do you mind if we get in the truck before we have this conversation?"

"What about my car?"

"Leave it." He steps back, pulling my door open. "Mark Summers is on his way to get it. We'll wait for him and hand off the keys. Where's your stuff?"

I gesture toward the back seat, and Garrett pulls the door open, retrieving my suitcase and duffel bag.

Scrambling, I grab my purse and shut off the car.

"Anything else?" he calls, shouting over the storm.

"That's it." We shut both doors and race toward his truck. By the time we reach it, I'm completely soaked. I may as well have been plunged into a pool as I tear open the door and step up out of the ankle-deep water.

I slam the door closed, and the world feels instantly quieted, though the storm is still raging. Garrett shakes his head like a dog, reaching in the back of the truck. He grabs two T-shirts and tosses one to me, then he uses the other to dry his face and arms.

He's tall and tanned, with more muscles in his ropy arms than I remembered. Each movement causes new lines of muscles and skin to appear underneath his drenched shirt, like a sculpture. I fight the urge to reach out and trace my fingers across him, to study him like the work of art he appears to be.

My throat is sandpaper as my eyes travel up his arms and across his collarbone. His chin, beard, lips. He's beautiful. Every bit as beautiful as I remember.

He clears his throat, and my eyes meet his, my cheeks boiling over with the heat of embarrassment. He just caught me staring. And not just staring, but drinking him in.

I avert my gaze at once and tuck a piece of hair behind my ear.

When I look back, hoping he won't call me out on what just happened, he holds up the fabric in his hands, nodding his head toward the shirt in mine. "It's clean, I promise."

"Right." I pat the material against my face, and his familiar scent hits me all at once. Fresh, like laundry detergent and soap, plus a mixture of something citrusy like bergamot and something else that's entirely male. Entirely him.

As I slide the fabric down across my skin, it's hard not to imagine it's him, that he's the one touching me. Especially with his scent invading my senses, his gaze now drilling into me as if in payback for the way I stared at him. We're too close here, too alone. I try not to think about the times, not so different from now, that we spent together in his truck. The times when I couldn't keep every inch of my skin from his.

When I check the mirror, the ghosts of those memories have painted themselves in scarlet across my neck and chest. I wonder if he's thinking the same thing.

I chance another look at him, just once, and he shifts his gaze away from me—*guilty, perhaps?* I turn back to my mirror, scraping the water off more than absorbing it with the T-shirt before drying my phone's screen.

When I'm as dry as I can get—which isn't saying much—I follow his lead by wadding the shirt into a ball and tossing it into the back seat. He turns the heat up, pointing the vents in my direction with a chuckle he fails to hide.

"What's funny?" I demand, though it feels pointless to ask. He's clearly going to call me out on what I've been thinking about. He's always been able to read me like that.

"You look like a drowned rat," he says pointedly.

Oh. "Well, you look like a wet golden retriever."

"Aren't they supposed to be golden?" His eyes meet mine and several lifetimes pass, neither of us saying a word, though I desperately want to. I just don't know what I would say.

I never thought I'd be in this position—soaking wet, sitting just inches away from Garrett again, having all his attention to myself.

Before I can work up the nerve to say anything, he blinks—moment over—and turns away. He checks his dark hair in the mirror as I feel the moment fizzling out like carbonation under my skin.

He closes his visor just as we're both distracted by a tow truck pulling into the parking lot. We are alone no more. Just like that.

"There's Mark. Give me your keys." He holds out his hand as the truck stops in front of us, and Mark Summers steps out and jogs through the rain, waving a hand over his head. Like Garrett, he has grown up well —*I can't believe we're all adults now*—and his kind smile is as familiar and warm as ever. He appears at the window, a black rain hood pulled up over his blond hair.

Mark has always reminded me so much of Will— pure sunshine in a bottle.

Garrett rolls down the window as Mark gives me a lopsided grin.

"Tessa Becker." He drawls my name, his eyes trailing the drenched outline of my body. "When Will said you were back in town, I thought he was pulling my leg."

"My brother?" I tease. "Never."

He tilts his chin upward as Garrett puts the keys into his palm with a little too much force. "Don't worry about the car. Just a little flat. It doesn't look like the rim is bent or anything. 'Course, I'll get a better look at it in the shop. Either way, we'll get you fixed up, good as new." He pauses, his eyes flicking from the car to me. "Maybe I'll bring it by once it's fixed, and I could take you to dinner? Will said you're staying at his place."

"Alright, Romeo," Garrett cuts in before I can answer, "why don't you just get the car fixed and try to play loverboy when my truck isn't getting drenched in the process?" To emphasize his point, he brushes a handful of water off the plastic piece of the door just inside the window.

"Fair enough. See you guys later." Mark backs up with a beaming smile before waving and returning to his truck. Garrett rolls the window up. We wait as Mark backs the tow truck up in front of my car, but when he's done and back out in the rain, he gives us a thumbs up, and Garrett waves at him again before pulling away.

For a while, the ride is silent, and I'm not sure if we're supposed to be pretending this is all very normal, or admitting that it's not. It's not like I haven't ridden in a vehicle with Garrett. As my brother's best friend, I've ridden in his truck more times than I can count.

Just not since everything went wrong.

"Thank you for coming to my rescue, by the way. I can't remember if I already said that." I pick at the skin next to my thumbnail for something to do.

"Come on, now." He gives me a look that says I should know better. "Of course I came to get you."

"I know, I just...I didn't expect Will to call you. I thought he was calling a mechanic. If he'd told me..."

"What? You'd have said no? You needed a ride, too. Not just the car picked up. Unless you were hoping to ride with Mark." There's an edge to his tone, even with the joke.

"You caught me." My hands go up in mock surrender. "Foiled my plan."

He's quiet for a long while, but eventually he says, "Well, ever so sorry, but it sounds like you'll have a second chance when he drops the car off."

I sway my head to the side. "Who would've ever thought little Mark Summers would grow up so well? He was so small back in school. Now he… Well, clearly he works out."

He gags silently.

I laugh, shoving his arm. "Dude, leave him alone. He's sweet."

"Mm-hmm. That's why you were ogling him. His *sweetness*."

"I was *not ogling* him."

"You were ogling each other." He cuts a glance toward me. "Makes sense. You always were into the teacher's pets."

I eye him. "That's not how I remember it."

His quick glance my way is pointed, but he says nothing else. We ride in silence for a while as I take in the familiar sights of my hometown. Nothing has changed here, and yet everything has changed. This place is a roadmap of my childhood—the empty lot where I learned to drive, the park where I played with my friends, my favorite Italian place that Mom reserved for the most special occasions, the doctor's office I visited when I was sick, and the streets Britney and I used to drive down at all hours of the night discussing everything from boys to the future to our parents.

Garrett slows the car before he turns into my brother's subdivision, and I can't believe how quickly that went. I'm almost sad to say goodbye to him again.

When the house comes into view, I'm hit with an odd pang in my gut, like missing something that was never really mine. Perhaps it's because Will isn't here. It's funny. Will is my brother and one of my best friends, and yet I've only been inside of his house once —the weekend he moved in six years ago.

The few times I have visited, I stayed with Mom, and Will would come there. Now, Mom's house has been sold to pay for her care, and this is all that's left.

I know it's unlikely, but the threat of her making a recovery that doesn't require facility care and learning that our home is now owned by someone else—that we have no real plans for where she'll go if that were to happen—keeps me up at night.

As if he can read my mind, Garrett clears his throat before saying, "Are you, um, gonna go visit your mom while you're in town?"

"She'd kill me if I didn't." I look worriedly at the house as something occurs to me, then squeeze my eyes shut. "Oh. *Shoot.*"

"What's wrong?" He comes to a stop in the drive-way, unbuckling.

I scrub my hand over my forehead, frustration running through me. "I just realized I gave Mark my car keys, which just so happen to be connected to the rest of my keys." I pause, looking over at him. "Which means I don't have my keys to Will's place. Mark does."

Realization sweeps through Garrett's features, his dark brows smoothing out, pink lips coming unpinched. "Oh." He shuts the truck off. "Okay."

"We'll have to go back to the shop and get them. I'm so sorry about this."

He takes his key out of the ignition, clearly still not understanding what I'm saying.

"What are you—"

"I've got a key."

"Oh." *Well, that makes sense.* "Okay. Cool."

He pauses, hands resting in his lap as he stares at me. A strange look comes over his face, like he's realizing something for the first time. His eyes go slightly wide, and he appears conflicted, but eventually, he pushes his door open without a word and grabs my luggage from the back seat.

We climb the concrete steps and find ourselves on the large front porch. The space is plain, and Will has made no effort to decorate, but I'm impressed to find it still looks kept up. He's even repainted the front door, which desperately needed painting when he bought the place.

"Well, thank you again for all of this," I tell him, reaching for my bags.

"Always happy to help," he says, sticking a key in the lock. He pushes the door open, and his eyes find mine. Something flips in my stomach, a deep tug like even my muscles want me to step closer to him, but I can't.

If I do, I'm terrified of what would happen. What I would let happen.

What I might *want* to happen.

"Thanks again," I stumble over my words, and from the look on his face, he read, highlighted, and notated everything that was just going through my mind. I step into the house backward and move to shut the door, but he doesn't budge. *Why isn't he leaving?* "I'll, uh, see you around, okay?"

A corner of his mouth quirks with an expression I don't understand. He sighs and looks to his right, talking to himself when he says, "He didn't tell you."

"Who? *Will?* What didn't he tell me?"

He puts a hand on the door and jiggles his keys in the air. "I, um,"—there's a bit of laughter in his tone—"I have a key to Will's place…" His chest puffs with a deep breath. "Because it's my place, too."

My brain sputters to a stop. "What?"

"Guess you'll be seeing me around a lot." His bright smile beams. "Roomie."

CHAPTER TWO

GARRETT

She didn't say a word for at least five minutes.

Chuckling to myself, I shut my bedroom door. In the guest bedroom next door, Tessa is unpacking in what would appear to be stunned silence. I pull my drenched shirt over my head and grab my phone, dialing my idiot best friend.

He answers quickly, his voice distant, clearly in the car.

"Yes?" he sings pleasantly. "Did you get her?"

"Oh, I got her." I scrub a hand through my hair, a finger tangling in one of my curls. "You didn't think it might be helpful to mention to her that I live here?"

"I thought you could break the news."

"You're an asshole."

He hums with laughter. "It's fine. You guys haven't seen each other in a few years. It'll be good to catch up, won't it?"

"I guess that depends on whether you define 'catching up' as me having to listen to Mark Summers nailing your little sister through the wall," I groan, letting that thought slip out before I'd prepared for it.

I hear him turning the heat down in the car as I pull my pants down and kick them aside before picking a pair of sweats from a pile of clothes I should really put away. Someday. "You're one to talk. Also, what did you just say?"

"You heard correctly." Pinning the phone between my cheek and shoulder, I pull the pants over my hips.

"Since when is Mark Summers nailing my sister?"

He should be angrier than this. Why am I always the one who has to play jealous—er, protective—big brother?

"He's not...yet. But he will be, if he has his way."

"If I didn't know better, I'd say you sound jealous."

"*Please.* More like disgusted."

He laughs again, and we both know he doesn't believe me. *What-the-fuck-ever. I don't need him to believe me. I need him to stop this before it happens.*

"Mark's a cool guy," he says eventually. "If he wants to date my sister, fine by me. But I'll tell her to keep it down. Better yet, I'll let you borrow my headphones."

I scowl, pulling the phone away from my ear to put my shirt on, and when I come back, he's saying, "...talk to her if it's weird or whatever. She can stay somewhere else."

That's even worse. "No, don't be stupid. I'm joking. It's fine. It'll be fine."

"Seriously. It's half your house too, man. Just say the word."

"I'm not going to kick Tessa out, dude, chill. It's fine. We can be civil, you know."

"Oh yeah? You should tell your voice that."

I bite my tongue.

"Oh, shoot. I'm getting a call from a client. Gotta go."

"Okay, well, if—"

The call ends before I can finish my sentence. I drop my phone on the nightstand just as I hear the shower kick on. As a sudden headache announces itself deep within my skull, I drop onto the bed and cup my temples with my palms, trying hard not to picture Tessa in the shower right now.

Fuck me.

CHAPTER THREE

TESSA — AGE 16

"What's up, Little Bit?" Garrett's voice draws me out of the video game I'm playing while I sit on my bedroom floor. I pause it and turn around to face him. He's sweaty from practice, a dark patch on the front of his blue shirt. If he turned around, I'm betting there's a matching one on the back.

"Oh. Hey. Smash Bros. You want to play?" I hold up a spare controller. "Britney's on her way, so we can both kick your butt."

He opens his mouth, but before he can answer, Will's voice fills the hallway and soon he appears in my doorway next to Garrett. Cory and Justin are close behind him. "We're going to the park to shoot some hoops with the guys. Where's Mom?"

I turn back around to the TV. "She took food to the church for Joan Margaret's granddaughter's baby shower. Aren't you supposed to do your chores after practice? *Before* you go anywhere?"

"I'll do them later," he says.

"We can wait on you," Garrett offers.

"It's fine," Will says. "Come on. Let's go. Brendan and Mark are probably already there."

"You can come with us if you want."

It takes me a second to realize Garrett's talking to me. "Thanks, but no thanks. Britney's on her way, remember?" Besides, no matter how much I actually enjoy hanging around my brother's friends, the idea of watching them play ball for hours on end is about as appealing as having my legs waxed, and I don't plan to do that anytime soon either.

Britney's always bragging that it's so much easier than shaving, but no thank you.

"I'll be fine here." When I look over, Garrett is the only one still standing in my doorway, watching me. "Have fun."

"Garrett, come on!" my brother shouts from out of sight.

"Coming." He jogs out of my doorway, and seconds later, I hear the boys running down the hall and out the door. Once it slams shut, I crawl across the floor to grab my phone, pressing one—Britney's speed dial number—to see where she is.

On my knees next to my nightstand, I can see out the window as the boys make their way down the street. My brother is in the center of the group, always the unofficial leader, with Garrett and Cory just next to him. Justin is lagging behind on his phone.

"Hello?" Britney sings in my ear, but I hardly hear it.

When Garrett turns his head back toward the house, glancing up at my window, I swear it's as if he's looking for me. Like he can feel me watching him— *them*. I was watching *them*.

"Tessa?"

I shut the curtain quickly. "Sorry, hey. Are you almost here?"

"Pulling in any moment. Sorry, Dad made me help with the pool before I could leave."

"No biggie. See you in a bit."

"Love ya." She makes a kissing sound into the phone.

"Love ya back." I end the call and sit back down to finish my game, making a mental note to do the dishes once this round ends. It's not my job, but there's no way they'll be back in time for Will to do them before Mom gets home.

As I play, my mind keeps drifting back to Garrett. I find myself doing that more often now, though I can't explain why.

He's always just been Will's friend. My friend, even. But always just Garrett. Now I'm noticing things about him I haven't before, like the dark hair growing on his face and chest and the way he puts more effort into dressing than my brother does. Or the way his voice gets all slow and soft when he's tired. The way his gaze seems to find me in whatever room I'm in. The way he actually listens to me, sometimes more than anyone else, even Will.

He's just around a lot. It's probably normal to think about him really. I think about Britney a lot, too. Not in the same way, but...

And Mom.

Will.

Yeah, totally normal.

My phone chimes, and I jump, instantly embarrassed. I'm expecting Britney, but the text is from Garrett instead.

> Save me a game when we get
> back, ok?

CHAPTER FOUR

GARRETT — AGE 17

> Save me a game when we get back, ok?

It's stupid, but it's also the third draft, and if I spend any more time on this text, Will is going to notice for sure. And then there will be questions.

"You sure Tessa doesn't want to come with us?" I cock my head to the side, trying to sound nonchalant and not at all stalkerish. Wearing an expression that I hope says *I don't actually care about your response, and in fact, I've nearly forgotten what I asked*, we make our way to the neighborhood ball court. It's rundown, with no net and a faded backboard that hasn't been replaced since my dad was a kid, but it works.

"Why would she?" Will scowls, stopping abruptly to tie his laces. They're always coming untied.

"Hmm? Oh. I don't know. Just seems like she's bored in the house all day."

"It's summer. She has Britney over, like, all the time. She's fine." He stands back up. "Besides, it's not like she's any good. We need a strong team."

I nod. He's not wrong, though I wasn't really suggesting Tessa play with us, just that she...*what? Watch?*

That's not really better, I guess, but I can't help thinking of her holding that controller out for me. I like playing video games with her. Will kicks both our butts most of the time, but it doesn't matter. He knows I can beat him when I'm not taking it easy on her.

When it's just the two of us, though, and she does that stupid little victory dance: hands in the air, wiggling fingers, spinning in a circle—

"What are you smiling about?" Will scowls at me from across the court, and clearly, there's been a whole conversation I've missed.

"Nothing. Let's play." He passes me the ball as we divide into our usual teams.

When I looked back at the house on the way here, I could've sworn I saw the curtain in her bedroom move. Like she was watching us. Probably just checking to make sure we were gone, but part of me wondered if she was watching us for another reason. Watching *me*, specifically.

It's stupid. This is stupid.

She's Tessa. She's like a little sister to me. She's

always been like a little sister to me. She's the one I taught to play freeze tag and the one whose hair I cut gum out of—though her mom wasn't too happy with me over that.

She's been my friend as long as I've known Will, and we can never be anything else. Period.

Maybe that's not what this is about anyway, these confusing feelings I've been having lately when I'm around her. Maybe it's just that I miss her sometimes. *As a friend.* We used to spend a lot more time together —all of us—but lately, I spend most of my time with the guys playing ball or out on dates with girls from class.

I feel like I'm seeing her less and less, and I have no idea why that bothers me. We're growing up and growing apart, which is normal. It's not like Tessa is my responsibility.

I just feel bad for her, I guess. My house is filled with my siblings and chaos, and hers always seems so empty and quiet.

My phone buzzes in my pocket with her response, but I don't dare check it. Still, the knowledge that it's there waiting for me, that she's home waiting for me, keeps my chest feeling tight the entire game.

CHAPTER FIVE

TESSA — PRESENT DAY

Fresh out of the shower, I pull on a black dress, a matching cardigan, and heels. I don't bother with more makeup than a bit of sunscreen and lip gloss. Between the rain and my tears, I know there's no point. Anything else will just be rinsed off.

While I'm thinking about it, I grab my phone and dial Will.

"Yes, dear?" he says playfully, his voice too chipper.

"Um, yes, hello, I'm looking for the asshole who didn't tell me he was sending Garrett to pick me up and also forgot to mention that Garrett lives in the house where I'll be staying while said asshole is away."

He chuckles. "Speaking."

I groan. "Seriously, Will? You didn't think that might be important information for me?"

"Remember when you used to wish for a surprise party for your birthday?"

"This is not a surprise party, and it is not my birthday."

"It's a...surprise," he offers. "What's the big deal anyway? You guys are fine now, right?"

"Define 'fine.'"

"Hey, Siri, can you look up the definition—"

"Will." I groan his name again, and he laughs.

"Fine. I didn't tell you. I thought if I did, you'd try staying somewhere else. You're safer at the house with Garrett."

"Safer?" The word throws me off guard.

"You know, from dangerous potholes and insistent old biddies who will want to measure the distance from your hemline to your knees."

"My hemline is just fine, thank you," I scoff, but I pull my dress down anyway, the thought giving me chills. It wouldn't be the first time.

"Besides." His voice is serious now. "After Brit's funeral, I thought you probably wouldn't want to be alone."

I swallow down the lump in my throat. "I wish you were here."

"Me too. I hate that I'm missing it. You'll give Kristy and Justin my condolences, won't you? I sent flowers from both of us. If there was any way I could miss work right now, I would, but I'm swamped—"

"I know," I cut him off, hating the sound of stress in his tone. It's so unlike him. "I'll tell them. They know you wish you were able to be there, don't worry."

"Alright. Thanks."

"I gotta go anyway. Be safe, okay?"

"You too. Don't give Garrett too much hell, okay?"

"Only the smallest amounts I can muster."

I end the call and quickly style my loose waves with mousse. I put a clip in on one side to help tame the waves, looking myself over in the mirror. I can't believe this is happening. I can't believe she's gone. My best friend for most of my life is just…gone. It's not fair, and I hate it. We were supposed to have so much longer. We were supposed to grow old and gray, and live in a beach house together, reminiscing about the good old days and complaining about our sore hips and the price of stamps. In the blink of an eye, every plan we ever made has been ripped away.

Just as I step out into the hallway, it hits me again that I don't have a car.

I'll have to call someone to take me to the funeral and forget about visiting Mom for the day. Just until my car is fixed.

How long will that take anyway? I should've asked.

As I run through a roster of people in my head who I'm still on friendly enough terms to ask such a favor, Garrett's door opens, and he steps out, dressed in black jeans and a matching button-down shirt. His fingers work quickly to fasten the top button.

"Look at that. Tessa Becker is actually on time." He beams.

"What are you doing?"

"Taking you to Britney's funeral." With his brows pinched together, he adds, "Unless you don't want me to."

"Um, no. That would be great, actually. I just had no idea you were planning to."

He pulls his head back a half inch, clearly shocked. "Well, I knew that's why you were coming into town, and without a car, I assumed you had no way there."

For some reason, this surprises me. He knew Britney well enough, sure, but I hadn't automatically assumed he'd go to her funeral. She was his friend by default, because we were always together, but the two of them never spent any time together without me as their glue. "Really? You don't have plans?"

His mouth plays into a cocky grin. "Consider them canceled, Little Bit."

The grin that escapes my lips is reminiscent of the many years we've spent tormenting each other. "Please don't call me that. I'm not so little anymore, in case you hadn't noticed."

He stares over my head, pretending he can't see me, and I swat his chest. He catches my hand, and the moment implodes into stark silence. Suddenly, all the feelings I've been fighting against, everything that I've tried for years not to feel, smack me square in the ribs. I can't breathe or talk or do anything except stare up at him, waiting to see what he'll do.

Golden flecks of sunshine shimmer in the dark depths of his cocoa eyes. There's a warmth there in the abyss, an ocean of things unsaid—the Pacific of dangerous truths.

I can't—

He drops my hand, stepping back and running that same hand through his hair. "We should probably get going, yeah?"

When he lowers his hand to his side, I catch his fingers flexing. The movement is stiff and rigid, like I'm coursing through his veins the same way he's swimming through mine.

"Right. Yeah." My voice is shaky—rollercoaster ride meets stage fright meets the flu—but he's gracious enough not to mention it.

We make our way out of the bungalow, off the porch, and down the walk in utter silence, both lost in our own thoughts.

It's always been terribly easy and dreadfully complicated with Garrett in equal measure. He was Will's friend, sure, but he was mine, too. In a way that none of the others were. For most of our lives, that's all we were. Friends. Comrades. We teased each other like siblings, played like teammates, and fought like family.

But something changed along the way, and we've never been able to find our way back to that path. That place. We're still in the woods of it. The same woods we've always been in—it's the same trees, the same streams we know like the backs of our hands. I look around, and everything looks just as it was. But something is different. *Everything* is different. Sometimes I think we're walking a parallel path, one where we can see the former path just beyond the trees—we can reach out and almost touch it—but no amount of reaching or sidestepping or backtracking will get us where we were.

We're the main characters who have been recast in season two, where the creators hope you won't notice. The same but noticeably different.

Checking his watch, Garrett looks back at me. "We have time to stop by your mom's. You feeling up for it?"

The shaky breath I draw in betrays me.

"Will doesn't like to go either." His weighty tone is a hug, even from a distance. He knows this isn't easy on either of us. The more I study the grave expression on his face, his pinched cheeks and somber, distant eyes, I wonder if it's hard on him, too.

I never really thought about it until now, selfishly, but Garrett was at our house almost every day from the time the boys became inseparable sitting next to each other in class in second grade. As he got older, he spent holidays at our house and skipped vacations with his family to stay over. He spent nearly as much time with Mom as we did.

"Do you visit her often?"

He hesitates and turns his head, waiting until we're in the car to answer. Something in his expression worries me. I suspect he thinks I'm going to be mad. Like I'll stick a flag in Mom and declare her *mine, not his.*

31

Nothing could be further from the truth.

Eventually, the conflict smooths out over his face, and he lands on, "I've gone by a few times."

"I'm glad."

The last wrinkle at the corner of his eye disappears. "Yeah?"

I buckle in and stare ahead as he pulls out of the short driveway. The house is oddly comforting. It's the Tom Hanks of houses. Familiar and ordinary, the same gray craftsman you see in every neighborhood no matter where you live. Four white pillars that run from the overhanging roof to the porch's brick pony wall. The ornamental grass bushes are a beard, overgrown and covering the entire front of the structure, aside from the stone steps. The four windows are eyes, met in the middle with the simple front door nose. It's simple and safe and so completely perfect for my brother.

With a solid nod, I glance at Garrett. "We should visit. If there's time."

He doesn't meet my eyes, but his smile betrays his relief as he says, "There's definitely time."

Ten minutes later, we arrive at Oak Meadows, the skilled-nursing facility where Mom lives now. It's a sprawling one-story building, tawny and plain. Its length spans the entire oversized parking lot, spreading out in every direction. Most of the windows are covered with blinds, concealing the patients' rooms. A few are open and exposed, however, the darkness beyond them still leaves everything a mystery.

The limited amount of grass they have between the sidewalk and the building is dying off, patches of brown fighting for real estate among the green.

"Do you want me to come with you?" Garrett asks.

"Would that be weird?"

He's already unbuckling and stepping from the car. "Not weird at all."

We make our way through the main doors, checking in with a receptionist named Becky, who chews gum loudly throughout our entire interaction and tells us we can sign the guest log, which turns out to be a mostly empty sheet of paper attached to a clipboard that's being held together with duct tape.

There are two nursing homes in town, and I was promised this was the best of the two when we chose it, but guilt is already starting to creep in. The place carries that ineffable scent you spend your life trying to avoid—a combination of death, industrial cleaners, and waste. The yellow floors glisten from a fresh wax, and the walls are decorated with bulletin boards covered in photos of the residents at recent events. I search for Mom's face among the memories but come up short. She's not there, but I shouldn't expect her to be. We're taking it one day at a time.

Guilt weighs on me when I realize I don't have the way to Mom's room memorized. I've visited only twice since we brought her here six months ago, both times right after her arrival.

I study the signs above our heads for direction, but Garrett takes the lead, guiding us through the labyrinth with little hesitation. I wonder if he judges me for visiting so little. Often, I've thought about moving back. I think I should, but...this place feels so different now. Without Mom being who she used to be, without the home where we grew up.

When we reach Mom's hallway, a nurse is just exiting her room. She's dressed in purple scrubs and has her blonde hair pulled up in a loose, low ponytail. She's our age, most likely, but I don't recognize her, which strikes me as strange. If you aren't from here, there is practically no reason to ever end up in this tiny town. She's probably from a town over and married someone from here, if I had to guess. I check for a ring, but if she has one she isn't wearing it. Her bright smile goes to Garrett first, then me.

"Hey there. Visitors?" She glances between us again. "I was just finishing up with her."

"Yeah, I'm Tessa. I'm Francis's—"

Her eyes bug out. "*Tessa?* Oh my gosh. You're Ms. Frannie's daughter!" She tells me this as if I might not know. "I recognize your name from her paperwork. Oh, wow. She's going to be *so* excited to see you. Come on." She pushes the door open, stepping back, and waves for us to follow her into the room. "Ms. Frannie, I'm back so soon. You certainly are popular today.

Look who came to see you." Her voice is loud and booming and overly cheerful as she leads us around the compact room, through the small eat-in kitchen, and to a slightly larger living space. It's about the size of a hotel room.

It's hard to see her world reduced to this. My once fierce mother, now reliant on others to do everything for her. She would hate it. She does hate it, I'm sure. She just can't tell us yet.

I'm still holding out hope that someday she'll be able to.

Mom sits in a padded chair facing the window, her hair cascading down her back. It's the first thing that catches my eye—her hair.

The silver of it hits just below her chin, where it melts into the dark locks I still picture covering her whole head when I pull her from memory. It's not fair. She's still young—just fifty-three. Not old enough to be here.

Not old enough to be like this.

She had so much left to do. And yet, there's a very real chance she'll never leave this room.

As if she has the same thought, the nurse eases toward Mom, brushing her shoulder first before combing her fingers through her hair, gathering it between her hands like she's preparing to pull it into a ponytail. She leans down next to Mom, looking at her so I can see the bright smile plastered on her face. "Ms. Frannie, it's Tessa. Tessa is here to see you."

She looks up, waving me toward them while the tennis ball currently seeking shelter in my throat is swallowed whole by a volleyball. I can't force it away, can't even breathe. All I can do is take a step forward, seemingly pulled by a magnetic force more than by choice.

Before I'm ready, I'm at Mom's side. Her face is blank, completely emotionless, as she stares out the window in front of her. The view is nice enough—a cluster of pine trees being used to block the street just beyond it. I wish it was sunny for her sake, rather than overcast, but I'm at least thankful the rain has stopped.

The nurse—Emma, based on her nametag—scurries in front of Mom and around behind me. She hoists a chair from the small kitchen table for two and brings it to me. "Here. You gals can sit and catch up."

I do as I'm told, grateful for any sort of direction.

Thankfully, Garrett seems to know what to do. "How is she?" he asks Emma as she backs up to give us some space.

Right, that's a perfectly logical question to ask. Why didn't I think of that?

"Good. Good." She says the words on a drawn-out exhale, then adds, "You know, she has her good days and bad days." Her voice is lower as she says the last part. "We're still doing a lot of protein and physical therapy to keep her muscles in good shape. A few mental exercises daily, too. She can follow things with her eyes"—she smirks—"but only when she wants to.

She's been able to blink to answer questions, but only a few times."

"Her doctor seemed to think she'd be talking by now," I point out, searching for the nurse in the dimly lit room.

When I land on her, she gives me a patronizing look. "Yeah. It's not a linear process, you know? We just have to be thankful for the good days and work through the bad. Build on what she can do and try a little extra each day. The important thing is she isn't regressing. Anything except that is progress."

"Has she tried to move at all? Fingers, toes?"

She wants to lie to me, I can tell. Everything in her seems to want to tell me she's moving and talking up a storm, but eventually, she presses her lips into a fine line and shakes her head. "I'm sorry, no. But she can hear you, like I said. She's aware of what's going on. She can open her mouth to eat when we ask her to, though it's still only pureed food and liquids."

I remember watching her eat pureed chicken the day we brought her here. Meat that had been blended until it was liquid. My stomach seizes at the thought.

Nurse Emma goes on, "And she follows commands with her eyes, like I mentioned. Blinking or following our finger or the light. Not always, but it's happened enough that we know she can do it. Those are all really good signs. We still have a lot of hope her recovery will go further than this, but there's no way to guarantee it.

I know this visit will do a lot to keep her spirits up, though."

Carefully, I lift a hand and brush Mom's hair behind her ear. "Hey, Momma. It's me. It's…it's Tessa."

"I'll give you two some time," Emma says, stepping back toward the door. "If you need anything at all, just press this button on the wall, and I'll be here. Otherwise, I'll come back in a little bit to see how we're doing."

"Thank you." Garrett nods at her as she shuts the door, then moves across the room to sit at the dinette with his back to us. It's his attempt to give us privacy, too.

"I'm staying with Will," I tell Mom softly, almost as if it's a secret. With a giggle, I add, "I know you must've never thought, when we were kids, that would happen intentionally, but it's true." I brush her hair back again out of habit, though it hasn't moved. For the most part, her gaze is empty. Every few minutes, she finds me, letting me know she realizes I'm here, but just as quickly, it's as if she forgets. "Actually, Will's away for work for a few days, so it's just Garrett and me staying at his house. Garrett told me he's been to see you a few times." I pause. "I'm, um, I'm going to Britney's funeral later." Reaching out, I take her arm, then her hand. "I wish you could go with me. I know how much you loved her." I narrow my eyes at her, willing her to say something. To give me some sort of acknowledgment that she's still in there.

"It's sad, you know? She's...well, we hadn't really spoken much at all in the last few years. You know that. We'd grown apart. She stayed here, and I was gone, and...it's no excuse." I blink away fresh tears. "I know you hated that I stayed away as much as I did, and it's no one's fault but my own, but I promise I'll be back more."

Her eyes drift to me slowly and hold my gaze.

"Do you understand, Momma? Could you...would you blink to tell me you understand?"

Anxiety is like a balloon bouncing across grass in my chest, waiting to pop as I study her eyes, waiting for her muscles to do their jobs, to give me a signal she understands what I'm saying. We don't have to talk, but we can communicate in some way. Her nurse said it's possible. Her stroke doesn't have to take everything away from us.

I stare at her face, studying every inch, watching for a twinge in her skin, but there is nothing. Her fingers droop loosely around my hand where I'm gripping hers, and her eyes go soft again as she turns her head back toward the window.

The anxiety quickly turns to anger. *Why did I even bother coming here?*

Then comes the guilt. *What sort of a daughter gets mad at her mother for having a stroke? None of this is her fault.*

I stand up and kiss her temple, afraid if I don't leave now, I'll start crying. "Okay. Well, we have to go to the funeral now so we aren't late, but I'll be back, okay? I love you." I turn away abruptly as tears sting my eyes.

Next to the couch, I spot a bookshelf. There are just a few books there—her Bible, worn and familiar, a family photo album, and a handful of novels. Odd, since she's never been much of a reader. It's the top of the row of books that catches my eye, though, and I cock my head to the side as I ease toward it, trying to make sense of what I'm seeing.

"Everything okay?" Garrett asks, his voice straining as he stands up from his seat at the table.

The scrap of paper on top of the row of books is entirely foreign to me, as is the handwriting found on it. Both are as out of place as if I'd found a polar bear costume in here. It was clearly torn from a notebook, a corner sliver of paper as if it was an afterthought.

The word scratched across it, however, is anything but.

Murderer

CHAPTER SIX

GARRETT — PRESENT DAY

"Mom, who wrote this?" Tessa asks, towering in front of her mom with the slip of paper. She waves it in the air, moving it closer to her mom's face, like I've seen Frannie do to Will over a bad grade. "Who was here?" She's scared, not mad, but either way, she's getting no response. "Do you know who wrote this? Blink, and I'll find a way for you to tell me. Just blink and let me know you remember."

Frannie doesn't. Frannie doesn't move. She doesn't smile. She doesn't acknowledge her daughter in the slightest. I'm not even sure she's looking at her anymore.

She's just…there.

She can't tell us who wrote the note any more than she could stand, dress herself, and walk out of here on a whim. It's terrible. I realize how I sound, even with thoughts no one else can hear, but that doesn't make it less true.

"Tessa, we should call the nurse," I say gently. When she doesn't argue or try to stop me, I move over to the button and jab a finger into it.

Tessa's wild, hazel eyes land on mine, and I feel that familiar jolt. A zing of lightning so potent it hits every appendage like static electricity from a dryer. It's the same feeling I've been trying to tamp down since I was a kid. She needs me, and I wish like hell I could make this better for her.

"Maybe she'll know what it's about or who might've left it," I say again. In her hand, the paper is wrinkled now from the way she keeps rolling it between her fingers.

"*Oh my gosh.*" Her lips form an O.

"What's wrong?"

"The nurse. When we came in earlier, she said Mom was popular today." Tessa takes quick steps toward me. "The nurse told Mom she was popular today." She waves the paper at me, and now I feel like I'm the one in trouble. "Someone else was here. Whoever it was that wrote this, they might've done it today."

The nurse's words float through my head, and I do vaguely remember her saying that. Maybe. But... "It's probably a misunderstanding."

"How could I misunderstand this?" She turns her head, studying the paper in horror. "Someone is calling her a murderer."

"That doesn't make sense." The look on her face tells me I should immediately rephrase what I said, so I do. "I just mean, for all we know, it was inside one of the books and fell out when someone took it off the shelf. Like maybe someone had been keeping notes on one of the murder mysteries or something." I had no idea my brain had even concocted that theory until it left my mouth. "We don't know what it means."

Before she can respond, there's a quick, light knock, and then Nurse Emma eases her head into the room, eyes wide when she sees how close we are to the door.

"Ope. Sorry. Did someone call for me?" Her cheeks flush as if she's caught us in an intimate moment, and it's only then I realize how close I'm standing to Tessa. So close I can smell the sweet coconut of her shampoo.

I step back, despite every nerve in my body rebelling. "Yeah, we—"

"Did someone else visit my mom today?" Tessa asks, cutting me off. It's a reminder this isn't my business. Not really. She doesn't mean it to be, maybe, but it's just the truth. Frannie Becker isn't my mom, no matter how much I think of her as one.

"Um, yes. Before you came by." Her smile falters slightly. "There was a woman who visited."

"A woman?" Tessa only sounds slightly deranged. "What woman? What did she look like?"

"I'm sorry, I don't remember. She was here bright and early this morning. I remember because your mom's room is the first on my rotation. I came in, but

43

when I saw she had a visitor, I immediately stepped back out to give them time. She was blonde, I think, but don't quote me. You could check the front desk and see if she signed in."

"Right. Okay. We'll do that." Tessa blinks, coming out of whatever sort of trance she's been in. She rubs her lips together, deep in thought.

"Is everything okay?" Nurse Emma asks.

Plastering on a sickly-sweet smile that rivals Nurse Emma's own, Tessa gives an affirmative nod. "Yes. Of course. We're just going to go."

We step out the door. Tessa moves faster in heels than I've ever seen her as she jogs down the hall and toward the lobby. We approach the window where we signed in earlier and wait for the receptionist to appear.

When she does, she walks around a corner from the back with a protein bar in her hand. "Checking in for a visit?"

Tessa taps the counter with her finger. "We're already checked in. I was hoping you could tell us about a visitor my mom had earlier?"

"Probably not," the woman says, but grabs the clipboard and places it in front of us. "If they signed in, it'd be on here."

"*If?*" I ask.

She shrugs. Not unkind, just indifferent. "We don't require visitors to sign in, but it's encouraged."

Next to me, Tessa scans the sign-in sheet. There are

just three listed before us, but none that I recognize. Eventually she puts it down.

"Oh. Okay. Thank you anyway." Her tone is soft and defeated.

"Thanks," I add, following her out the door with more questions than answers. We both know why this has upset her so much—echoes of the past play in my ears. This isn't the first time accusations have been thrown at this family, and with a new death in town, the first in years, I hate to think it could start up again. No one could think Ms. Frannie had anything to do with Britney's death. She's been in the nursing home all this time. Still, it feels like I've eaten something rotten, the contents of my stomach rumbling with warning.

In the car, she unfolds the crinkled paper in her hands, staring down at it. "My mom isn't a murderer."

I can't tell if she's talking to me or herself.

CHAPTER SEVEN

TESSA — AGE 16

My door bursts open like a firework, boys exploding in every direction. I sit up in bed, closing the book I'd been reading, and eye them. Will, Garrett, Justin, Brendan, and Cory pant heavily, faces red as they slam the door shut. It's as if they were running from something.

"What are you dweebs doing in my room?"

Like he just realized I'm here, Will's expression goes serious. "I need to talk to you." He crosses the room and sits on the end of my bed. The other boys linger near the door. I'm used to this—the house dripping with my brother's friends. The understanding that they might pop up at any moment.

It's something I learned to ignore years ago. Besides, I like Will's friends, for the most part. With only one year's difference in our ages, it means we've always gotten along well enough. I was never the baby sister annoyingly tagging along. At least, if I was, they hid it well.

My eyes flick to Garrett without thought, and his face is serious. Stoic, even. He doesn't smile, just stares back at me.

When I look back at my brother, there's no hint of a smile on his lips either. My stomach flips with worry.

"Well?" I prompt.

"Did you hear about Amber Allen?"

My stomach drops. Amber Allen is in my grade. Is she pregnant? Did she run away from home? She's not really someone I'd consider a friend—we've never hung out outside of school or anything like that—but in a town this small, everyone is pretty friendly with each other. We don't have room to be choosy, and even if we did, I like Amber. I don't want her to be in any sort of trouble.

Will licks his lips, huffing another deep breath. "You can't tell anyone we told you."

"O-okay." I put the book down, adjusting onto my knees. Whatever it is, it's serious.

"Amber and her mom were..." Checking behind him, almost for confirmation from his friends that he should keep going, he nods. "They were found dead this morning."

I get that sick feeling I have in health class when we talk about illnesses and diseases. My fingers hurt. My muscles are sore. Nothing about my body feels right. "What are you talking about?" It's too horrible to be true. This is the most disgusting prank Will has ever tried to pull. I shove him off my bed. "Stop it. Don't be awful!"

"He's serious, Tessa," Garrett's voice cuts through the chaos, and I stop yelling at my brother long enough to listen.

"He can't be." Someone is sitting on my chest. *Two* someones. It's ice cold, and I can't draw in a breath. "You're lying. All of you."

But I know...somehow, I know they're not.

"Why would you say that? How would you know?" I ask finally.

"Everyone's talking about it." Will moves to the window and pulls back my curtains, lifting a blind to stare outside into the darkness. "The sheriff just announced a curfew, chased us off from the basketball court. No one can be out past dark anymore while they're investigating."

"Why?" I move next to him, looking out the window too. "What happened to them? Two people don't just drop dead at the same time unless..."

His eyes dart back and forth between mine, and there's a confirmation there, even before he nods. "Yeah. I know. They think someone hurt 'em, Tessa. They think they were murdered."

It's as if someone traces their cold finger down my spine. "Who told you that?"

"I already told you. Everyone was talking about it

down at the park. Tye Prince and Aaron Harper and Brett Johnson."

"How would any of them have known?" I sneer, but I know he's not lying. I just hate that he's not.

"Aaron's dad is friends with Sheriff Ward," Cory says, wiping sweat from his brow, his skin glistening in the glow of my overhead light. His gaze is fixed on me, willing me to understand. "Aaron overheard him talking to his mom about it."

"No one's allowed to go out. The cops are patrolling the streets," Garrett adds. "Like he said, they made us leave the ball court and told us we had to get home. We all came here to wait for our parents since your house was the closest."

"Parents. Oh no. Where's Mom?" I ask, as a sudden weight sinks in my chest. "Does she know?" She's worked as a cleaner for the Allens for years. "She'll be so upset."

"She's fixin' dinner," Will says. "She was on the phone with someone when we came in. Sounded like that's what they were talking about, though. Everyone will know by morning."

"I have to call Britney." I grab the pink Razr on my nightstand and flip it open, about to speed dial her.

Will snaps his hand over mine, closing the phone. "Are you dense? You just heard me tell you not to tell anyone."

"Oh, come on. It's Britney. She's not going to say anything to anyone."

"Yeah." He snorts. "Okay."

"She won't. Besides, who is left to tell? You guys already know, which means a lot of other people do too. You said everyone is talking about it."

"Yeah, but Aaron wasn't supposed to tell us. He could get into big trouble if his dad finds out he ran his mouth. You gotta keep quiet until Mom tells you."

I groan. I couldn't care less about what stupid Aaron Harper gets in trouble for, but whatever. "Fine." I drop my phone back onto the table and flop down on the bed. "But get out of my room. You guys stink like gym socks."

They mumble in agreement, shoving each other on their way out of my room. A few minutes after the door shuts, unexpected tears sting my eyes. I don't know why I'm crying. Amber and I weren't friends. We weren't—

My door opens again, and I turn my head, trying to hide the evidence that I'm crying. "What do you want?"

"I wanted to make sure you're okay." The voice isn't the one I expected.

I sit up to find Garrett lingering in the doorway, his messy, dark curls pillowing around his head. One corner of his mouth twitches, like he's trying to decide what to say. "Will said you and Amber aren't, er, *weren't* friends, but I've seen you two at school talking, and well, I just wanted to…you know."

"Thanks." I dry my eyes quickly with the backs of my hands. "I'm okay. It's just…sad." It's pathetic really.

That's the best word I can come up with at this moment. Sad. "It doesn't feel real."

"I know." He runs the toe of his sneaker over the powder-blue carpet. "Nothing ever happens here. Not like this."

"Exactly. The closest thing we have to actual danger is, like, that time Jimmy Saltz got arrested for punching Dallas Green over a parking spot he was aiming for."

A corner of his mouth twitches again, this time with a hint of a smile. "You sure you're okay?"

"Yeah, I'll be fine," I promise him. Still, he lingers in the doorway. I feel like there's something else he wants to tell me, but I have no idea what. What could be worse than this?

It's always like this with Garrett, though. He has one of those faces that always feels as if he's waiting to say or do something else, like he's brimming with it. The way he looks at me, full of fascination and expectation, you'd think I often randomly burst into song to entertain him or something.

"Do you have plans Friday?"

"Plans? Friday? Next Friday?" I practically squawk, my voice so loud and pitchy it grates on my own nerves. *No plans here except talking to Britney on the phone, eating buckets of popcorn, and digging into the latest Sarah Dessen novel.*

He nods.

"Not yet." I trail a finger across the threads of

pattern in my comforter. "Britney and I might do something."

"Yeah?" He scratches the back of his neck.

"Why do you ask? Do you have any *fun plans?*" I tease.

"Nah, not really." He seems to think, twisting his lips, then adds, "Actually, I'm having a party."

"A party?"

A laugh escapes his lips on a breath. "Are you a parrot? What's with the repeating?"

I grab a pillow from behind me and chuck it at him, narrowly missing as he ducks. Laughing, he picks it up, but instead of giving it back right away, he holds onto it. "I, um, it's my birthday party."

My stomach twists itself into a zillion knots. That's right. His birthday. "Sweet eighteen," I muse. My cheeks must be the color of the wine my mother allows herself a single glass of once a week.

He nods, and to my surprise, his own cheeks give mine a run for their money. "Somethin' like that. Anyway, I thought if you didn't have anything to do... it'd be alright with me if you came." His gaze zips across the wall and over the ceiling, like he's preparing to paint in here, before falling back to me. "And invite Britney, too. If you want. Or...whoever."

"I could invite anyone?" I jump off my bed, crossing the room and snatching the pillow back from him. "Like my boyfriend?"

Once tomato red, his skin has quickly returned to its usual tan. "Since when do you have a boyfriend?"

I shrug one shoulder, and his gaze falls to it, then jerks back up. He swallows. "Since now."

"Who?" he demands.

"Why do you care?" With a fist shoved into my hip, I push the pillow into his chest, but he catches it with both hands, tugging it and me forward until we're toe to toe. Refusing to let go of the pillow, my knuckles rest against his chest.

Anticipation builds like an inflating balloon. His dark eyes zip back and forth between mine like he's interrogating me, and I can't quite think straight.

Guilt takes hold of my insides when I realize what I just said to him. I don't know why I lied. It was just a joke, really.

He blinks, releasing the pillow and swiping his fingers over his lips. "I don't. I just thought you should tell your brother. So he can...look out for you, or whatever."

I take a step away from him, shaking my head to clear the fog. Whatever that was, it was weird. *Why is he looking at me like that?* "I'm perfectly capable of looking after myself, thank you very much. Where's your party, anyway?"

"My house. Well, the guest house, actually," he says, bobbing his eyebrows before he scratches at the place in between them. "Anyway, it's super low key. No gifts or anything like that." He scowls. "But if you want to come, cool. If you want to bring someone, go for it. If not, no biggie."

"Okay. I'll think about it."

"Cool. Just, um, let me know. If you want."

"Sure."

"I'm really sorry about Amber, too." He pats the doorframe. "It sucks."

"Yeah." Like me, he doesn't seem to know what to say about the situation. Any way you phrase it, it doesn't feel like enough. Neither of us is equipped to deal with anything of this magnitude.

Without waiting for me to get out of my thoughts and say something else, he moves back into the hall, and with that final, familiar look that tricks me into thinking he's going to say more, he's gone.

CHAPTER EIGHT

GARRETT — AGE 18

By the time my party rolls around on Friday, the news of Amber's death has hit every corner of our town. Rumors range from a wild party gone wrong to an attempted kidnapping to a murder-suicide pact, but I think that last one is because the drama club just put on Romeo and Juliet, and the play is fresh in everyone's mind.

The air around the school went from being charged with sadness, to worry and fear, and now, only a few days later, it's nearly forgotten. We had a memorial for her at school where her friends said some nice words, and they had a photo of her blown up and placed on a poster for a week, but that's basically been it.

I'm not sure how to feel about it. On one hand, there was a moment when I worried my party was going to have to be canceled, and that would suck. But on the other, two people literally *died*—people most of us have known our whole lives—and we're all at a party.

So…that kind of sucks, too.

I've never known anyone who died, strange as that is. My parents are alive, and their parents are alive. I knock on the wall next to me to ward off any jinxes over the thought and catch a strange look from Will, but I shrug him off, pretending what I just did is normal.

Mom and Dad zip into the room. He's a few feet in front of her, as always. It's not that he walks in front because he has to be in charge or anything weird like that, he just always moves like he's in a hurry, and my mom couldn't be bothered to hurry on her best day.

Mom's eyes scan the room, looking pleased. "Well, how's everything—" Just then, a soccer ball zips through the air. Dad's hands shoot out to the side, and he lunges, catching it seconds before it smashes into a family photo on the wall.

I have no doubt who the culprits are, but it takes several seconds for them to appear, looking guilty as sin as Dad waits with his hand on his hip. Their eyes are wide as they peek up from the ground, dark brows drawn together. They're three years apart, but they may as well be carbon copies of each other.

"Henry, Isaiah." Mom scolds my brothers, crossing her arms. "You boys were told to wait at the house with your sister. Where is she?"

"Mo-*om*," Henry whines, displaying his missing

front teeth. "We just wanted to see the party. Why does Garrett get to have all the fun?"

"Because we love him the most, obviously," Dad teases, to which both brothers just groan. Henry slaps a hand to his forehead.

"Jenny's always on the phone with her *boyfriend*," Isaiah says, singing the last word in a disgusted voice. "*And*, as the fourth oldest—who is now *officially* in double-digits, I might add—with Corbin at practice and Jenny on the phone and Garrett at his party, doesn't that make me in charge?"

"It doesn't while your older siblings are still in the house." With a sigh, Dad puts one hand on Henry's shoulder and the other hand on Isaiah's shoulder, then looks at me. I already know what he's going to say before he says it. Frankly, I'm shocked it took this long. "Sorry, Gare. I'm going to have to take these two knuckleheads home. Think you can handle the party without your boring ol' dad?"

I nod, not expecting any less. "Yeah, sure."

"No drinking, no drugs," Dad warns, his tone teasing. "Your body is a temple and all that jazz."

"Yeah, yeah." I can't help laughing with him, even when I'm disappointed.

Dad turns his attention back to my brothers, leading them through the crowded room. "Where is your baby sister? Did you leave her in her playpen?"

"Jenny was with her," Henry says.

When they've fully disappeared in the sea of my

friends, I look back at Mom. Her lips are pinched together. "I'm sorry, bud. I know little brothers sometimes ruin all the fun."

"It's fine," I tell her. She really does look upset, and I hate that. "Honestly. I'm just ready to hang out with my friends. It's not a big deal."

She eyes the door, and I know she's thinking she needs to get back to the house and help Dad. Probably before he drives away in the golf cart back to the main house, leaving her to have to walk.

"You can go, if you want. We'll be fine."

She breathes a quick sigh. "Are you sure? I don't mind staying." Clasping her hands together, she bends at the knee like I've just given her the greatest gift.

"Positive. Go ahead."

"It's just…you know how your father is. Those boys will be knee deep in ice cream if I don't catch up to them now. And it's nearly their bedtime." She winces. "You probably don't want to hang out with your mom anyway, do you?"

"It's cool," I say. "Promise."

She hesitates for just a second longer before brushing a hand over my cheek and pointing a warning finger at Will. "Keep him out of trouble."

He salutes her. "Yes, ma'am."

With a nod, she hurries out of the room in a rush to catch up with my dad, her heels clicking across the wood floor.

"God, your mom's hot," Will says, watching her leave. "No wonder you have so many siblings."

"Gross. Shut up." I shove him and turn away, just in time to see my mom zip out the door. Before it shuts, Tessa slips inside.

I suck in a breath involuntarily, almost choking on it as I wait to see if she has brought anyone with her.

"What is *she* doing here?" Will asks, stepping up next to me.

"I invited her." It's hard to see her through the crowd of people who keep walking in front of me, so I shuffle side to side in place, trying not to make it obvious what I'm doing with occasional glances in random directions.

When she finally closes the door behind her, and I realize she's alone, something unclenches in me that I'm pretty sure has been clenched for a while.

Will steps into my line of vision, waving a hand back and forth. "Um, hello? Earth to Garrett. I asked why you invited my sister to your party without telling me?"

I blink, suddenly very aware of my hands and the placement of my tongue in my mouth. It's like I want to crawl out of my skin, like nothing fits where it belongs anymore. "Sorry, um. I…what?"

He sighs, looking back over his shoulder. "Jesus, she saw us." He rolls his eyes. "Now she's going to want to hang out with us, and I'm going to have to play big bro all night. This was supposed to be our night." He raises his brows, darting his gaze toward the group of girls chatting away in a corner. "Cassidy is supposed to be here."

"She'll be fine, dude. Chill. You can have your fun. I'll handle Tessa."

"That's not fair. It's your birthday." He's not mad, I know. Will and Tessa are closer than any siblings I know. But he's right. I didn't entirely think this invitation through. She'd just looked so sad in that room when I came back to check on her, and... I can't explain it.

She makes me act like an idiot most of the time.

"I don't mind."

"Whatever, fine, but remember you offered." He passes me a fake baton, patting my chest. "She's yours tonight. You hear me? This is on you. I'm not playing babysitter."

At least I think that's what he said. Something like that. I'm not sure, because my entire brain short-circuited over him saying Tessa was mine. I know what he means. My responsibility. But even at that... Something warm hits me from the inside, like I've drank hot soup.

This is wrong.

She shouldn't be here.

She shouldn't look like...that.

For the first time, I take in the way she's dressed. No different than any other girl here, I guess. Jeans and a shirt that shows off a little bit of skin on her stomach. A little more makeup than I'm used to on her. Her dark brown hair is different. Curly and sort of...big? Like it gets when it rains, except not like that at all.

She looks pretty, I realize, with an agonizing sense of dread.

I mean, she always looks pretty, but this is different. And it seems everyone here knows it, too. Before she makes it to us, Brendan steps into her path, holding his hands up. He's practically leering at her. *Jesus. Wipe your drool, bro.*

She looks up at him, and everything in me holds a breath as I wait to see how she'll react. But how else did I expect her to react other than... *Oh god. She's laughing.*

She's laughing at stupid Brendan and his stupid, fucking joke. I hate him. Why did I invite him anyway with his stupid hair and his stupid rich parents and his stupid jokes?

He's not even that funny. I've heard his jokes.

Plenty.

Oh my god, I sound like my sister.

"Dude, what is wrong with you?" Will's back. Or maybe he never left. Honestly, I have no idea because I feel like I'm on another planet right now watching this all play out on a TV show called *My Worst Fucking Nightmare* starring me and Tessa Becker and my douchebag ex-friend, Brendan Taylor.

"What the hell does he think he's doing?" I ask with

a wave toward the absolute car crash happening in front of me.

"Who? Brendan?" Will, on the other hand, is completely unfazed. Cool as a cucumber, apparently. La-dee-fucking-da. "Talking to my sister, I guess. Why do you look like you haven't shit in a week? He's a good dude."

"You're okay with him talking to her?" The floor beneath my feet is gone, and I'm falling. Dropping. Plummeting. "Seriously?"

"Why wouldn't I be? Tessa's only a year younger than us, so it's not weird. I date girls in her grade all the time. I mean, obviously, if he breaks her heart, I'll pummel him, but I'm not about to be one of those obsessive big brothers who tries to control who she dates." He wraps an arm around Cassidy Cole, stopping her dead in her tracks. She looks shocked to see him at first, then registers who he is and relaxes. "Besides," Will adds, "I've got my hands full."

I'm pretty sure I've lost my hearing because there's this ringing in my ears I can't seem to dull, and the entire room is spinning. But nope, it's not, because Emily Gray just wrapped her hands around my waist and I'm here, on planet Earth, but also not planet Earth. Just hell.

As in, what the *hell* is wrong with me?

"You look like you saw a ghost, birthday boy," she says, planting a kiss on my cheek. I'm not looking at her, though—at the girl I was into not that long ago—I'm looking at Tessa.

And for the first time in my life, she's not looking back at me.

CHAPTER NINE

TESSA — PRESENT DAY

Sunset Cemetery is one of five cemeteries in our town, but easily the largest. It's also located next to the town park. As a kid, I was both terrified and fascinated by its proximity. Childhood in this town isn't complete without at least a single time of you sneaking away from the playground, racing across the paved drive of the cemetery, and daring to touch a headstone without getting attacked by zombies or ghosts, all while your friends watch and cheer you on, fists clenched with hope you make it back alive. More importantly, that you don't get caught by a parent. Any parent.

This is still one of those towns I hear people wistfully lamenting about *nowadays*. The ones that are truly a village. The ones where, if any adult sees any child doing something wrong, they won't hesitate to get on to them as if they were their own child. And chances are, before you make it back home, they'll have already called your parents, so you'll be hearing it from them, too.

Most of us got caught by someone's parent while sneaking into the cemetery at least once, but a few legends made it without anyone noticing.

I even heard a rumor that one kid spent the entire night in the cemetery, but I have yet to be convinced he didn't start that one himself.

As we got older and had less parental supervision and even less interest in the playground if it didn't involve writing our initials on the plastic equipment, kids moved from the playground to the cemetery to seem edgy, getting drunk or making out—usually both —against a gravestone.

Most of us didn't know anyone who was buried here. For the rare few of us who knew someone who had died, it was usually a grandparent or a much-older family member, and their deaths at that age felt less impactful. Will and I were one of the rare exceptions, with our dad's passing, but he was cremated, so still, whether or not we were being respectful of the graves wasn't something any of us concerned ourselves with.

They were just stones. Meaningless names. Until they weren't.

When people started dying, when we started putting people we knew in the ground here, everything started to feel different. It didn't change anything. People still came here to get drunk and fool around, but suddenly it wasn't without a stop by a gravestone of the girl you used to sit by in chemistry or without putting a flower next to the grave of the kid you once considered a best friend.

Driving around the cemetery isn't without its pangs of nostalgia, but mostly, this place just feels sad now.

"We may have to park at the playground and walk," Garrett says, jutting his head in the direction of the ball court where my brother and his friends once spent so much time. It's clearly been fixed up now, with a new goal and painted concrete.

"That's fine." I don't love the idea of walking across so much wet ground, but it doesn't seem like we'll have a choice. There is no parking lot here. You either have to park at the playground and walk over or park on the road that encircles the cemetery. We're on our second lap around when Garrett notices a spot.

It's a tight squeeze, but we make it.

I glance down at my hands in my lap, then look up at the sight in front of me.

Britney was so loved. The thought hits me square in the chest as I further take in the crowded street and large gathering in the center of the hill just ahead, everyone huddled together near the blue tent.

I step out of the car and directly into a puddle. Water floods my heel, and I curse under my breath, then feel guilty over doing so. If any of the ladies from church had heard me, I'd get scolded.

Luckily, no one is close enough to hear except Garrett, who snickers to himself and holds out an arm to help me across the puddle. I keep hold of him long enough to balance on one foot and pull my shoe off my foot, dumping the cold water on the ground like a coffee that had been left in my car.

With the still damp shoe back on my foot, we slowly make our way up the large hill. I scan the crowd of familiar faces, though everyone seems to be looking straight through me. Despite the cloudy day, most faces are clad with sunglasses, and the ones that aren't still stare into space with devastation etched into their skin. Pain seeps from the pores of everyone here and fills the air like the moisture from the storm.

The service hasn't started yet, but Garrett and I stand near the back, peeking in between people to get a glimpse at her casket. Pastor Charles is at the front, wearing a black suit—like he wears from the pulpit on Sundays and Wednesdays—and a solemn expression.

My heels keep sinking into the muddy grass, so I balance on one foot then the other, fighting to stay steady. Next to me, Garrett notices, offering his elbow, which I loop my arm through without much thought, clinging to him and hoping my shoes don't end up stuck in the mud when I finally give in and ignore the sinking sensation.

"Friends…" Pastor Charles's soft voice breaks through the whispers, and they taper off quickly. His chin quivers as he looks at Britney's family sitting in the front row under the tent. "I'll never understand it." His voice cracks. "This will never get any easier." Next to him, his wife, Mabel, puts a hand on his shoulder, drying tears of her own. She's impossibly pretty, with buttery-yellow hair and crystal-blue eyes. "Britney Davis was a beautiful, loving member of our community. She was a sister. A teacher at our elementary school. A daughter. A devoted member of our congregation. A friend. A wife. A mother." Tears line his green eyes, and he puts his head up toward the sky. "Britney Davis was loved, and she loved." He clutches a hand to his chest, patting. "Oh, did she love. Anyone with a child in her class, whether in Sunday school or first grade, can attest to that." He pauses, eyes scanning the crowd. When they land on me, there's a hint of recognition in his eyes I haven't found in anyone else's. "She was the best of us." He nods. "And she went home to see our Father before any of us were ready. I know there is a celebration going on in heaven right now."

"Amen," someone in the crowd calls out.

Pastor Charles is silent for several long seconds, his eyes scanning each of us like they do from the pulpit. Finally, he drops his head. "Let us pray."

When the service is over, everyone lines up to offer their condolences to Britney's family. Garrett and I are near the back of the line when I notice Pastor Charles moving toward us around the crowd.

"Tessa Becker." He's close enough now to keep his

voice low, but still, some people turn their heads around to see. He holds out his arms, and I sink into his familiar hug. As I do, the sadness hits me again. He strokes my back gently, his cheek resting on the top of my head before he pulls away. "I hadn't heard you were back in town."

"Just for this." I shrug, tears springing to my eyes before I can finish the thought. "I couldn't miss...saying goodbye to her."

His head falls forward, bouncing with a nod. "She was a good one. I know you two were close."

I sniffle, but if I say anything else, I know I'll start crying, and I desperately don't want to do that.

"We've been missing you in church, Mr. Campbell." His tone is soft when he looks at Garrett. "How's your family? That little one must be growing like a weed."

He clears his throat. "They're good."

Pastor Charles turns his attention back to me. "And your momma. How is she? I've been meanin' to get by the nursing home and visit. She'll be on my case about it once she's feeling better." His smile is sad, despite the attempted joke.

"She's okay. We were just there to see her before we came here."

"Good. That's good. We're all praying for her every day. Things just aren't the same around here without her." Something catches his eye. "Oh. The family needs me, but"—he puts a hand on my shoulder—"we're all here for you, honey. And Will, too. If you need anything, all you need to do is call, okay? And I mean that. You say the word, and I will make it happen. Your momma raised half this town. We're all just looking for ways to repay the favor. Promise me you'll let me know if there's something we can do."

I meet his kind eyes with a nod. "Thank you. I will. I promise."

With that, he steps away with a nod of acknowledgment and a little wave. I turn back to Garrett, who slips an arm around my shoulders.

When there are only three people ahead of us, Britney's sister, Kristy, notices me in the line. Her eyes widen, and she turns to Mabel, whispering something to her. Mabel nods and steps into Kristy's place in line. Looking back my way, she rushes toward me, arms outstretched, sunshine hair flying behind her. I catch her in my arms seconds before she starts sobbing, and my world collapses once again. I never realized how many ways hearts have to break.

I pat her hair, squeezing her against me, and for a moment it's like having my best friend back. Kristy and I were never particularly close. She was three years younger than Britney and me, and she often tagged along just because Britney's mom forced us to let her.

Still, I wrap my arms around her with everything I have, rubbing a hand along her back. "I'm so sorry," I say, low enough that only she can hear.

She pulls away, drying her eyes. "Thank you for coming. It would mean a lot to Brit that you're here."

I brush her hair back, strands of it clinging to her wet cheeks, and tuck it behind her ears. "Of course. I wouldn't be anywhere else."

"She always loved you." Fat tears roll down her cheeks, and I brush them away. "She still talked about you all the time. In the big city. She was so proud of you." She sobs. "But she missed you a lot."

"I know. I missed her, too. And I loved her. I love both of you." It's the truth. The painful, devastating truth. I missed her, and I will miss her for the rest of my life.

She hugs me again. "I can't believe you're here. You have to come see Justin and the kids. They'll be so happy you're here. I don't know how to explain it to them, you know? How do you tell kids that someone could do this to their momma? How does anyone explain that?"

Her words stab me in the chest. "What?"

"I just don't know how to do it." She grabs my hand, dragging me away from the line. "You were her best friend. What would you say to them?"

"Wait. Are you telling me someone hurt her? That she was..." I can't finish the sentence, can't bring myself to think about the possibility. No one gets hurt here. Not since the murders back then. This place is supposed to be safe again.

The obituary didn't mention anything, but everyone online kept calling her death an accident. I hadn't wanted to seem insensitive by prying, and without Momma to tell me what was happening and Will perpetually out of the rumor mill, I didn't know. *A terrible accident* they kept saying. I just assumed it was a car crash.

Her blue eyes widen. "You didn't know?"

My world has shifted. "Didn't know what?"

"Britney's death wasn't an accident." She's crying again as she takes my hands. *Impossible.* "She... Someone *killed* her. Like they killed all the others." She falls into my arms again, shaking my entire world to its core.

CHAPTER TEN

GARRETT — PRESENT DAY

She's quiet on the way home, staring out the window, and she keeps wringing her hands together like she always does when she's stressed.

"I'm sorry." My voice feels foreign cutting through the silence. "I just assumed you knew. Kristy must've, too."

"I just saw her obituary on Facebook. It never mentioned..." She isn't looking at me as she says it.

"Right." Will should've told her, but I'm honestly not sure if he knows. He's gone so often now—only home on the weekends—that he doesn't really talk to anyone around town except when he runs errands, but most weekends he's too exhausted to get out much at all. I should've mentioned it to one of them, I guess, but how do you even bring that up? It's been so long since the last murder, I guess we're out of practice. "I forget the rest comes with being in town. The gossip spreads here, but Justin and Kristy fought to keep the details out of the paper to protect the girls. Perks of being in a small town, I guess. You know Ray down at the paper will do anything for Kristy."

I don't know if that was meant to be a joke—the small-town bit—but I want her to smile again. It's horrific seeing her sad, always has been. I can't imagine anything worse than the look on her face right now, the devastating truth that there's nothing I can do to take her pain away. Being useless is not something I handle well, especially when it comes to Tessa. It makes my skin crawl.

"Without Mom around to talk to, I'm pretty out of the loop, I guess," she says eventually. Adjusting in her seat, she tucks her hands under her thighs. "It's true, then? They're saying someone killed her? Do they think it's somehow related to all those girls when we were growing up?"

"I don't know," I admit. There's a balloon of air in my chest that I can't quite breathe out. With every new breath, it seems to grow bigger, more uncomfortable. "Her family would know more than I do, but what I've heard around town is that she died"—I wince as I say the word, hating the way it feels on my tongue—"by gunshot."

"She was shot." She winces, then eyes me. "Where? At home? Where was Justin?"

"I haven't spoken to him directly. I called and left a

message with my condolences once the news got out, but he hasn't responded. Understandably. He's got so much on his plate right now, I can't imagine having time to return calls. And the house has been so busy with people visiting I haven't wanted to intrude. But, from what I've heard, he was on a business trip, and Britney was home with the girls. Justin's dad, Anthony —I don't know if you remember him, but they still live next door to Brit and Justin—he woke up and said he thought he'd heard something, but he couldn't be sure it wasn't a dream or a car backfiring or something. His wife was out of town visiting Justin's aunt, so he couldn't check with her to see if she'd heard it. He looked outside but didn't see anything. At that point, he wasn't even sure which house the sound might've come from, you know? The next morning, he went around to check and make sure everything was okay, and he, well, he found her. The girls were still in bed, thankfully."

"He waited all night? Seriously?"

"He just didn't know." I can't blame her for the judgment in her voice, but if he hadn't checked at all—like none of the other neighbors did—those girls might've been the ones to find her. I can't imagine anything worse. "Based on what other people are saying, he thought he'd dreamed it, but it was still bothering him when he woke up. He couldn't shake the worry."

She turns her head to look out the window, clearly annoyed. "So do they have any suspects? Surely someone knows something. Whose gun was it?"

"I think I heard it was registered to her dad, but it was passed down to Britney when he died a few years ago. Like I said, this is all rumor-mill whispers, but the police seem to think it was self-inflicted—"

"She wouldn't."

"Yeah, her family doesn't think so either."

She inhales sharply, then bites her bottom lip in thought. "How is it possible we still don't have answers about everything that happened back then? Six people died in less than a year, all moms and daughters, and we never got answers. We all just...moved on."

I swallow, gripping the steering wheel. "There were suspects, but not enough evidence. Anyway, whoever it was, I think we all assumed they were long gone. Until now. And we still don't know if it's even connected."

"No one else has ever died here. Not violently like this. There are twelve hundred people in this town. How big of a chance is there that there's not some connection between what happened back then and what's happening now?" Her eyes pinch, and she massages the place between her brows before looking my way urgently. "Someone needs to protect her daughters."

"Kristy is staying at the house for now to help Justin. I think everyone had the same thought, but they're much younger than any of the other girls who were killed. Plus all of those daughters were murdered on the same day as their mothers. There really doesn't seem to be a connection between then and now, but I agree it's unsettling. I don't want this to all start up again."

"Well, we can't just let this go. We have to...to do something. Someone has to know something about this case and all the others, too. I owe it to Britney to get answers."

"You're stubborn enough. If anyone can figure out what's going on around here, my vote would be on you." I hope I sound as if I believe what I'm saying. I just don't know how any of us can find out more than the police. Then again, I also don't see how we could find out *less* than the police.

She gives me a small smile. "Thanks, but this has been going on for years. As much as I want to get to the bottom of everything, I just don't see how I could with only a few days left here."

That's right. She's leaving. She's going away again, and I can't stop her. "When do you leave?"

"I'm freelancing, so technically I can stay for a while, but I don't like to leave my house for too long. Realistically, I plan to leave in a day or two. I just want to see Will before I go back."

"Maybe a day or two is all you'll need." I bump her arm with mine. "Either way, you have a place here as long as you need it."

She draws one side of her mouth in. "Britney wouldn't have done this."

She doesn't seem to be looking for a response to that, and I'm not sure I have one, so I just reach across the console and squeeze her hand. "You know I'm here, right?" I'll leave it at that, let her take what meaning from it she will.

Her smile is soft and sad when she looks up at me, her hazel eyes locking with mine. "I know."

CHAPTER ELEVEN

TESSA — AGE 17

I'm walking out of the school and toward the parking lot when hands fall over my eyes, cloaking me in darkness. I squeal, grabbing the fingers to pull them away, when I feel his breath tickle my ear.

"Happy birthday."

A wave sweeps through the lowest part of my stomach. "Garrett?"

He drops his hands with a laugh, and I twirl around to face him. "You sound surprised."

"Not in a bad way," I tell him. "I just thought you were Brendan."

His shoulders fall, and he drops his gaze to his hands. "Oh. Right. I saw you guys hanging out at my party, but I hadn't seen you together since." When he looks back up, he's squinting one eye from the sun. "Are you, like, dating him or something?"

I smile to myself. While we haven't actually said

what we're doing, it kind of feels like that. I wonder what Brendan has told him about us. "I mean, we... well, yeah. I think so. Sort of."

"You think so, sort of?" His dark brows pinch together.

"Well, we didn't say we're boyfriend-girlfriend or anything, but we've been talking on the phone at night lately, and he walks me to class most days and sat beside me in church last week."

"Right," he says, glancing back at the school. "Well, cool, I guess." His tone is flat, almost like he's annoyed. He's never really talked to me like this.

"What? You don't think it's a good idea? I thought you guys were friends."

"No. It's not that. He's, I mean, it's whatever. It's not like I spend any time thinking about your love life." He scowls, and now I feel dumb. This isn't Britney. Garrett doesn't care about whom I'm dating any more than Will does. "What are you doing for your birthday?"

My cheeks heat with flames of excitement. I finally have actual plans to share when he asks this. "I'm going to Britney's parents' cabin at the lake. They're letting us spend the whole weekend up there alone."

"Oh?" His eyes study me, and I know he can read my guilt like a book.

I cover my face and rush out the words. "Okay, and Brendan might stop by. No big deal. Like you said: boring."

Something twitches in his jaw. "That sounds like a really big deal, actually. Does your mom know?"

"No, and you can't tell her." I warn him, wagging my finger in his direction. "Swear to me you won't tell her."

"Why should I?"

His harsh tone surprises me. Garrett has never been cruel to me. He teases me, sure, but he's always been a friend first. And I've lied to Mom for the boys so many times.

He pinches his nose between his fingers. "Look, I won't tell your mom. Duh. You know me better than that. Have you at least told Will?"

"No. It's none of his business. Besides, it's not like anything is going to happen. We're just hanging out."

"Fine. Then we're coming, too," he says, his voice as firm as if he's stamped the words right into the concrete below us.

I stop short, jumping in front of him to stop us from walking any farther. "What? *No!*"

"Yes." He's unyielding, his jaw tight.

"Garrett."

"Tessa." My name is soft and warm on his tongue. His eyes flick down to my lips and across my face before they slowly rise to meet mine again.

"Garrett."

"Tessa." He's unfazed and, apparently, amused.

"Why?" I whine. "I shouldn't have told you."

"Oh, that would be a mistake because Brendan *definitely* would've told us."

Warmth hits my cheeks again.

"We're coming with you to make sure you're okay," he adds. "I'm not negotiating."

"I'll be okay. I'll be better than okay, in fact," I tell him. "Totally fine. He's just coming by to hang out, and Britney will be there the whole time. It's super casual. And, like we said, he's your friend. More than that, he's Will's friend. Do you think Will will let him continue to live if he does anything to hurt me?" The attempt at a joke falls flat.

He looks like he's either going to yell at me or throw up. Either reaction confuses me so badly. "We're coming, Tessa. You two don't need to be in a cabin with Brendan alone, whether he's our friend or not."

"Why? I'm alone with you all the time. What's the difference?" I demand, stepping closer to him in what's meant to be a challenge, but he catches my waist, and I feel more off balance than I ever have.

His eyes flick down toward my lips and linger there. *Do I have food in my teeth? Jesus, why does he keep looking at my mouth?*

"Guess we'll find out, won't we?" he mutters, barely a whisper. Then he releases me, and he's gone.

When the weekend comes and Britney's parents drop us off at the cabin with enough food to last two weeks rather than two days, we unpack everything and rush to get ready before the guys get there.

"I can't believe we're having a *real* party," she squeals as she pulls a soft pink cami on with her black skirt. She's only three months older than I am, but she looks closer to three *years* older with her thick, black eyeliner and long, tan legs. Being best friends with the pretty, popular girl means I'm usually the third wheel when we're together. Guys we meet gravitate toward her first. Guys I like ask me if I could get her to go out with them. It's just the reality, and it's something I've become used to, but this time, for once, it's me the guy is coming for. I'll be the one with someone to kiss tonight.

At that thought, my stomach balls up in a knot, and I feel like I'm going to vomit. I look over the clothes I brought to choose from. Everything in my pile that's name brand is a hand-me-down from Britney, and most of the rest came from clothing donations to the church.

It's not a good feeling to walk through town and know that anyone you pass might've been the original owner of what you're wearing. I'm far from the only kid in school wearing hand-me-downs, but it gets to me sometimes.

I know Mom does the best she can on her own, but just once I'd like to be able to afford what Britney can.

"Oh. Can I borrow this?" Britney asks, snatching a long necklace with a key attached to it.

I nod, not really paying attention. "Sure. What should I wear?"

She muses over my options, tapping her finger to her chin. "Oh, how about this?" She grabs a navy strapless top and some of her blue jean shorts.

"I can't wear your shorts. You're smaller than I am."

"Please." She scoffs, shoving them toward me. "You want them to be a little too small. Trust me, you're going to look so hot, Brendan won't know what hit him."

"I don't know. My brother is going to be here," I remind her hesitantly.

"And Garrett." She wiggles her butt. "Why do you think I picked this skirt?"

"Disgusting," I spit out. It's exactly how I feel, but not because I find Garrett disgusting in the slightest. It's just that the idea of Britney and Garrett together makes me want to die. "Since when do you like either of them?"

"I didn't say I liked them, but they're hot." She shrugs at my dramatic grimace. "Sorry, but they *are*. And Tyra says flirting with cute boys never hurt anyone."

She's wrong because I feel like I've been split down the center with a scalpel. "Garrett doesn't really date anyone. Or flirt, for that matter. You can have Will."

She pauses her process of sorting through jewelry to look up at me. "Why?" A smile plays on her lips, then suddenly she's launching across the bed toward me.

"Oh my god, Tessa Becker, *spill.* Right now. Do you *like* Garrett?" She drops to her stomach, fists under her chin as she waits for the hot gossip.

"Gross, no." The response is instant and impulsive. And a complete lie. Except I didn't realize it until right this moment. I've never let myself consider the fact that I might *like* Garrett. "He's my brother's best friend."

"That doesn't make him ugly." She grins with her tongue pressed between her teeth.

"I mean, yeah, he's not ugly," I admit, my insides swirling. What does this even mean? How am I supposed to look at him again? How am I supposed to be in the same room with him? He's going to see it all over my face.

"But?" Britney prompts.

"But I have a boyfriend."

"Mm-hmm. So you don't care if I make out with him tonight?" She rolls off the bed and stands. With a pointed look, she rests a hand on her hip and waits.

She knows the answer. I can see it all over her face. I'm positively mortified and don't know how to process any of this, nor do I have time to. Why didn't I see it before?

I stare at her, rage and fear washing through me as images of Britney kissing Garrett flash in my mind as if flicking through channels. "I mean...you can do what you want, I guess—"

She bursts out laughing, mouth open, and smacks

the air. "*Girl!* Why did I not know this before? You've got it bad!"

"I do not!" I cry, but it's no use. She knows me. I cover my cheeks with my hands, trying and failing to hide my blush.

She purses her lips. "Maybe we should cancel on Brendan and tell Garrett he was sick and couldn't make it. After Garrett gets here, of course."

"Don't be silly. If Garrett and Will get here and Brendan's not here, they'll just leave. He's the only reason they're coming. Besides, I like Brendan."

"Okay, sure." She gives me a look of mock sincerity.

"I'm serious."

"No, totally." Her cheeks are pink with delight as she beams, then she rushes to her bag, grabbing a strapless bra and tossing it to me. It's the kind of push-up bra my mom would never allow me to wear. "Here. Put this on. Garrett—oops, I mean, *Brendan*—will love it." She winks at me.

I scowl, tossing the bra across the room. "You're the worst."

She picks it up and hands it back. "Trust me, you'll be thanking me later." Once I've slipped it on, she admires me like a proud big sister. "And so will he." She whistles just as the doorbell rings downstairs. She doesn't bother to elaborate on which *he* she means.

CHAPTER TWELVE

GARRETT — AGE 18

"Dude, chill," Will tells me, ambling up the hill as if we're on our way to afternoon tea and not to protect his sister from some creep. Okay, he's our friend, but he's also a creep. "She's still going to be there whether we break our necks running up this hill to get inside or not."

Brendan's red Pontiac sits just in front of where we parked, telling me he's already here. Of course he is. Can't be on time for practice, but *by god*, he's early for her.

I shouldn't care.

Damn it, I don't care.

Not any more than is normal. She's like my little sister.

Biggest lie I ever told.

I rap my knuckles against the door, listening carefully to the sounds inside, though it would be easier to hear if Will wasn't in the background breathing like a damn wild boar as he ascends the hill.

"It's not that steep, you big baby," I snap behind me.

He's laughing, because that's what Will does. Nothing is ever serious for him. Not even his sister's safety.

When the door opens, it's Tessa who greets us. She's wearing makeup like she wore to my party, though I rarely see her in it at school or around the house. Some gloss on her lips, dark stuff around her eyes. Extra pink on her cheeks, though maybe that's from drinking.

Shit, is she drinking?

"Are you drinking?"

She balks. "*What?* No."

Her top is low cut and gives me a perfect view of just how much she's grown up. Jesus, I feel like a creep. Maybe *I'm* the creep.

Fuck. Do those shorts even qualify as shorts?

My throat is tight. *Is this what anaphylactic shock feels like?*

"What are you wearing?" Will asks, and thank god it didn't have to be me this time.

"Clothes." She steps back. "Are you coming in or not?"

Will walks around me, nudging my shoulder with his as a way to apparently bring me back from my stupor. Inside, the house is warm and smells of something spicy, like chili or cheese dip.

Who can think of food at a time like this?

"There they are!" Britney squeals from another room before she comes bounding in, throwing her arms around Will first, then me. The hug is brief, but it comes with a cloud of flowery perfume. "Thanks for crashing the party, you two. We needed extra people anyway." She grabs Will's hand and nods toward me. "Tessa, can you show Garrett around really quick? Brendan's getting the stereo hooked up, and I need Will's help in the kitchen."

"I don't think he needs a tour," Tessa says begrudgingly.

"I'd love a tour," I argue.

Britney looks at me as if I've just put the star on the Christmas tree.

"He'd *love* a tour," she repeats. "Did you hear that?" Before she walks out of the room, she narrows her gaze at Tessa in a way that makes me feel like this house is booby-trapped, à la *Home Alone*, and I'm about to fall for it.

"Fine." Tessa steps forward, pointing around lightning quick. "Kitchen. Living room. Bedrooms are down the hall. Bathroom is at the end of the hall."

I shove my hands in my pockets. She's uncomfortable, and I hate it. It's not supposed to be like this with us. She's mad at me, though I don't blame her. I don't know why everything has changed for me lately. I don't know why I can't look at her legs in those shorts without feeling as if I'm thirteen years old again, getting hard when the wind blows just right.

I don't understand what's happening with me. It's just Tessa. Except, there's no *just* anymore.

It's Tessa.

I clear my throat. "Well, that wasn't much of a tour. You can count on my one-star Yelp review."

She snorts with laughter, then covers her mouth with her hand. She's always hated her snort, but it's cute. "Fine, whatever. Come on." She leads me into the living room from the foyer, pointing to where Brendan is bent over, plugging speakers in behind the TV. "Living room."

He lifts up to wave. If he's mad we're here, he doesn't show it. "'Sup, Campbell?"

"Hey." I barely look his way, my eyes trained on Tessa as she leads me into the kitchen, where Britney has Will stirring something in a pot on the stove while she supervises. Seeing us walk past, she gives me a mysterious smile, and suddenly I'm uneasy.

What in the *Parent Trap* is going on here? Is she trying to set us up? Or maybe Tessa asked her to make me uncomfortable so I'd leave.

She ought to know better. I'm not going anywhere.

In the hallway, when it's just the two of us, Tessa slows her pace enough for me to admit, "I feel like I'm about to walk into a trap."

She looks back. "What? Why?"

"Because Britney keeps looking at me like she's a hunter waiting for me to step on that suspicious-looking pile of leaves."

She laughs again—*there's the snort*—and shakes her head. "She's just...it's nothing. That's just Britney."

"I've been around the two of you plenty of times, and she has *never* looked at me like that."

She spins around, grasping my arm. "Do you trust me?"

"Of course." The words leave my mouth like a cough, a reflex. It's not even a question.

"Then don't worry about it." She drops my arm. "Bedroom's here." She points to a room with clothes scattered all around on the floor and across the floral bedspread. Her clothes. My eyes land on the bra on the floor and—*Jesus H. Christ, what is wrong with me?* My body is a sauna.

I have seen her bra before. Hell, I've helped Will put away laundry before.

I've seen her wearing a bathing suit, too, which is basically a bra.

And *fuck*, now my mind is there, and I'm half hard.

I'm losing my mind.

I'm losing my damn mind.

"Bathroom's there," she says, and I realize she's farther ahead of me because I'm standing in place like an idiot. I shake the clouds from my head and jog to catch up. "Her parents' room is here." She touches one of the doors that is shut. "Off limits, obviously. And there's the laundry room, guest room, and this is storage." She raps her knuckles on the last door. "Any questions?"

"Will there be a quiz?" I tease.

That earns me a look of annoyance. "We should get back out there."

"Of course. Can't keep *lover boy* waiting."

"Nope," she quips, and the lack of denial kills me.

"Are you two still…"

"Since this morning?" she asks, stopping in her tracks, her voice deadpan. "Yeah, we're still."

A lump settles in my stomach, and suddenly, I'm mad. And stupid. I'm mad and stupid, and it's a dangerous combination. "So, uh, does Britney like Will?"

"I don't know, why?" Her brows draw together in a perfect line.

"I don't know." I shrug. "Just asking."

"Do *you* like *her*?" she asks, arms folded across her chest. I detect a hint of jealousy in her tone.

Upper hand firmly in place, I give an exaggerated frown with a look that says it's possible. "She's cool."

"Well, she likes Will," she says, her voice pitchy and weird all of the sudden. "So…sorry about your luck."

"Eh, I'm hotter than Will. Guess we'll just have to see who has her attention by the end of the night, won't we?"

Her eyes could melt glass as she stares at me. She doesn't even blink. "Guess so."

I fight the smile on my lips and step around her, making my way into the living room. I should be better than this, but I'm really not. Had I known Will wouldn't care about his friends dating his sister, I'd have...done...something. Probably. I mean, I think I'd... Obviously. Right? She'd... I mean, it would make the most sense, of all of his friends, that she'd be into me. If I was into her, which—we're friends. But like, maybe also—

What is wrong with me? My internal monologue sounds like that show Jenny watches all the time. What is it? *Gossip Girl* or something?

Well, anyway, the point is, I need to fix this before she goes too far with Brendan. Before she falls in love with him.

"Pepsi or Dr. P?" Britney appears with two plastic cups.

"Dr Pepper, obviously," I say, taking the second cup when she holds it out.

"Obviously," she teases.

"Thanks."

She takes a sip of the drink in her hand, looking around. "So, nice tour?"

"Very nice," I tell her. "This is a cool place."

"Thanks. That's right, I forget you guys haven't been here before. Tessa and I come here a lot in the summer with my family, but this place rarely gets used in the fall, so I thought it was the perfect chance to get out here with our girl." She nods her head toward the doorway, where Tessa is lingering, pretending not to listen. "She looks pretty tonight, hmm?"

"She's always pretty." Tessa's eyes find mine, clearly

shocked, and I don't know if it was a mistake to say that. Either way, it proved me right. *She cares.* Even if she likes Brendan, even if she's here with him, she cares what I think. She cares about me. Maybe more than she realizes.

"Got it all set up," Brendan says, clapping his hands just as the music kicks on. A JoJo song plays through the speakers as he walks over to her, pulling her into his arms and planting a kiss on her lips.

I'm going to vomit or kill him.

I'm going to vomit *and* kill him.

The sound of plastic crumpling draws my attention, and I loosen my grip on the cup in my hand before I crush it. When my eyes find Britney, I'd nearly forgotten she was still there. She's staring at me like I'm a science experiment, her eyes gleaming.

Something is definitely up with this girl.

"What's that look?"

"Nothing," she says, her voice ringing with pure glee. "Very interesting, that's all."

"What's interesting?" I scowl.

Before she can respond, Will appears in the room with a bowl of chips. "There's food," he tells me, mouth as full as his hands are.

I don't think I'll ever eat food again. When I look back over at Tessa, Brendan's hand is on her jaw, talking to her so low none of us can hear it.

"Okay." Britney claps her hands together, calling loudly, "I think we should play a game."

"What game?" Tessa asks, pulling away from Brendan to eye her best friend with suspicion.

"Let's see, we've got Truth or Dare, Spin the Bottle, or..." Her eyes light up, and she leaps to her tiptoes. "Seven Minutes in Heaven." She shimmies her shoulders. "Ooh. Yes, that's the one."

"What? My sister is here!" Will argues before the rest of us have time to point out why this is such a bad idea.

"Don't worry." She puts a hand up, crossing the room into the kitchen and returning moments later with a sheet of paper and a plastic cup. "We'll draw names. One boy, one girl. If it's a relative, we'll redraw. Obvs."

"That only leaves you," Will pouts.

Britney looks at him as if he slapped her. "Is there something wrong with me, Will Becker?"

He chuckles and pats her head. "No, Brit. Obviously not. I guess I can kiss you or whatever."

"You'd better say that. You should be so lucky." She huffs, but it's playful. At least, I think it is. "I know where you sleep. If you think I won't put Nair in your shampoo bottle the next time I spend the night at your house, you don't know me at all."

He pulls her into a hug, scrubbing the top of her head with his knuckles. "Shut up. You know you're hot."

She lets out a little *hmph* and goes back to scribbling our names in a line on the page. Then she tears each name out, folds the scraps of paper, and drops them into the cup.

"What if she gets someone besides me?" Brendan asks, gesturing toward Tessa like a caveman. He may as well be grunting. *Her. Mine.*

"It's just a game," Britney says, holding her hand over the top of the cup as she shakes it around. "It's not like you guys are official or anything yet, right?"

Brendan hesitates, running a hand through his hair and looking down at Tessa. "I mean, no. I guess not. Are you okay with this?"

To my surprise, her eyes slip from his momentarily, and it's clearly not intentional when they find mine. I'm not even sure she realizes she's done it. Then she looks at Will. "As long as I don't have to kiss my brother, I guess." She fights against the growing smile on her lips, but so do I because—*holy shit! She didn't say she doesn't want to kiss me.* I'm fire and ice all at once as that realization hits me.

"Don't make me barf," Will says, his mouth full of chips again.

"Could you, like, stop eating for just a second?" Britney asks, her upper lip curled as she digs her hand into the cup, swirling it around. "If I have to kiss you, I swear to God, I'm making you brush your teeth first."

Will leans forward, puckering up and shaking his head back and forth slowly, taunting her. "Come on, babe, you know you want to kiss these cheesy lips."

She squeals and jumps back, pulling the first name

out of the cup. She unfolds the paper slowly, building the tension as her lips curve into a smile, and she scans each of our faces. I feel like I might explode if she doesn't say something right now.

What am I going to do if she says it's him? If Tessa goes into a closet with Brendan? This game is so fucking dumb.

Why would anyone want to pla—

"Tessa's up first," Britney cries, holding up the name so we can all see it.

Tessa's hands come together in front of her, and she bounces up on her toes, not out of excitement but out of nerves.

"And…" Next name. I swear my heart is pounding so loudly I can no longer hear her. My ears burn hot as I watch her read the name, then fold it back up. Her eyes gleam as they flick up to meet mine. "Garrett."

Everything explodes.

CHAPTER THIRTEEN

TESSA — PRESENT DAY

Back at the house, I take another shower, letting the warm water wash away the mess of the day. I'm exhausted and conflicted about staying. The more I dwell on it, I'm finding I'm just as conflicted about leaving.

I want to see Will, of course, and won't leave before he's back in a few days, but I'm also sad about the fact that Mom's alone so much. With Will traveling, Garrett and I are all she has, and it's not fair to expect Garrett to do the most of any of us.

Where does that leave me?

Aside from that, I'm torn about Britney. Whatever happened to her, it's not my business. I left town after graduation for a reason. I don't know her as well as I did anymore, but that doesn't mean I don't love her and want answers and justice for her family.

And then there's the note I found in Mom's room. I

still want to find out who left it and why. There's a chance Garrett is right, of course, and it wasn't anything, but what are the odds?

It's too much of a coincidence, especially if Britney's death is related to the others. And if someone knows what happened back then...

I can't leave without knowing. I have to go back and visit her again. Try to get some answers for Mom's sake, to keep her protected. At least that'll give me some sort of closure. Maybe I can even get Will to go, too. That'll be my goal.

Now out of the shower, I dress in sweatpants and a Gracie Abrams T-shirt, running a comb through my wet hair before heading into the living room. Garrett's there with two bags of takeout waiting on the coffee table.

"I ordered from Domenico's. Thought you might be hungry." He stands there, watching me, waiting to see what I'll say as if he thinks I might be angry.

"Starving, actually." I haven't eaten since breakfast in the car on the way down here. "Thank you."

He holds out two bags. "Meatball or Turkey?"

I purse my lips, knowing he doesn't need to ask, and he smirks, handing me the bag with the meatball sub. "Oh, did you—"

"Yes, I asked for extra pickles and tomatoes, you monster."

"You're amazing." I squeal with delight as I tear into my bag, flopping down on the couch and kicking my feet up onto the table. "Oh my god," I say after my first bite, my mouth still full. "I forgot how much I missed this place."

He drops a napkin in my lap and sits down next to me. "It missed you, too," he says.

"Does that mean *you* missed me?"

"Please." He scoffs, taking a bite of his own sandwich and grinning when I have to dab a smear of marinara sauce from my lips. "I'm counting down until you get the heck out of Dodge."

"Just for that, I'm staying forever." I wiggle my toes. "Get used to it."

He huffs out a breath of laughter through his nose, shaking his head.

"Why do you live here, anyway?" I fish a pickle in danger of falling out of the sub. "With Will, I mean. I didn't ask earlier in all of my shock."

After he swipes his mouth with a napkin, he places his sandwich on the paper in his lap and dusts his hands, finishing chewing before he answers. "Well, I don't know what all he's told you, but you know after college I ended up staying in Nashville for a few years. But then when I decided to come back home during the pandemic, I was looking for a place to buy, and Will had just started with his new company that was supposed to be permanently work from home."

I nod, rolling my eyes at that *little inconvenience*. My brother left his job of three years, a job he liked, for a company that promised him better pay and that it would be fully remote. Once the pandemic restrictions were lifted, they quickly changed their tune, which meant he had to travel to Huntsville during the week to be in an office and do the exact same work he was easily doing from here.

"Anyway," Garrett goes on, "no one was really selling their houses here during that time, so Will said I should just stay with him until things went back to normal." He rolls his eyes. "Whatever that is. And then when he started having to go to Huntsville, I guess it was nice having me here to watch things. And this house is too big for just him, so right now, until one of us decides to retire from the ol' bachelor life, settle down, and have two-point-five kids and a golden retriever named Scout, I guess this is home."

I take another bite, then reach for one of the lemonades he got us. I know he's mostly joking, but I remember a time when Garrett had been certain he'd never have kids. There's no doubt he loves his siblings, but I also understand the frustration with having such a big family at times. I wonder if he's changed his mind about kids or if that's still the plan.

"Well, that makes sense." I pause, my mind looming over what he said. "Speaking of retiring from bachelor life, any updates on that front? For Will, mostly. But, you can tell me about yourself too, if you really want to."

He smirks. "You trying to ask if I'm single, Tessa Becker?"

"Please. What monster would want to tie you down?"

With a growl, he leans forward and takes a bite of my sandwich without warning, smirking at me.

I blink down at my food and then up at him. "You did not just do that."

Wiping his mouth, he grins. "Did too. Better watch that smart mouth before I eat something else."

The air in the room shifts, taking me with it. My face flames with what he's just said, my ears ringing. "What?"

"Dessert." He nods toward the bag, then winks. "What'd you think I meant?"

I roll my eyes and return to my sandwich, my body alight with something electric. He's always been able to do that to me, and I hate it. But only because I love it so much.

"Anyway, what about you? Will said you haven't dated anyone in a while."

"You keeping tabs on me?"

He shrugs without comment.

"I date, but not seriously. Guess I was always just waiting for Mark Summers to come sweep me off my feet."

With a snort, he wads up a napkin and tosses it at me. "You're such a brat."

"Am not." I stick out my tongue. "Hey, I'm thinking about going to visit Mom again tomorrow. I know you have to work or whatever, but would you want to come with me when you get home?"

"I'm happy to."

"You don't have to if it's weird or if you have plans or anything."

"Nope. I said I'm happy to, Little Bit."

I take the last bite of my sandwich and crumple the paper, dropping it into the bag before I stand up, step over his legs where they're propped up on the table, then drop down over him, straddling his lap.

He freezes, his sandwich just in front of his mouth. With a swallow loud enough I can hear it, his Adam's apple bobs.

"I told you," I say, leaning in toward him slowly. Without warning, I take a bite off the back of his sandwich. His eyes flick to my mouth, then back up to my eyes with a questioning stare. "To stop calling me Little Bit." I lick a bit of mayo off my lip, and he drops his sandwich, scooting it away from him until there's nothing between us.

"Oh yeah? What are you going to do about it?"

I bounce on his legs playfully. "Prove I'm not so little anymore."

His hand goes to my hip, stilling me with a not-so-playful look in his eyes. "You'll always be little to me, Tessa Claire."

"I'm practically crushing you, Garrett *Daniel*."

"You couldn't crush me if you tried." He smirks, holding me too tightly. "But I'd welcome the challenge."

103

His fingers flex on my hip, and I swear I feel something underneath me. *Him.*

I feel him underneath me, where he wasn't before. My cheeks flush hot, but I force a laugh, though it sounds more nervous than gleeful. "God, you're such a pig."

He shakes his head. "Don't be a chicken."

"What would make me a chicken, exactly?"

"You started this." He lifts his other hand to my side, sliding his palm slowly down to my hip. "Not me. Here I was being a perfect gentleman."

"You've never been a perfect gentleman a day in your life."

"Trust me, I have."

"Well, I never asked you to be."

"You didn't have to ask. You're…Will's sister."

Despite feeling as if I were floating just moments ago, his words send me crashing to the ground and into our sobering reality. "His sister." I nod. "Your friend. Right. Yep, you've made that very clear."

"Tessa…"

The warmth I felt blooming in my chest moments ago dissipates in seconds, and I stand. "Thanks for dinner."

He lifts his hand and takes my fingers, but I pull them back. "You don't have to go."

"I know." His eyes are sad, but he doesn't follow me as I make my way across the room. "But I really should get some sleep. I'll see you in the morning, okay?" And then, because it's him and because I really don't want to leave things awkward and uncomfortable, I add, "By the way, now that I've had both, my sandwich was *way* better."

He tosses his head back against the couch with a silent laugh, and we're back to normal. Just like that.

CHAPTER FOURTEEN

GARRETT — PRESENT DAY

Holy fuck.

I thought we'd left all of that in the past. I thought she'd moved on, thought I'd moved on, but what was that? Why did she…

Why did I…

What the fuck was that?

I stand, staring toward the hallway, prepared to bang on the door and demand that we talk this out or…sort things out another way.

Preferably without clothes on.

In her bed. My mouth on her…

Jesus, I need help.

How am I supposed to spend the next few days in this house alone with her? There is still so much between us that we've never resolved, and I'm ready to resolve it now.

Except…

My eyes fall to my phone, where there's a text from hours ago waiting from Will. I pick it up and call him, eager for a distraction and a moment to cool down.

"Yeah?" he asks, voice groggy like he's been asleep.

"We've got a problem."

"What's that?" He sounds more awake now.

"Tessa and I went to visit your mom today. How long's it been since you went by there?"

"Come on, dude, don't start with that right now. It's been a long day and—"

"It's not that." I stand up and move into the kitchen, lowering my voice. "Someone else had visited her and left a note."

"What kind of note? For us?"

"No. Well, I don't know. It was just this little torn slip of paper that said 'Murderer.'"

He's quiet, but I know he understands the gravity of what I'm telling him.

"Tessa took it, so there's no chance the cops will get it, but," I pause, heaving a breath before I say the sentence I hoped to never utter, "do you think it could be about…"

"Yeah." His voice is dry and emotionless. "Yeah, I do."

CHAPTER FIFTEEN

TESSA — AGE 17

"Garrett," Britney repeats, looking back over her shoulder at me. She wads the paper up without showing us, and I know exactly why she does because I saw my brother's name on that slip, not Garrett's.

I should say something. Not that I want it to be Will, obviously, but in the name of fairness, I should make her redraw, right? My eyes linger between the boys, trying to think as Britney zips down the hall to the storage closet between her parents' bedroom and the laundry room.

"Right this way," she sings, holding out a hand, and I refuse to look at Will. The awkwardness of this moment—my brother watching me inch toward the hallway, knowing what I'm about to do—is finally settling in.

I could stop all of this right now, have a chance to be with the guy I came with, but…when I find Garrett's eyes looking at me, I know this is a chance I might not get again.

A chance to kiss him without worrying about what he'll think or what Will might think. And he seems into it anyway. Or at least not repulsed by the idea.

Everyone is silent as they watch the two of us meet near the entrance to the hall, Garrett's eyes on me. "Are you sure about this?"

Britney rushes back. "Come on, you two."

"It's just a stupid game," I say with a sigh. "And if we don't do it, she'll just find an equally stupid game to make us play."

"That's right," Britney sings again, tapping me on the nose with her finger. She takes my arm and pulls me down the hall. "Now, we'll start the clock for seven minutes when I get back in the living room. Have fun."

I step into the closet first, followed by Garrett. The room is spacious, as far as closets go, and filled mostly with towels and bed sheets rather than cleaning supplies, which they keep under the sink. As far as places to spend seven minutes, it's not the worst.

It smells of laundry detergent and stale air, in that order. When Britney shuts the door, I hear her footsteps fading as she hurries away.

"Should we turn on the light?" Garrett asks, and to my surprise, his voice is shaking.

"Why? Are you afraid of the dark?" I tease.

He huffs a shaky breath. "You know we don't have to do anything if you don't want to, right?"

"Obviously." My heart sinks with what feels like rejection.

"I'm sorry I'm not Brendan."

"Are you?" I lift my face to look in the direction of where he's standing, though I can only see a vague outline of him in the darkness as my eyes adjust.

"Are *you?*" he challenges.

"I asked you first."

"Fine. No. I'm not sorry it's me in here with you and not him. If you want to know the truth, there it is."

It's impossible he just said that, isn't it? Unless he just didn't want me in here with Brendan because he doesn't want me doing anything at all. I'm starting to think he's more overprotective than Will *and* Mom. "But you...don't want to do anything."

"I never said that."

My fingers are ice cold, and I wring them together in my palms. "You said we don't have to."

"Unless you want to."

"Do *you* want to?"

"Do you?"

I press my lips together, thinking. "I don't know. I mean, it's a game. It's just a game, right? And you're just a guy."

"And you're just a girl," he agrees.

"And it would just be a kiss."

The breath he releases is loud, like he's been holding it in for a while. "Do you want me to kiss you, Tessa?"

"Are you just going to tease me about it with Will later? Say I don't know what I'm doing, or I have chip breath or something?"

His hands come to my sides, holding me so gently it's like a whisper against my skin. "I wouldn't do that."

I know it. Despite the question, I know he wouldn't. "Okay."

"Okay?" His fingers flex against my skin, and I can see him a bit better now. "Okay what?"

"Okay, we probably just have a few more minutes, so we should get this over with."

"What a ringing endorsement. Is that how you woo all the guys?"

"Just the ones I like."

He steps closer until I can feel his chest against mine, each rise and fall of his breath pushing us closer together. "I meant what I said earlier. And I know you heard me."

"What are you talking about?"

"You look pretty tonight. You always do."

I don't know what to do with my hands—this is Garrett we're talking about—but I can't keep holding them in between us, so I put them on his shoulders like we're about to slow dance. "Are you nervous?"

"Kind of," he admits. "I, um, I haven't, I just want you to know I haven't, I mean, I don't, like, I haven't done this with a ton of girls, you know? I don't want you to think it doesn't mean anything."

"Seven minutes in heaven?"

His hand lifts to my face, thumb caressing my cheekbone. "Kissing you."

"You haven't kissed me yet."

"I'm aware."

"Why haven't you kissed me yet?"

"Have you…kissed a lot of guys?"

"You're seriously asking me that right now?"

He laughs, resting his forehead against mine.

"No," I answer. "I've only kissed one other person besides Brendan."

He nods against my skin. "Okay. Are you ready?"

"Been here waiting."

"Can you not make me laugh right now?"

"What would you rather me do?"

"I have a few ideas."

He's either too nervous or worried I'm too nervous, but if one of us doesn't act, we're going to run out of time. I push up against him, shoving him harder than I meant to, and his back hits the wall of shelves. He groans and lurches forward as several quilts fall from their places, knocking us to the ground. Outside, I hear Britney squeal while Will teases, "Don't forget you're not alone if Jesus is in there."

We're both laughing from the impact and looking around at the damage when I realize Garrett is on top of me now, his body balanced over mine. Slowly, his head turns toward me, and we're face to face, just inches apart. I can feel his warm breath on my lips. The rest of my body tingles with the same sensation I get when my arm falls asleep. "Are you okay?" he whispers, but he's not moving.

"I didn't mean to shove you that hard." I'm whispering, too, but I don't know why. We're safe in here, in our cocoon. The world out there doesn't exist. Consequences. Awkwardness. Dealing with our feelings. For now, everything can wait. All that exists in this moment is him and me and the racing of our hearts.

"I'm not complaining." Slowly, ever so slowly, his arms bend and he lowers himself closer to me, stopping only when his nose is brushing mine. "I'm going to kiss you now before I chicken out."

"I knew you were afraid of the dark."

"Shut up." He eases his body weight down on top of mine, silencing every single joke in my head as his hand brushes hair from my face, his thumb smoothing over my cheek. I feel his touch all the way down to my toes.

This is actually about to happen.

I'm going to kiss Garrett Campbell.

I close my eyes, despite the darkness, and hold my breath as I feel his lips inch forward slowly, too slowly. They brush mine, feather light and not nearly enough. My heart is racing so fast my chest is going to explode and then—*light.*

"Time's up!" The door swings open, and our cocoon evaporates.

CHAPTER SIXTEEN

GARRETT — AGE 18

I can't sleep.

I can't fucking breathe, let alone sleep. How am I supposed to sleep after what just happened? It was real, and she was real, and I was…

I shake the thoughts out of my head, angry with myself for reasons I don't totally understand. Will thinks it's funny more than anything, but he has asked for absolutely no details so I can't talk it over with him.

Not that I would want to, I guess.

Yet another con in the column for choosing to have feelings for my best friend's little sister.

Choosing doesn't feel like the right word for this. The feelings just *are.* They exist with or without my consent to them being here. Besides, is that what this is? Like, legit feelings? Do I want to *date* her?

I've never wanted to talk to my own little sister this much in my life. Jenny would know what to do. Other than some initial awkwardness with Brendan where nobody seemed to know if they were still a thing, and none of us addressed it, the rest of the party went off without a hitch. After we left the closet, Britney decided she didn't want to play the game after all, which didn't actually fool any of us, so we broke out a few board games, and Will and I kicked their butts at each and every one.

I've never had such an uneventful Friday night in my life.

But I've also never had a better one.

I scrub my hand over my face. If this is the best night of my life, and I didn't even get to kiss her, what would *more* feel like? Would I survive it?

I roll over on the air mattress, bumping into Will, who groans and swats me. "Just go talk to her, bro. You're keeping the neighbors awake with all that loud pining."

"I am not pining." I glare at him.

"Dude." He props his head up on his palm. "You're pining so hard you're a tree."

"You're an idiot."

He chuckles. "Just go talk to her."

"You realize you're officially the worst big brother ever, right? You're supposed to pummel me and say we can never be friends again for even looking at her."

He studies me, going serious. "Is that what you think?"

"It's what I know. If anyone ever looked at Jenny—"

"Well, people *do* look," he says simply. "And they will." He quirks a brow.

I slam a hand into his shoulder. "She's fifteen, you asshole."

"Hey, easy." His hands go up in surrender, then he uses one to rub the place I hit him. "I'm not saying *I* look, obviously. I'm not a total creep. I'm just saying it's going to happen." He's quiet for a moment. "And the way I see it, if I can't always be around to protect her, the best thing I can do is make sure I fully trust the man who is. If I didn't trust you to be with my sister, I wouldn't want you as a friend."

His words shock me, both because of what he's said and because of how serious he is when he says them. "Thanks, man." I clear my throat, the moment too heavy and weird. "I don't even know if she likes me like that. It was just a game."

He flops onto his back, staring up at the ceiling. "Maybe she doesn't."

Ice forms around my organs. "You think?"

"She doesn't really talk to me about that sort of thing, but there's only one way to find out."

"Just ask her?" Even as I suggest it, I'm feeling and sounding equally skeptical. "Maybe it's weird. I should just pretend it didn't happen."

He groans, covering his face. "So we can continue to not sleep? I need my beauty sleep, Garrett. I don't know if you're aware, but your mom doesn't like me for my brains."

"Last I checked, she doesn't like you at all."

"That's not what she was saying last night."

I jab an elbow at him, and he dodges, laughing. "Kidding, kidding." He pauses, then adds, "It was two nights ago."

I shake my head against the pillow, then swallow, the moment going serious. "What if I ruin everything?"

He's quiet for a long time, so long I think he might've fallen asleep. I turn my head to look his way and see him staring at the ceiling, too, deep in thought. "Well, then," he says eventually, "I guess it's been nice knowing you."

I scowl and shove him, nearly knocking him off the air mattress. "Asshole."

"You're not going to ruin everything," he says with a dry huff. "If anything, you'll just make things super awkward for, like, a week or two, and then we can all laugh about that one time you sort of fell in love with my sister."

Love. That word hangs in the air between us, heavy and real. So real it feels impossible.

"Now," he says, "go find her and tell her you've pissed the bed or something and need to talk to her. Then drag her out onto the porch and confess your love, but for the love of God, do it quietly so I can go to sleep." With that, he flops over. "Oh, and if Brit needs some company while Tessa's gone, tell her she knows where to find me."

I bound off the air mattress with extra force,

causing him to plunge toward the ground. He yelps, then pulls the covers up over him, still chuckling as I ease down the hall, stopping and backtracking six or seven times, practicing what I'm going to say like I'm fucking Romeo in the school play.

This is so stupid.

It's Tessa.

It's just Tessa.

I can do this. No big deal.

When I reach the door where the girls are sleeping, double-checking that it's not the door to the guest room where Brendan stayed, I drop my hands to my sides, shaking them out with a long, slow breath.

Here goes fucking...everything.

I knock softly before whispering her name. "Tessa?"

When she doesn't answer, I pull my phone out of my pocket and send her a text.

> Can we talk?

Inside the room, her phone chimes, but I get no response. Maybe she's asleep, apparently much more at peace with this whole situation than I am.

Carefully, I ease the door open. "Tessa?"

As my eyes adjust, I can see their bed, but my heart plummets when I realize neither girl is in it. The comforter is thrown aside, and both pillows still have indentations from their heads, but they are nowhere to be found. I step farther into the room, spinning to look behind me. Their phones are charging with cords against the wall, but they're just...gone.

What if she's in Brendan's room? It doesn't answer where Britney is, but—

I dart out into the hall, seeing red as I move in a haze. When I spot a door down the hallway to my left. I freeze.

What the...

Moonlight shines in through the storm door from outside the back doorway of the house. I step closer. It's standing wide open, and it definitely wasn't before.

I would've noticed.

The images of Amber Allen's memorial flash into my head, her photo suddenly replaced with Tessa's face. Without a single thought, I race out the door, shoeless and shirtless, in a rush to get to her.

The night is quiet, the air cold and foggy. It's a perfect night for whatever horror movie I'm apparently about to live out.

Where did you go? I scan the surroundings, making my way across the wooden deck and down the stairs. My socks are soaking wet and muddy as I stomp down the yard. Britney's car is still here, parked in front of Brendan's, which is in front of ours.

So they either didn't leave, or they didn't leave alone.

I'm about to dash back inside and get Will's help when a sound shoots through the air. I freeze, every hair on my body standing at attention.

I hold my breath, trying to listen.

Several seconds pass before I hear it again, but when I do, it's unmistakable. The sound of Tessa's laugh sends warmth through my veins, and I rush toward it.

She's okay.

She's okay.

She's...naked?

"What the hell do you think you're doing?" I demand, sounding more like my father than I ever have as I stalk toward the lake. The shore is covered in clothes, discarded here and there haphazardly, and Tessa and Britney are swimming in the murky water, apparently naked.

Both girls squeal and cover themselves, though I can't see anything except bare shoulders.

"What are *you* doing?" Tessa whisper-screams. "Go back inside."

"Like hell. Do you have any idea what time it is? It's not safe. The town has a curfew for a reason."

"There's no one out here," Britney says. "Relax, *Dad*."

"There's a murderer running around our town, and you guys are out here skinny dipping on a dark and foggy night. Have you two seen, like, any horror movie ever?" I wave a hand toward the house. "Why didn't you tell us you were sneaking out of the house, so we could've at least kept an eye on things?"

"Because you would've spied on us or tried to join us, and we didn't want either," Tessa says. "We're fine."

I cross my arms. "It's freezing. You're going to get sick."

She splashes water in my direction. "We're fine. Go away."

"Get out of that water before I come in there and make you come out."

"That's what you want to do anyway, isn't it?" Britney taunts. "Maybe I should just leave you two alone."

"No!" Tessa cries.

I bite down on my cheek so hard it hurts. "Are you scared of me, Tessa?"

"No," she says, but her voice quivers. It's not for the reason it seems, though, and we both know it. She's not scared I'll hurt her. She knows I'd sooner die. She's... she's scared of what might happen if we're alone. If we'd had a few more minutes in that closet.

"Get out of the water before I come and get you."

"You're not the boss of me."

"You're acting like a child."

"You're acting like a parent."

Britney laughs. "Okay, okay. Turn around, and I'll get dressed and go inside, and then you two can work this out however you see fit."

I do as I'm told, closing my eyes as I hear splashing in the water and then squishy footsteps behind me. There are a few hurried breaths, and then Britney sighs right behind me. "Okay, it's safe."

I turn back around to find Britney dressed. She

wrings water out of her hair before heading for the house. "Alright, you two. Play nice, you hear me?"

Tessa's stubborn ass is still in the water. She crosses her arms and sticks out her tongue at me. "Party pooper."

"I'm not being a party pooper. It's not safe."

"We were perfectly fine until you came along."

I click my tongue. "I disagree. It's freezing. You're probably going to get pneumonia. Come on. Get out of the water."

"Oh my god." She lifts defiant fists and slams them into the water. "Is this what it's going to be like now?"

"What?"

Behind me, I hear Britney shut the door to the house, but I barely register it. All I can focus on is the fact that Tessa is just feet away from me and completely naked.

I try to think of something else. Anything else.

Sweet potatoes. Spongebob. Books. Socks. Mr. Feffernan. Gym class. Toe rings. Toes in general. That one time I fell on stage during the class Christmas pageant in front of the whole school.

"We kissed, and now you think you can control me?" Tessa has moved closer, so now I can see just a little bit more of her and the view is intoxicating. I can't even pretend to look away.

"I'm not trying to control you," I balk, though to be fair, I guess I am. "Or if I am, it's because you scared the shit out of me. Whoever killed Amber Allen and her mom is still out there. The parents are scared. The police are scared. When I realized you were missing, I just…" I puff out a breath. "Panicked. You're so stubborn, it drives me mad sometimes."

"Maybe that's why I do it." She's fighting a smile, but I see it in her eyes.

"Yeah, I kind of thought so." I wrinkle my brow, waving a hand at her. "And, for the record, we didn't kiss."

She purses her lips. "That's what you're thinking about right now? God, you're such a guy."

If you had any idea what I'm thinking about right now… "I'm just saying. What happened in the closet was a kiss I'd give my grandmother, and even that was interrupted."

"Whatever, Garrett. The point is that I'm not a child. I'm not your little sister. You can't boss me around."

"I can, and I will if it means keeping you safe. Now I'm going to turn around, and you're going to get dressed so we can go back in the house and get warm."

"Fine. Go inside. I'll meet you in there when I'm good and ready."

"Like hell."

"Then I guess you're going to have to come and get me."

I lock my jaw. If I get in that water, we both know what's going to happen. "Is that what you want?"

"No. I wanted to swim with my friend. But since you ran her off, I guess you'll have to do."

"If I get in that water, there won't be any swimming." My throat is as dry and scratchy as sandpaper. "I'm going to haul you out of there and take you inside."

"And then what?" She stares up at me with big doe eyes, and I can't believe this is actually happening.

I swallow, looking above her head. "Tessa."

She takes another step closer, and the water is barely covering her breasts. She's shivering, too. The heat in me instantly shifts, offering a semblance of relief. "You're cold."

"I'm fine." I know she's trying to fight it, but she can't. It's fifty degrees out here, and I know that water is probably colder. Why won't she just admit it?

I'm done. I march into the water, and it's freezing. Somehow colder than I imagined. It's waist deep before I reach her, and I'm pure ice when I stop in front of her. "Out of the water. Last warning."

She blinks.

I bend down, wrapping my arms around her waist and hauling her out of the water. I don't look—much— but the feeling is enough. The sensation of her against me sends firecrackers through my brain, every nerve in my body on high alert. I don't think I even take a breath until we reach the shore.

To my surprise, she looks pleased. We're face to face, nothing but my soaking-wet clothes between us, and this girl doesn't look scared at all. I guess I'm terrified enough for the two of us.

"Did you peek?" she whispers, teeth pressing into her bottom lip.

I clear my throat, but my voice still comes out as a croak. "I'm really trying to be a good guy here."

She shrugs one shoulder. "Since when?"

Carefully, I ease her down onto the ground. Her feet squish in the mud beneath us. "Get dressed, okay?" Even as I say it, I don't let her go. My hands are still around her waist, still holding her close as she shivers against me. She twists her fingers up into my hair, staring right back. It's like she's begging me to look, and at this point, how could I not? "You're going to catch a cold."

"Only because you insisted on bringing me out of the water. I was perfectly adjusted to it."

I press my lips together, shaking my head. "You're impossible, you know that?"

"So I've heard."

"Now, clothes. Please. And if you want to go swimming, go during the day, okay? Preferably in summer. And, at the very least, let someone know you'll be out here, okay? If not me, then Will. At least until they catch the killer."

She grabs her clothes, thankfully, pulling on her sweatpants. I keep my eyes on the sky, though I don't turn away. "Why? Why does it matter to you so much?"

I can't help looking at her then, but it's her eyes I

find as she pulls a shirt over her head. *What a silly question.* "Because...you're you."

"I'm me," she repeats, nodding as she gathers her hair in her hands and squeezes the water out. "Your friend."

"My friend," I say slowly. This feels like a trap, and suddenly, all the courage I'd summoned moments ago feels like a distant memory. "Among other things."

"Like?"

"You're...you know what you are."

"I'm your best friend's little sister," she says slowly. "That's what I know." She pauses. "Unless you tell me differently."

"Do you...want me to tell you differently?"

"I want you to do whatever you want." She blinks up at me, waiting.

"I—"

"Yo!" Will's voice cuts through the night, and I don't know whether to hate him or thank him. "Get inside."

Something's wrong.

"Give us a minute, Will," Tessa begs.

He rounds the house, barefoot and holding his phone to his ear. "It's Mom, Tessa. Someone else died. Emily." Even in the darkness, I know he's looking at me as he says her name. "Emily Gray was just found dead."

CHAPTER SEVENTEEN

TESSA — PRESENT DAY

The next day, I lie in bed for far too long trying to convince myself last night never happened. Staying in this house and in this town is dangerous, and not just because of the killer who may or may not be on the loose. Staying here with Garrett feels like scraping open an old wound with my fingernails and digging deep within it, pulling out my insides and laying them on the table for examination.

I thought we were over this. I thought everything that happened between us was in the past, and we were evolved adults who had moved on, but after last night, I don't know where my head is.

I can't explain what happened to me other than to say I had a momentary lapse of sanity. All I know is that I'm relieved I left when I did, before things went too far.

Garrett is already at work, so I can dwell on it in

silence while I have my morning coffee and create a plan for the day. I still don't have my car back, though I need to check on it soon. Without a car, I can't visit Mom yet, but Britney's parents' house is within walking distance of Will's, so that's where I'll go.

When I arrive, the house is just like I remember it. A well-preserved tudor with a cobblestone circle drive and wrought-iron fence. There are a few people standing outside, and at first, I assume it must be Britney's parents, but I soon realize I'm wrong. Of course I'm wrong.

The weight of that is agonizing—the ripping away of a reality in such a brutal manner I know it will never exist in my mind again. There was *before*, when I knew they were gone but hadn't had to experience their absence, and *now*, when it's front and center and unescapable.

Britney's parents died a few years ago within months of each other. In a cruel twist of fate, cancer took them both just before they could meet their first grandchild.

Nearly to the house, I spot the cop car parked next to the overgrown shrub in the center of the driveway. From this distance it's easy to recognize that the woman talking to the officer is Kristy. Her sunshine hair and delicate features mean she looks so much like Britney, but they were always inches apart in height.

At once, whether it's because I've caught their

attention or inadvertently made a sound, both the officer and Kristy turn their heads toward me.

It takes a second for recognition to register on Kristy's face, but eventually it does. "Oh my gosh!" She rushes over to open the gate, and I can see now there are tears staining her cheeks. "It's like you can sense when I need you most." She throws both arms around my shoulders, collapsing into our hug. When she pulls back, she dries her eyes, sniffling. "What are you doing here?"

"I was coming to talk to you, actually," I say, looking up at the officer. When I do, my heart skitters to a stop. I hadn't recognized him from afar, but now, up close, it's obvious. Even though it has been a few years since I last saw him, it couldn't be anyone else.

"Sorry, we're just finishing up." Kristy waves toward him, noticing me staring. "Tessa, do you know—"

"Brendan." I nod, jaw slack.

He looks equally shocked to see me, but eventually he shakes his head as if to clear the fog and steps forward, outstretching his arm for a hug. "Tessa. Wow. I heard you were back in town."

I lean into his hug briefly. "Yeah. For the funeral."

"Right." He folds his hands in front of him, looking back up at the house. "It's awful. Britney was... It isn't right. She was one of the good ones."

"Have you got any leads?" I ask, probably overstepping, but it's hard to feel the boundary with Brendan when we were once a bit more than intertwined.

"We're following up on some things." He gives me a wary look, then bounces his gaze to Kristy. "I'll leave you two so you can talk." He's hesitant. "If you need anything…"

"I'll call," Kristy agrees. "Yeah, of course. Thanks again, Brendan."

With that, he takes a step back, one hand in the air. "You guys be safe, okay? It was good to see you, Tessa."

"You too." He's grown up well. Somehow, as he matured, he's even more handsome than before. There's a sad sort of nostalgia between us now. Not necessarily regret, but wonder. Did I make the right choice back then? Was there even a choice to make?

When he's gone, Kristy lowers her voice. "So you said you were coming to talk to me? Is everything okay?"

"Yeah. Er, well, as okay as it can be. Nothing new is wrong anyway." She visibly relaxes. "I just wanted to check in on you and see if there's anything I can do." I want to hug her again, to tell her this is unfathomable, that Britney deserved the very best investigation, and I'm going to do all I can to make it happen.

But none of that will help.

"That's sweet of you. Thank you." She sniffles, looking down. "I'm staying here for a few days to help Justin with the girls, but I'm not sure I'm any help. I kind of feel like it's me who died, you know? Is that awful to say? I don't…" Pausing, she dabs her eyes again and sucks in a ragged, shaky breath. "I don't know how to go on without her. I don't know who I am without her. I need my sister. My nieces need their mother. I'm not enough for them. I can't be. I can't fix this." Tears stream down her cheeks as she sniffles and looks away, her chin quivering.

I don't know what to say or do, but I have to do something for Britney's sake. Guilt gnaws at my stomach over the thought of her daughters. I should know them. I should be their aunt, too, like we always planned. Instead, I've only seen pictures.

"They're lucky to have you." I touch her arm gently. "You're the only one left who can tell them all the crazy stories about Britney as a kid. Like all the times we tried to build Six Flags parks in your backyard by, like, attaching kiddie pools to lawn mowers and asking your dad to pull us around."

Kristy laughs through her tears. "And then using that same pool to bob for apples."

"Exactly." I twist my mouth. "Brit lives on through you. She would want you to be okay. Those girls need you to be okay, you know?"

She's still drying her tears when she says, "I meant what I said to you at the funeral. She always loved you. She was so proud of you for getting out and paving your own path."

"I should've come back more," I whisper, tears blurring my vision without warning. "I should've called."

"You had a life to live, too." Now she's the one comforting me. "And so did she." She smiles through her tears. "She had a really good life." She draws in a deep breath, drying her eyes with the backs of her hands. "Do you, uh, do you want to come inside?"

"Oh." I don't know if I can handle it, but I nod anyway. "Yeah, okay. Sure." Dread swells in the pit of my stomach like those gel beads in a vase of water as she leads me into a house that used to be as familiar as my own. The scent hits me all at once. It's nothing I could ever describe—soap and warmth and love and happiness—but it's been here all my life, as tangible as the pictures on the walls. A piece of this house as much as the roof is.

Tears spill over onto my cheeks as I study the pictures of Britney's life on the walls. Her childhood. Her motherhood. It's not fair. None of this is fair. The fact that we grew apart, and I never tried to fix it, the fact that I'll never have a chance to tell her how much I love her. The fact that she's gone.

Kristy leads me through the entryway and into the small sitting room where Britney practiced piano taught by Justin's mom from next door when we were kids. I can't help smiling remembering how much she used to complain about it afterward.

She was never the type to sit still long for anything, and Mrs. Davis tried her hardest to work with that, but the hobby was doomed from the start.

Together, we sit on the couches opposite each other. She grabs a tissue from the box and dabs her eyes. "You'll have to ignore me. I don't think I've stopped crying since we found out she was gone."

I wave away her concern. "Don't be silly. Of course you haven't."

"It's just not fair." She presses her lips together, chin quivering as tears overflow down her cheeks. It's uncanny, their resemblance, and I find myself missing Britney more the longer I'm here. The house is too heavy, too full of memories. I don't know how she can stand to be here. She dabs her eyes.

"Can I ask what you think happened?" I prompt, leaning forward over my legs. "And feel free to tell me to mind my own business if you don't want to talk about it."

She sniffles, drying under her nose and grabbing a new tissue. "I don't mind talking about her. Already, no one really wants to. It's too hard, even for me, but I don't...I don't want to stop talking about her because it hurts. It shouldn't be easy."

"No," I agree, turning my attention to the rug under my feet. I wish it were as simple as asking these walls what happened. The fact that her last moments were here, that a home I once considered a fortress of warmth and safety, and where we ate chocolate-covered popcorn by the fire while we watched *Gossip Girl* and cheesy Hallmark movies, is now the place where something precious was stolen from us all. Thinking of Britney here, terrified and alone, hurt—it's a pain like no other. She's right. None of this is easy, because it shouldn't be. The pain is the price we pay for getting to know and love her.

"No one's really asked me what I think," Kristy says finally, breaking the silence. "They all think I'm too stupid or emotional to know anything."

I wait, letting her process her thoughts aloud.

"But I knew my sister. She was my best friend. She was my cheerleader and the person I went to for advice." She drops her head forward, staring into her lap. "You know how she was."

"I do." She was everything. Britney was *everything*.

"She was happy," Kristy says. "The cops are looking at Justin, but it wasn't him. They were happy." Her tone is so matter-of-fact it's abrasive.

From what I remember of Justin, I can't see him ever hurting anyone. One of the last times I saw her was when I came home to be in their wedding, and I still remember the way he doted on her.

It's not lost on me, though, that secrets often lurk behind closed doors. I squint, remembering what Garrett told me about the night Britney was killed. "I thought he was out of town when it happened."

She nods. If she's shocked I know that, she doesn't show it. In a town this small, we're all used to everyone knowing the tiniest of details about each of our lives. There are no true secrets here, not for long.

"Yeah, he was, but the police can't verify his alibi because he was driving alone. And I realize that sounds so sketchy, but Britney and Justin were good, you know? I just don't believe he could've hurt her. She would've told me if things weren't good." Pausing, she leans forward over her legs, clasping her hands together on her thighs. "And everyone loved her. Everyone at the school, everyone in town. She was always trying to help people. They looked into parents in her classroom and families that went to dance with her girls, then they looked into Justin and his family, and me, of course, because clearly, I'm capable of evil like this." She scoffs through her tears, which only seem to be getting more inconsolable. "And they said maybe she was having an affair, but when they couldn't prove that, it was back to square one, which is nowhere. And then they started saying maybe she'd done it herself, and...and..." She's sobbing too hard to finish the thought, covering her mouth with her hand. I move to sit next to her, pulling her over onto my shoulder and rocking us back and forth.

"It's going to be okay." I want to say it's impossible that she could ever do this, but we both understand that I don't know Britney anymore. Even if I once knew her better than anyone in the world.

Eventually, Kristy pulls back, sniffling as she says, "I don't know if it is. I don't even know if I'm allowed to tell you this, but Brendan was here earlier because he had a search warrant for the house. They were looking for any signs that either Britney or Justin had been having an affair."

"And did they find anything?" I ask when she pauses.

"Well… They…" She drops her head into her hands, sobbing.

"Shhh…" I soothe. "What is it?"

She aggressively rubs her eyes, like she's frustrated with herself. "Do you remember Cassidy Cole's death?"

The question catches me so off guard it takes several seconds to process it. "Of course." She was the third girl. Both she and her mom were killed on the same day, just like Amber Allen. Unlike Amber, Cassidy and Mrs. Cole were the first and only ones who were killed in different locations. Amber and Emily were both with their moms when they died.

"I don't know if you'll remember, but there was a necklace and bracelet that both went missing the night they died. Some big thing. I remember my parents talking about it."

"Right." I remember the robberies with startling clarity, but I can't admit it to Kristy.

She sniffs and meets my eyes. "The police looked everywhere for the necklace because her dad swore it was a robbery gone wrong. But Cassidy wasn't at home when she died, so it never made sense. And they never found the necklace."

I remember some people thought she'd taken it with her the night she died. Along with… "They found the matching bracelet, right? It went missing too."

"Yeah." Her blue eyes search mine, and her mouth

drops open, but at first she seems unable to speak. Finally, she utters, "Britney didn't do it, Tessa. I swear to you she didn't—"

"What are you talking about?" I put my hands on her shoulders, trying to understand.

She massages the space along her jawline and under her ear slowly. "They, well, the police, they found the necklace here. When they were searching the house just now, Cassidy's necklace was in with Britney's things. And they were asking me questions. I think...I just, I got the impression they believe she had something to do with the murders."

CHAPTER EIGHTEEN

GARRETT — PRESENT DAY

When I get home from work, I half expect Tessa to have packed her bags and disappeared, leaving me behind again.

Instead, I find her pacing in the living room, phone to her ear. "Well, can you please check the security footage? It's very important— No, I understand that, but what I'm saying is— I'm not accusing you of anything, sir. I just need to know who was visiting her." She pauses, catching sight of me. "It's for her safety. I mean, my brother is her medical POA because he's the oldest child, but he's not here right now. I don't even need to know anything about her medical care, though. I just need to know who visited her yesterday. One of your nurses said it was a woman, but she couldn't remember anything else about her. I don't understand why it's so complicated." She sighs loudly, not hiding her frustration. "No, I guess that was it. I just hope you realize we have other options for her care, and I'm happy to take her somewhere else if I feel like she's not safe there." With that, she pulls the phone away from her ear and ends the call, releasing an exasperated groan.

"Everything okay?"

"If by everything, you mean nothing, sure." She flops down on the couch. "How quickly can you be ready to go?"

"I just need to change." I gesture toward my slacks and polo.

"Okay, cool." She's not really listening, I know. She's in her own world, thoughts swirling.

In my room, I change into jeans and a sweatshirt before we head to the nursing home. Once there, Tessa leads the way straight to Frannie's room. This time, there are no nurses around to usher us inside, so Tessa knocks gently before opening the door.

"Momma?" She eases her head inside the room. "Momma, it's me. It's Tessa." Pushing the door open the rest of the way, she enters and crosses through the kitchen. Frannie is lying in bed, and at first, I think she's asleep, but once I'm closer I can see that her eyes are open. Tessa sits down on the edge of her bed and rubs her mother's leg.

"I told you we'd be back soon." She kicks her feet, swinging them slowly. "We went to Britney's funeral yesterday. I wish you could've been there. Will should be back soon, and I'll try my best to get him to visit you." Sliding her hand up, she takes her mom's hand. "I wish you could tell me who's been visiting you, Mom. I wish there was a way you could talk to me and tell me who it was. Someone left that note for you. Were they...were they threatening you? Or warning you, maybe?"

I walk up behind Tessa. The last thing I want to do is overstep or intrude, but I want her to know I'm here should she need me. *I would do anything for this girl.*

I resist the urge to reach out and touch her dark hair, to connect with her in some way. It might be what I need—to discuss last night, to find out where her head is and if everything is as fuzzy and confusing now for her as it is for me—but this isn't about me. Or us.

If I ever want to have that conversation, I can't be selfish with her now.

"I'm going to find out, okay? I'm going to get to the bottom of whatever's going on." She trails off with a breath. "I'm not going to let anyone bother you, okay? I promise. I'm here for as long as I need to be to understand what's happening. This place, the staff here, aren't particularly helpful, but I'll find out. I, um, actually, there's something else I wish I could talk to you about. Your doctors say you can still hear me when I talk to you, so I need your help. The police are investigating Britney's death, but they found something that connects her to one of the deaths back then, which I guess makes her a suspect for all of them. She didn't do it." Her voice cracks. "I know she didn't, but I don't know how to prove it. They found a necklace that makes her look guilty, and—"

I don't hear the rest of what she's saying because my brain has short-circuited. I take another step toward her. "What did you just say?"

She looks up at me, brows drawn down. "They, the police, they found Cassidy Cole's necklace at Britney's house. Do you remember the one that was missing?"

My throat is so thick and immovable it may as well be filled with concrete. I nod, or at least I think I do, then step away to the window to look out.

Why would Britney have Cassidy's necklace? *The* necklace.

Cassidy's mom was an actress years before she had Cassidy, and she'd been given the necklace by a director. It was worn by Marilyn Monroe at one point, or so they told everyone. It's worth more than most of the houses in our town.

"Yeah, of course." Cassidy bragged about it every chance she got, but on the night she and her mother died, it and its matching bracelet were discovered missing. Most people in town think their murders were somehow related to the missing jewelry.

"I'll be right back, okay?" I tell Tessa, crossing the room with a sharp ringing in my ears. It's as if someone stood next to me and screamed at the top of their lungs. My whole head is spinning with this news.

"You okay?" She stands.

I cut a glance back at her, not missing the deep line

in her forehead that tells me she's worried, and I'm only adding to it. As badly as I want to reassure her that everything's fine, I can't stay here. I need air. Now. "Fine. Just realized I forgot my phone in the truck."

I dash away from the room and down the hall, waiting until I exit the building to pull my phone out of my pocket and call Will again.

"Yes, dear?" he teases.

"They found the necklace."

"The necklace?" His voice shakes as he asks, and I know he's hoping I mean any other necklace in the world. But I don't.

"Britney Foster, er, Davis now, I guess. It was at her house. They've already connected it to Cassidy. Dude, you need to come home. It's only a matter of time before they—"

"Don't say it," he warns, his tone sharp. Then, lower, he adds, "Trust me, no one will ever know we had it."

CHAPTER NINETEEN

TESSA — AGE 17

When Will and I get home from the lake house, Mom is waiting at the door, dressed in her long nightgown. Her dark hair is loose around her shoulders, her face makeup-free and wrinkled with concern.

"Get inside before anyone sees you. They'll crucify me if word gets around you two were out of the house after dark. I'll be all the talk at church," she grumbles, shutting the door and locking it behind us. Growing up, our doors were never locked. Friends of ours and Mom's came in and out at all hours, most often without needing to knock. Now, things are different. There's been a definable shift from a place with nothing to fear to suddenly seeing danger everywhere.

"What happened to Emily?" I ask Mom, studying her expression to see if she knows more than she's going to tell me. "Was it a car accident?" It's ridiculous, really, that that's what I'm hoping for. Something we can easily write off rather than a new reason to add to the terror spreading like ivy across the town, suffocating us all.

"No." Mom releases a long breath through her nose. "No, it was not a car accident." She weaves between us, moving slowly. Her arthritis is acting up again—she gets it in her knees and ankles from years of cleaning houses and businesses for a living.

"Do you need me to get you some medicine, Momma? Are you hurting?"

"Don't worry about me." Gently, she eases down onto the couch, both hands out to slow her descent to the cushion. Once she's in place, she pats the cushions on either side of her. "Come. Sit. We need to talk."

Will and I do as she's told us, sitting next to her. This feels strange. Mom looks more serious than usual.

"What's going on?" It's Will who asks, though it's the question on both our minds.

"I want you two to be careful about what you hear, okay? And what you say. Something bad's going on in town, and I don't want the two of you mixed up in it."

"What are you talking about?" I ask. "Something bad?"

"I know you've heard the rumors. We all have." Mom's eyes are somewhat distant as she looks between us.

"People think it's a serial killer. That someone is targeting people," Will says. "But it's ridiculous, right?" He tries to laugh, but Mom doesn't join in. "I mean, why? Bad things don't happen here. This is the most boring town to ever exist."

"Oh, plenty of bad things happen here." Mom gives us an affirmative bob of her head. "Yes, they do. People in small towns—not just ours, but all of 'em—are better at covering up the bad, keeping it quiet. You got to, if you want to be able to look your neighbor in the eye, you know? See 'em around town."

"What are you talking about?" Will asks. "Bad things? Like what happened to Dad?"

Mom squeezes her eyes shut. She doesn't like to talk about our dad's death, except to say it was an accident at work, and that it was quick and he never suffered. He died right after I was born, and it kills me not to know more about him, but I know it's hard on her.

Will and I don't know a life where he exists. We don't have many memories with him. It feels selfish to push her, to cause her more pain when our wound is just an empty hole—a scar rather than the ever-present burning ulcer that remains for Mom.

Still, I always hope someday she'll tell us more about him.

Mom looks over at one of the few photos we have of our dad in the house, right after I was born, holding me with a one-year-old Will sitting next to him. "It was a bad thing, yes, but that's not what I mean. What happened to your dad wasn't anyone's fault. I don't want you to go getting any ideas about—"

A knock on the door interrupts us, and Mom's brows draw together as she turns her body to look out the window, wincing at an apparent pain. Will moves faster over to the door. He checks the window first, something we never do, even on the rare occasion someone knocks.

"It's Sheriff Ward." His eyes find mine, full of fear.

Mom rubs her hands over her thighs. "Well, go on. You two get to your rooms." She shoos us, standing up slowly and releasing a hiss of pain as she does. "I'll handle this. Get to bed."

I look at Will, who doesn't seem to want to leave any more than I do, but without a choice, we amble toward the hallway.

"Sheriff? What's going on? Is everything okay?" Mom pulls open the door, her soft voice gone at once. Suddenly, she's professional and courteous, the only way anyone in this town sees her except us. "What's he doing here?"

I freeze, wondering what he she's talking about.

"I'm sorry about this, Francis," Sheriff Ward says. "Ed says you were at the house earlier."

"Cleaning, yes." Mom's voice is sharper now, defensive. "What's that got to do with anything? When I left, they were— Well, when I left, everything was fine. I'm sorry about your loss, Ed. Emily and Pearl, they were real fine people."

"Don't you dare talk about them," Edward Gray

says, his voice strained like he's trying not to cry. The words set my arm hairs on end.

"Ed," a new voice cuts in. It's Pastor Charles. "Francis is not the enemy here. Your heart is broken, but let's all keep our heads about us, shall we?"

"What's happening?" Mom asks again, her voice guarded now. Suspicious.

"We need to come in and take a look around, Frannie," Sheriff Ward says. "Just to be sure everything's okay."

"Meaning?" she snaps.

"Some expensive china went missing today during the time Pearl and Emily Gray were murdered," he tells her. "Ed says you were the only other person in the house today."

"Is that right? I was in that house today the same as I have been every Friday for sixteen years. You really believe I stole something from you now? Or that I'd ever..." She trails off with a gasp. "You think I hurt them, don't you? That's what this is really about."

"Francis, we all know you didn't do this." That's Pastor Charles, his voice calm and demure. "But it would help Ed's peace of mind just to check, and then they can be on their way. The Lord is testing him right now, as He tests all of us. You understand this loss. You have every right to be hurt by this, but I believe you can find grace in your heart for Ed. Can't you?"

From where I'm standing, I can see Mom wavering. She shifts her feet in place.

"It's not personal, Francis, but we're starting to see a pattern. The Grays' china is missing, just like the Allens' coin collection went missing the day Amber and Jill were killed. The coincidences—you being the cleaner for both families, you being one of the people in both houses on the day—are surely just that, coincidences, but we need to come inside to prove it."

"Tommy Ward, we've known each other since we were both running around in diapers, and this is how you're treating me? You all know this is wrong. You know I'd never—"

Sheriff Ward cuts her off, his voice stern. "We'll come back with a warrant if you don't let us in willingly. Judge Thornton won't be happy to be woken up, but with four dead people on our hands, you have to understand that people in this town need to see some sort of action. See reason, Francis. We're talking murder here. If you're as innocent as you say, all you have to do is let us inside so we can prove it and move on."

Mom clears her throat. "I won't let you wake my kids. Their bedrooms are off limits, you hear? Come back with a warrant for those if you have to. And for goodness' sake, take off your shoes before you come into my house. This is not a barn."

"You heard her," Pastor Charles says. "Shoes off, boys, and let's be respectful of Sister Francis's time. It's late."

"Thank you, Charles," she says finally, reaching out

to take his hand and squeeze it. Will and I dart to our rooms and close the doors quietly. I stand on the opposite side of mine, back pressed to the wood, listening.

"They're just going to take a quick look around, and they'll be on their way." That's Pastor Charles again. "It's all going to be okay."

He says it over and over again as I hear the sheriff moving through our small home—turning things over, opening and closing drawers. His heavy footsteps make his path easy to follow.

It's going to be okay. I want to believe him, but I can't. How can any of this be okay? How will it ever be okay again?

CHAPTER TWENTY

GARRETT — AGE 18

The science club at school is spending the first two days of fall break at a ski lodge in Indiana. I don't want to decide what the most depressing part of that sentence is, but there we go.

I'm still not sure what the science club is, and I don't think anyone else knows either. For the most part, science club, as we know it, consists of about thirty students hanging out in the chemistry lab while our teacher reads a book or chats with the teacher across the hall.

It's not a bad deal, and it counts toward extracurriculars, which I need for college next fall. Still, I've never been so glad to have joined the science club than I am when I step onto the bus and see Tessa there waiting for me.

Okay, so technically she's not waiting *for* me. She's

on the bus that I just happen to be getting on myself, but either way, it'll make this trip more interesting.

Will *is* actually waiting for me at the back of the bus, but the space on the seat next to Tessa is empty, so I hold up a finger at him and drop down beside her.

"Hey there."

"Hello, Garrett," she deadpans. She's still irritated over what happened at the lake house I see. More specifically what *almost* happened.

"Since when are you in the science club?"

She turns her head to look out the window, nonplussed. "I've always been in it, I just don't go to the meetings."

"Interesting. And what if I told you meetings are a big part of it? Kinda the whole thing, actually."

"If you must know, the science club meets on Tuesdays after school, which is the day Mom has me volunteering at the church. The same day *my brother*"—she says the word extra loud and with force, clearly meant for him to hear—"is supposed to be volunteering, but he never shows up."

"That doesn't sound like him at all."

"What do you want, Garrett?" she asks, turning her head finally to look me squarely in the face.

I can't help it. My eyes flick straight to her mouth, her lips, before returning her gaze. "I wanted to see if you're still mad at me. You haven't been texting me back."

"I texted you back," she argues, mouth wide with indignation.

"Once, maybe."

"Well, I was busy."

"With what?"

"Homework. House stuff."

"I saw you Friday. You don't do chores on the weekend. And we're on fall break. Try again."

She sighs, but I'm right, and she knows it. I know her better than she realizes. "Fine. I'm still mad at you."

I grin. "I knew it."

Narrowing her gaze at me, her lips press together with confusion. "Why do you look happy about that?"

"Because I now have two whole days in the mountains to make you *not* mad."

"That sounds like a horror movie waiting to happen."

"Don't be silly. With looks like these, I'm *way* more cut out for rom-coms."

She pats my cheek. "Garrett. Sweet, sweet, Garrett. You wouldn't know romance if you met it, had its babies, built it a house with your bare hands, and spent the next seventy years disappointing it in bed."

The phrase leaves her mouth so casually, I open mine to respond but have to stop myself to process it. I chuckle. "I guess I get to prove you wrong."

"Do you want to prove me wrong?" she asks, the question eerily reminiscent of the one she asked me Friday night.

"I always want to prove you wrong. It's one of my three favorite hobbies."

She drops her head back, then pretends to stand up. "Is it too late to get off this bus?"

I grab her arm, pulling her down. "Sit, woman. You aren't going anywhere."

She drops down beside me, and the smile washes from her face in an instant. She swallows, eyes traveling to where my hand is still on her arm.

I should let go, but I can't. Not yet. Instead, my fingers run down the length of her skin, goose bumps lining every surface.

"Are you still dating Brendan?" It's the question I'm desperate to have answered but am terrified to know the answer to.

She's quiet, like she's trying to gather her thoughts —or maybe prepare me for the blow of her response— and finally, she says, "We got engaged actually."

Time stops.

"And I'm having his baby."

Then a smile.

"You're an ass."

Her smile cracks open wider as I shake my head, clutching a hand to my chest.

"Are you trying to kill me?"

She opens her mouth to answer, but Mrs. LeClere calls our attention to the front of the bus where she begins to remind us about the rules for the trip. They range from "don't wander away from the lodge" to "don't hit your classmates with ski equipment." She looks at Will specifically when she says that last one.

As she's taking attendance, a wad of paper hits me in the back of the head, and I whip around just as Mrs. LeClere shouts, "Becker, do I need to kick you off the bus before we even leave the parking lot?"

I snicker as Will ducks behind the seat in front of him and calls back, "No, ma'am. Sorry. I, uh, sneezed. My bad."

The bus rattles with laughter, and Will lifts up finally, meeting my eyes and pointing to a blonde head sitting next to him in his seat. Cassidy Cole.

I nod, understanding that my original seat is now taken, and I'm staying right here. I steal a glance at Tessa, knowing I hadn't truly planned to go anywhere. A corner of her mouth draws inward as she tries not to look at me, not to smile.

Oh, this is going to be fun.

CHAPTER TWENTY-ONE

TESSA — PRESENT DAY

With Garrett out of the room, I pick up the brush from Mom's nightstand and run it through her hair slowly, remembering how she'd do the same for me so often as a kid, even when I was much too old for it to be necessary. For a long time, the minutes right before bed were spent sitting on the couch just in front of Mom while she brushed and braided my hair. Never in a hurry. Never too busy to do it. Looking back, those moments were when we had our best talks. It was easier to ask her the hard questions or say the embarrassing things when I didn't have to look her in the eyes.

I can't remember now when that stopped or why. I suppose it was inevitable we'd outgrow the practice someday, but I wish we'd known which time would be the final one.

Mom's eyes scan the room, like she's searching for something.

"What is it?" I ask this without expecting a response, more out of habit than anything.

As the words leave my mouth, Mom's eyes freeze, then lock on mine.

"Mom?"

Her eyes are wide, unblinking. Fearful.

"Mom? Can you hear me? Is something hurting?"

I stand to press the button and call the nurse, worried something is seriously wrong, when her fingers wiggle. I stop.

"Did you do that on purpose?" I move back toward her, taking her hand, holding my palm just under her fingers. I think the nurse said something about this yesterday, but it's all such a blur I can't be certain. "Can you move your fingers for me again?"

She's still looking at me, watching me with a blank, fuzzy expression, but her eyes haven't wandered off again. I'm taking that as a good sign. She's listening. Trying.

I clasp her hand in mine. "Can you hear me? Do you know who I am? Squeeze my hand, Momma."

I wait, holding my breath and feeling for a single twinge of her muscles to let me know she's attempting it, that I'm not imagining all of this.

I run my finger across hers slowly, moving over her knuckles. She twitches, a single bump of her finger, and my chest tightens.

I release a shaky breath and sit down on the bed again. The doctors have always said they're hopeful she'll make more progress, but I was beginning to lose hope. Intentional movement of any kind would be huge. "I'm here. I'm right here." I try to think, remembering what the nurses have told us about her better days, how she responds by blinking about a quarter of the time. She wouldn't do it yesterday, but maybe... "Can you blink once if you can hear me?" I hold my breath, waiting and watching. Still, her eyes are locked on mine, but she isn't—

Blink.

It's slow, like she's drunk, but it was definitely something, wasn't it?

"Do you know who I am?"

There's another long pause and then, *blink.*

Tears spring to my eyes, and my breathing hitches, my voice going so high I'm practically a cartoon character. "Hi. Oh my gosh. Hi." I sniffle, collecting my thoughts though they feel a bit like scattered change. "Um, are you in pain? Should I call a nurse?"

Nothing. I double the time I waited before. Triple it.

She's saying no. I really think she's telling me no.

"Will will be back soon," I tell her, stroking her hand. "He'll be so happy to see you. We're both going to visit as much as we can."

Blink.

This time faster. She's happy, I think. She's saying yes, she wants us to visit.

"Mom, has someone else been visiting you? Someone besides me and Garrett and Will? Do you remember? Do you know what I'm talking about?"

Blink.

"Did they write this note?" I pull the wrinkled piece of paper out of my pocket and unfold it. "Murderer?"

She stares at me, not the paper, without blinking. I move it closer to her face. "Someone left this in your room. Do you know who?"

Blink.

I search the room. There has to be a way to have her tell me who it was without me rambling off every person I know. "Was it...Sheriff Ward?"

I'm thinking back over that night, over the accusations I don't think she's ever been able to let go of. Over the hurt on her face the next morning when she tried to pretend it hadn't happened.

She doesn't blink. That's a no.

"Ed Gray?"

Again, her eyes are still, unblinking.

"Pastor Charles?"

Nothing. She's so still she looks as if she's been carved from stone. I don't know who else it could be. I'm sure so many people heard the rumors back then. Once Mom had been accused of stealing—of murder, even—things were never quite the same. Even though she was never officially charged with any crime.

"It's all going to be okay, okay? I'm going to make sure you're safe. I'm going to fix this."

Blink.

My heart stutters. "I'll tell them no more visitors except us. Me and Will and Garrett. We're going to figure this out. I promise you."

Blink.

I cross the room, searching for something, anything, that might help. Could she hold a pencil? Probably not. I need to keep asking her questions, keep trying to get answers while she's able to give them to me. I grab my phone, scrolling through my contacts to come up with a list of suspects.

When the door opens, I look up, expecting Garrett, but find the nurse from yesterday instead.

"Oh. Well, hey there. I was just coming to check on her." She pauses at the door, turning to look at Mom.

"She's awake," I tell her. "Responsive. She was talking to me."

"Talking?" She balks. "Are you serious?" She hurries across the room to Mom's bed.

"Blinking," I amend. "She was blinking and answering my questions, and she moved her hand."

The nurse looks back at me as I move around to get a better view of Mom just to find her eyes closed.

No!

Approaching her bed, I touch her shoulder. "Mom?"

The nurse checks her pulse and pulls out a thermometer, swiping it across her forehead. "Ms. Frannie, are you there, honey?"

Something about the nurse who is closer to my age

than my mom's calling her 'honey' doesn't sit well with me, but I ignore it. "Mom, open your eyes again. Show her." *Is she doing this on purpose?* I can't help the suspicion that has begun to creep in.

The nurse gives me a pitying look. "It takes a lot of her energy when she's lucid. We usually only get a minute or two out of her, so it sounds like you were pretty lucky. I'll call the doctor to do a full exam, but just try to remember that any progress is progress."

I feel like everything has been swiped from me, like none of it was even real. "Mom, please," I whisper, knowing I look and sound like a child. I can't bring myself to care what the nurse must think of me.

"Here, let me show you something." Nurse Emma crosses into the kitchen and opens a drawer next to the sink, pulling out a laminated piece of paper. "I keep this in the drawer. You're welcome to try it next time she's awake." She holds up the sheet, revealing a printed alphabet. "I ask her to blink when I point to each letter to help her spell things and answer questions that aren't yes or no."

"Has she been able to do that?"

Her brows draw together. "Not completely, no, but that's expected. She loses her train of thought a lot, but to be able to do anything at all is an improvement. I've talked to patients who came out of things like this who tell me they were doing math problems in their head most of the time to keep their brains active. Or spelling words, recalling trivia, that sort of thing. It's all about rebuilding those muscles. It just takes time."

The door opens, and this time it's Garrett. Emma puts the paper back in the drawer.

"What's going on?" Garrett crosses the room, running a hand over his pockets like he's searching for his keys or phone, both of which are there.

I look back at Mom, feeling equally hopeful and completely let down. "She was awake and aware for a minute or two. She knew who I was."

His jaw drops. "What? *Seriously?* That's amazing, Tessa."

"We should probably let her get some rest for a while," Emma whispers, flipping out the light above the bed.

"Sure." With a final look at Mom, who seems to be sleeping peacefully, I slip out of the room with Garrett just behind me, so filled with questions I'm bursting.

CHAPTER TWENTY-TWO

GARRETT — PRESENT DAY

"There's something I have to tell you."

We're at the small kitchen table when she says it, sitting miles apart, which feels fitting. Ever since we left the nursing home, she hasn't been here with me, not really.

Seeing her mom awake, I'm sure it messed with her, but I don't quite understand the sadness I see in her eyes. Getting her back and then losing her again, maybe? *I can relate.* But progress is progress.

I set down my slice of the pizza we grabbed for dinner on the way home. "Okay, sure."

She mindlessly picks at a piece of pepperoni on her plate, not looking at me. "You, um, you might already know this. I'm not really sure what Will told you about back then, but the night Emily Gray died…"

So much about that night sticks in my memory, but it's hard to tell where she's going with this.

"Well, right after we got home, the police came by." Her face is completely emotionless and unreadable. "Sheriff Ward, Pastor Charles, and Ed Gray, actually. They accused Mom of having something to do with what happened to Emily and Pearl. And maybe even Amber and Jill Allen. They ended up searching our house for some stuff that went missing from their homes."

Her words feel about as believable as a fable or fairytale. The ghost story that comes before the flashlight flicks off and someone yells, "Boo." It's inconceivable. Frannie wouldn't steal, and she certainly wouldn't hurt anyone. Anyone who knows her can attest to that. "You're not serious."

"Yep, I am. They didn't find anything, obviously, but it was really hard on her, you know? She'd been working for the Grays and Allens for years, since right after Dad died, and it was such a betrayal." She squeezes her eyes shut. "I know our problems were far from important that night and that Mr. Gray was just upset, but it really affected her, you know? And all of us, I guess. It blew over when they didn't find anything, but she never went back to work for them. And slowly some of the other families started firing her. They'd blamed it on something else, of course, but we always knew. Pastor Charles gave her a raise and more hours at church, but without him and Mabel, we might've lost everything. And then...and then when Cassidy and Mrs. Cole died, Sheriff Ward came back to have them search for the necklace that they just found at Britney's." She drops her head forward, thinking. "I guess that's why finding the note was so hard for me. I've never really shaken the feeling of being accused of something like that, even indirectly. They thought our family was bad, that we'd had something to do with something so horrible. It eats at you, you know?"

"No." I'm up out of my seat and around the table in a second. I sit down next to her, putting a hand on hers. "No one who knew anything about your mom could ever think she was involved. That she'd ever hurt anyone. Do you hear me? Those people, whatever they did back then, it's because they were hurting, but it's not an excuse. They should be the ones who are ashamed, not you. Not her. Look at me." Slowly, her eyes lift to find mine, broken and empty in a way that shatters me. I hate that I didn't know about any of this until now. "Your mom is the best part of this place, okay? You all are."

She gives me a patronizing look as if I'm just being nice, but I'm not. It's true. Sometimes I think the Beckers are the only reason I survived growing up in this town.

"Well, thanks," she says softly. "I just don't want anyone to think she had something to do with Britney's death. Especially Kristy. It would kill me."

"She doesn't." I can't know this, but I have to make her believe it. "Your mom and Britney were still close, even now. Kristy won't forget that."

When she speaks again, her voice is soft and strained. She's trying not to cry. "I'm just so afraid someone might try to hurt her when she's alone and helpless. If someone like Ed Gray *does* still believe she was guilty back then, right now's the chance to get revenge when she can't fight back." Her voice catches. "Not to mention we still never got answers about her stroke. The doctors couldn't say for certain if the head injury came before or after by the time Will found her. What if Ed broke into the house and attacked her—"

"You can't go there," I warn.

"You weren't there that night, Garrett. You didn't hear the way he talked to her."

"I don't need to, okay? Trust me, if you start to play the 'what if' game, you'll go down a rabbit hole and never come back. All we can do now is try to protect her. You told them she's not allowed visitors except the three of us when we left. That helps."

"In theory, sure. If they actually monitor who's coming in."

I sigh and smooth a hand over my mouth. I wish I had the answers right now. "It's all going to be okay. Maybe we should talk to Sheriff Ward, though. Especially about the note and your concerns with Ed Gray. He could help us keep an eye on him."

"No." Her response is swift and assured. "Sheriff Ward is one of the ones who accused her back then, too. He was right there with Ed. I don't trust him either. Part of me always thought he hoped he could find a reason to actually convict her so the pressure would be off him. People were so angry with him for not getting answers."

"He was doing his job. I'm sure he knew your mom was innocent and just needed to appease Ed."

She sighs, rubbing a hand over face. "Yeah, maybe."

"There's, um, there's something I should tell you, too, actually."

Her bright eyes find mine, so filled with conflicting emotion they're unreadable. "Yeah?"

I open my mouth to tell her something, anything— the awful, awful truth—but we're interrupted by the sound of a knock at the door.

CHAPTER TWENTY-THREE

TESSA — AGE 17

The lodge is just as you'd picture it—snow-capped mountains and gray skies providing a perfect backdrop to the warm amber of the wooden building. There are tall windows along the front, giving a perfect view of the inside, bustling with people in front of tall fireplaces. Outside, skiers are gathered in droves and lines in various stages of their lessons. From a distance, they're just black dots, some zooming and others wobbling their way across the white blanket of snow.

It's perfect—and it had better be for the amount of fundraising we had to do to make the trip happen in the first place.

The sight of the ski lift carrying people to the peak does something funny to my belly. I've never been a fan of heights.

Next to me, Garrett is sitting up straight, wiggling in place as we edge closer up the mountain. He tosses me a cocky look, one that he's practically famous for, and pulls out his phone, checking the time.

He's had to pee for the last hour, and each bump is causing him agony, though I'm enjoying myself quite a bit. At least it's kept him occupied so he's not...doing whatever it is he's doing lately.

I don't know what this is, this weird, flirty thing that's gotten into him. I thought I understood at the lake house, but when I'd pushed him to admit what he wanted, he froze. Either that, or I seriously misread things.

If I'm honest with myself, I don't know how I feel about him. I can't stop thinking about us in the closet or the way it made me feel to have his eyes on me in the lake. I'm not going to pretend I don't find him gorgeous and kind and funny and easy to talk to, but he's also maddening. Aside from Britney and my brother, Garrett knows me better than anyone in the world, but despite my best efforts, he's not the best at letting me know *him*. His wall is miles high, and I've scaled it, picked it apart, and blown it to smithereens, but as soon as I think I've made progress, he rebuilds.

Besides, he's...*Garrett.* Maybe there has always been something between us—the way he sticks around to talk to me for a few seconds after Will leaves the room, the way he texts me to ask something random even though sometimes it feels like maybe he just needed an excuse to check in, the way we constantly seem to find each other in crowded rooms—but without proof, I shoved any suspicions I had away and suffocated them.

Now, we spend our time dancing around the subject, and I won't be the first to say it. I can't. Especially not after the way he shut down at the lake and refused to tell me what's in his head. Even before we were interrupted by Will, he had plenty of chances to tell me what he wants. *And if that's me.*

If I'm misreading this somehow, I'll be the one who will have to live out the remainder of the year flooded with embarrassment.

There's also the fact that I know how Garrett is. He goes out with a lot of girls, but I've never actually seen him date anyone seriously, as in for more than a week. The wall thing again, I guess.

He's not a player necessarily. Not the type of guy who'd intentionally hurt anyone. He's just...wild. A wild animal that doesn't let anyone get too close, that will never let anyone tame him.

At least I'm not foolish enough to think *I* could be that person.

When the bus stops, we collect our bags, file off, and find out our room assignments. Will and Garrett are paired together thanks to their last names being similar, but I'm paired with Kinsey Bell, who is nice enough but pretty shy.

Inside the lodge, we're given keys to our rooms and sent to check in before being told we can meet back outside afterward to get our ski lift ticket and rent our clothing and equipment.

Kinsey and I unpack in relative silence, except for the CMT music videos playing on the TV.

"So, you like Garrett, huh?" she asks, pulling on a sweater over her shirt.

"We're friends." The words are automatic after years of practice, but this time they don't feel honest. At this point I don't know what we are—don't know what I want and don't know what he wants—but friendship might not be enough for either of us anymore.

I'm just not sure how I feel about that.

That night, our bodies are sore and exhausted from hours of skiing. Or, in my case, attempted skiing. I never made it to even the entry level of the lessons— the bunny slope—because I couldn't make it past the training on the conveyor belt without falling over. My brother, on the other hand, was skiing on the level just under that of a professional skier before the sun set.

Once everyone has returned their equipment and changed into warmer clothes, we meet outside to hang out before bed. Most of us gather around the oversized fire pit outside, while a few people kick off their shoes and stick their feet in the hot tub. Others walk around the mountain, taking in the views. Kinsey is on the phone with her mom.

I'm alone near the fire, mind drifting to thoughts of sleep and the long ride home tomorrow when I feel him behind me. *Feel* him. It's the strangest thing. I hear his footsteps, maybe, but there's a lot of noise so it's not just that. Something in my body seems to sense him in the way I've always imagined mothers must know where their children are. The way Mom always knows when I'm up to something without glancing my way.

I turn my head just in time for him to drop down next to me in the snow.

"So, how'd it go?" he asks, teasing. He knows how it went. He skied circles around the conveyor belt I was practicing on at least ten times.

I go stone-faced. "Great, actually. You missed it, but I was just invited to join next year's Olympic team."

His smile is a warm sort of sarcastic. "Really? Wow. Don't forget about us little people. I can't wait to tell everyone I'm friends with someone famous."

I pretend to struggle to place him, squinting. "Sorry. What was your name again?"

He throws his head back with a laugh. "See, this is the problem with fame." He taps my temple. "Straight to your head."

"I've already ordered a bigger hat." This is when I'm the happiest. When we're being silly together. I'm grateful it's a piece of this that hasn't been lost or changed. Garrett understands my humor better than anyone, and he always has a comeback ready. "I take it you guys did better?"

"Your brother kicked my butt, but I wasn't too bad." He shrugs. "I don't know. Maybe skiing isn't my thing, either. I think I'd rather be somewhere warm."

"Hot tub's free." I jut my chin toward it. It's built into the ground with such thick steam rising up it looks like soup.

"Yeah." He chuckles. "You first. I prefer my appendages to stay thawed, thank you."

"Tell me about it. I'm starting to worry I'll never get warm again. Our room has a big bathtub, and I'm counting down until I can go back to the room without looking antisocial. I plan to soak until the feeling starts to come back."

When I look at him, his eyes are sort of fuzzy and distant. Like he's not really listening to me. He swallows a gulp of coffee before meeting my gaze again. "Yeah. Same," he croaks.

"Sorry. Am I boring you?" I ask, not nearly as offended as I sound.

He laughs. "No. The opposite, in fact." His expression falters a bit, the playfulness washing away, and he looks entirely serious as he says, "You're keeping me way too entertained lately. It's becoming a problem."

I blink. "Explain."

He shakes his head, looking around, and now it feels like we're in a covert conversation. "This is all so weird, Tessa. I have no idea what we're doing."

At least he finally said it so I know I'm not alone in this anymore. But even as I agree, it stings to hear him call this that word. 'Weird' isn't exactly a compliment. I start to leave, to tell him we should just forget it, but he takes my hand, stopping me before I can stand.

"But I do know I...I want to find out." He twists each of my fingers in between his slowly, almost caressing me.

It *does* feel weird, I can admit—if only to myself—but it also feels weirdly right.

"What do you want to find out?" I ask slowly, pacing myself because I'm almost afraid of the answer.

He huffs out a breath. "Everything." His hand moves to scratch the back of his neck like he does when he's nervous. "Turns out, I'm, uh, pretty obsessed with you."

My eyes widen. I didn't expect him to be so blunt. It's not like him. "You are?"

Behind him, the sky is getting dark, and the light from the fire reflects on his face as he studies me. He runs his tongue over his bottom lip before pushing up from the ground. "Will you walk with me?"

He holds out his hand, waiting.

It takes a few seconds for me to process the request and a few more seconds to agree to it. I slip my hand into his and let him pull me up.

He nudges his head toward the right side of the building, where we took lessons earlier today. Now that it's getting dark, the area is deserted.

"You've never just been Will's little sister to me, you know?"

He's still holding my hand. His fingers are laced

with mine, and I have no idea what to do about it. This all feels like a dream.

"I mean, obviously you were that. *Are* that. But you were—*are*—also my friend. And, for a long time, that's the only way I saw you. You were this friend who was always around, and when something good would happen—or something bad, I guess—you and Will were the first people I wanted to tell. As much as we annoy each other, you are someone important to me, and I never want to lose that."

We're walking slower now as we round the building and near the fence that blocks off the training area.

"I don't want to either," I tell him. The seriousness of the conversation is uncomfortable when I'm so used to joking with him. At the same time, I very much want to see where this is heading.

"And then I started to…to see you differently."

"You mean I got hot."

At that, he snorts. "Yes, Tessa. You got hot. But you also got…interesting in a way I wasn't expecting."

I cock my head to the side. "Whereas before I was boring?"

"Before, you were just *you*. And suddenly, you were different. Er, I was different. I don't know. I started to think about you, you know? Really, really think about you. Not just when we were together, but…" He looks away. "All the time, I guess."

"You thought about me, how? Like you really

wanted me to kick your butt at Smash Bros? Or more like you really hoped I would stop leaving books in the hallway for you and Will to trip over when you sneak back home at night?"

His eyes go dark while he studies me, the thought so clear on the end of his tongue I can practically read it. "Like I *really wanted you.*"

His words wash over me as if each one is a finger tracing along my collarbone.

"Oh." I puff out a breath, shocked by his fearless honesty. This is such a different conversation than I'm used to with him. Such a different version of him.

He looks away. "And you were still Will's little sister."

"Right. Doesn't change." I try to laugh, but it falls flat. There's nothing funny about the way he's looking at me.

"Right. And no matter how badly I..."

"Wanted me," I remind him, though this time there's nothing teasing in my words. I want to remind myself it's real.

"Right. No matter how badly I wanted you, the idea of ever bringing that up to Will was terrifying. I thought he'd kick my ass and never let me come over to the house again. I thought he'd tell me you were off limits."

"Will isn't the boss of me."

We've stopped now, just along the wooden fence.

"I know. But he could ask me to stay away, or start coming to my house rather than having me over, and the idea of losing all of you in that way was enough to keep me quiet." He rushes to add, "Not that you weren't worth it, you know? It was just that you guys are my family, and if I couldn't visit anymore—"

"No, I get it," I cut him off. "Truly. You're at our house more than yours, and well, we've never really talked about it, but that doesn't mean I don't notice."

His jaw is tight as he nods, and this seems to be the first uncomfortable part of the conversation for him, which is crazy to me. I know his family is large. He's one of six kids, and they just found out his mom is pregnant again. They're busy and overwhelmed, but they don't seem like bad people.

Our house probably feels like an oasis, though, ordinary as it is. At least it's quiet most days.

"Then I saw you at my party talking to Brendan, and I thought Will would be furious, but he just, well, he wasn't. He said he was a 'good dude.'"

I chuckle as Garrett does a convincing impression of Will with those last two words.

He looks down at me, eyes warming at my laughter. "And when I asked him about it, he just blew it off. Said he wasn't the kind of brother who'd try to control who you dated and a bunch of other stuff that made me realize I'd had it all wrong. I was planning to talk to you about it, but then you were with Brendan and I panicked. Will was right. Brendan *is* a good dude, as much as I hate it, and I didn't want to make enemies with him or hurt you if you didn't feel anything for me. So, I guess I thought if I could just keep you from falling for him—" He rubs his lips. "I don't know what I thought, honestly. And then we played that game, and it seemed like if you had any feelings for me, even if they were way, *way* down, it might help you realize you were with the wrong guy. But then we got in the closet and it was so real. I'd forced my way into the party because I was jealous of Brendan, but I had no idea what to do once I had a real shot with you. *If* I had a real shot. I chickened out."

"You were scared of kissing me?"

His eyes flicker down to meet mine, and his chest puffs with a deep breath that he slowly releases. "Terrified. I mean, I've kissed a few people before, but this is different. This is you. It means something *because* it's you."

Warmth blooms in my chest, spreading like an ink stain. I bend over, setting my cup of cocoa down and wiggling it in place to create a space for it in the snow. I take Garrett's without asking, setting it next to mine.

"Can I ask why you're stealing my coffee?"

"Because." I pinch my tongue between my teeth, twisting the cup until it stands in the snow on its own. "We are getting a do-over."

"A do-over?" His brows wrinkle together.

"Unless you don't want to."

"No, I do," he rushes to say.

I take both of his hands, holding them in mine. "Look, I don't know what this is either, but I'm just a girl, Garrett. I'm just me. You can't be scared of me."

"I'm scared to hurt you. I'm scared to mess this up."

"You won't. I trust you."

He closes his eyes, drawing in another long breath. "What are you saying?"

I lace my fingers with his. "I'm saying kiss me. And please don't take seven minutes this time."

Something changes in his stature. His shoulders and body language go from languid and nervous to dominant like the flick of a switch. He squares himself to me, stepping forward until our bodies are pressed together. His hand comes up to my cheek, thumb resting under my jawbone as he tilts my head up just a bit more. He runs his tongue over his bottom lip at the same time as he brushes mine with his thumb.

His eyes are dark and drunk with something heavy and hot, something I feel on every inch of my skin. The confidence I knew seconds ago is a distant memory as his eyes lock on my lips.

Then, oh so slowly, his lips descend on mine. The kiss is soft at first, testing, but his hands are on opposite sides of my head. Even when he's gentle, he's in control. Directing me, holding me, making me feel everything all at once until I'm dizzy.

I'm a feather floating through the air as a growl

comes from somewhere deep in his throat, and then, without warning, he moves forward, easing me back until I'm pressed against the gate.

There's nothing innocent about this now—nothing that feels like a first kiss with someone new. This is someone I know. Someone I want. Someone I feel like I've been meant to kiss all along.

Long, sure fingers tangle in my hair, and he turns my head, kissing my jaw before his hands are on my waist. His warm palms slide down my body. Stopping his descent, his thumbs press into my hip bones, shooting a jolt of lava through my insides. He lifts me up, and I gasp. He smiles against my mouth, and nothing has ever been so perfect and magical as this kiss, surrounded by chilly white tundra while my insides rage hot. He places me down on the top horizontal post of the gate, slipping his body between my legs, hands back in my hair.

It's like he can't get enough of me, and I revel in that power.

I wrap my legs tighter around him. Now's my chance to tangle my fingers through his hair, the curls I've always loved so much. He groans, kissing me harder, holding me against him with such fervor it's as if he's afraid he may never get the chance again.

When I feel like my heart may explode, I place a hand on his chest, pulling back and gasping for air. No one has ever made my heart race the way it is right now. I've never been kissed like that. Never been looked at the way he's looking at me.

I can't help grinning over the sight of his red lips, wild hair, and the faraway look in his eyes, both of us drunk on whatever is happening here.

It's magical with him. All-consuming.

He smiles, resting his forehead on mine. "Well, we definitely should've been doing that in the closet instead."

The way he's looking at me is something unexpected. Fiery hot, but intensely captivating. Lust and admiration rolled into one. If I had a mirror, I'd imagine my expression is eerily similar.

I don't think I've ever seen him look at anyone else this way, but at the same time, I'm realizing I think he's *always* looked at me this way. I don't know why it took either of us so long to notice.

"We should probably get back," he says eventually. "While I still have enough willpower to say that."

I tug on the collar of his shirt. "Please don't use words that contain my brother's name right now."

He kisses me again, quickly this time, then turns to pick up our cups and hands mine to me, offering his hand to help me down from the gate.

"What does this mean?" I ask him, locking my hand with his as we walk through the snow and back to join our classmates. Without the warmth of his body on mine, everything feels so much colder. "Like, are we just…people who kiss each other now?"

I expect him to say we don't need to define it or that he's not sure, like Brendan and so many other guys have. Instead, he squeezes my hand, his eyes drilling into mine with a boyish grin playing on his lips.

"I hope it means you're mine. Because I'm sure as hell yours."

CHAPTER TWENTY-FOUR

GARRETT — AGE 18

That night, by the time I make it back to our room at the lodge, Will is already there, and it's no surprise that he's broken the rule about having girls over. As I open the door, two guilty heads whip around to face me.

Cassidy Cole is standing next to the bed, her blonde hair wild and messy, lipstick smeared. She looks at Will, who just shrugs with a deep frown and quick shake of his head that tells her everything's fine and not to worry. She sets back to work buttoning her jeans.

"Sorry, bro. Were you waiting for us to finish?" Will asks, tossing a boot across the bed to Cassidy.

"What? Oh. No. I was…out." I'd planned to tell him about Tessa right away to relieve the last remnants of my guilty conscience, telling me this is too good to be true, but that'll have to wait until we're alone.

Cassidy pulls her boots on, then stretches across the

bed and plants a kiss on Will's lips. "Text me, okay? And save me a seat on the bus ride home in the morning."

He squeezes her boob, and she swats him with a loud laugh. "Okay, I will."

Once she's gone, I drop down on my bed and kick off my shoes. Will's smile is bright enough to light a city. I smirk when his gaze finally drifts from the door to me, as if he just remembered I'm still here. "So, I guess that's a thing now."

He drops back on his pillow, arms under his head. "Yeah, something like that."

I open my mouth, prepared to tell him about Tessa, when he speaks before I get the chance.

"Hey, you know that jewelry she's always bragging about? The really expensive stuff from that director with the weird name?"

Everyone in school knows about Cassidy's Hollywood necklace, because she's brought it up every chance she could since around middle school.

"Sure. What about it?"

He props up on one elbow, his face serious. "We're going to steal it."

CHAPTER TWENTY-FIVE

TESSA — PRESENT DAY

As I round the corner into the living room, I see the head of the person waiting there through the glass of the small windows.

"Mark!" Strangely, I'd nearly forgotten about my car in all the madness going on. He grins, holding out a pair of keys, and I spot the tow truck in the driveway.

"I thought you might like to have this back." He looks over my shoulder. "Hey, Garrett."

"Hey," comes Garrett's distant reply.

Mark places the keys in my hand. "Realized after we got it fixed that no one had your phone number. Figured I'd come rectify that."

"Oh my gosh, you're right." I slap a hand to the side of my face. "I totally forgot to give you my number. I'm so sorry."

"Nah. Not a problem." His smile is warm and innocent. Mark was around quite a bit in school, not part of

Will's main circle, but close enough that I know him well. He's always been sweet, if a little quiet. "Wheel and rims were fine, by the way. Luckily. We just replaced the tire, aligned and rebalanced, and you're good to go."

"Thank you. Truly. What do I owe you? Do you have a way to take a payment? I don't have checks or anything." I can't recall the last time I wrote a check. "Or should I call in or stop by to pay? I'm sorry. I feel so bad I didn't call to check in. Life has been..." I release a drawn-out breath, not sure how to finish that sentence. Thankfully, he doesn't wait for me to.

"Eh." He waves me off. "Don't worry about it. It's just one tire. Consider it a favor for Ms. Frannie's daughter. I was really sorry to hear about her accident."

"Thank you, seriously. Is Ernie okay with that?"

"Ernie retired last year, and I bought the shop." He shrugs. "It's no problem."

"I feel bad. I should really pay you something. Especially after you had to drive out here, too."

His lips curve. "It was worth it." He takes a step forward, leaning an arm against the frame. "Besides, if you really want to pay me back, I'd love to take you to dinner."

Behind me, I hear Garrett shutting the pantry door with a little extra force.

"Dinner would be great. When were you thinking?"

"Well, if you don't have plans tonight, I thought we could go to Joanie's. You were always crazy about their cookies." He watches me closely, his eyes hopeful. I don't bother to correct him, but it was Will who was a sucker for Joanie's cookies. I preferred the ones from the other bakery in town, Overflow. Still, it's a sweet offer.

"Good memory. I love Joanie's."

"Yeah? I could go home and change and then come back for you. Say around seven?"

I glance behind me to see if Garrett's there, but he's not. He's probably not even listening. He doesn't care. I don't know why I feel guilty. Garrett and I decided a long time ago that this would never work between us.

It's why I hear myself saying, "Yes. That sounds perfect."

"Perfect," he repeats, patting the doorframe and taking a step back. "I'll, uh, see you around seven, then?"

"See you then." I shut the door and turn around, dropping my keys on the coffee table and going back to the kitchen. Garrett is next to the sink, pouring bourbon into a tie-dyed silicone cup. "Well, that was nice of him."

He looks over, like he hadn't heard me enter the room. "Super nice." He lifts the cup, taking a sip.

"It feels good to have my car back." I stroll past him and stand on my tiptoes, leaning up to reach for a plastic container to store the remainder of the pizza in. Will and Garrett are so much taller than me. Nothing in this house is accessible.

Garrett leans over me, his body pressing on mine without warning as he grabs the container I'm reaching for. Every inch of his body is touching mine, and I'm very aware of it. My breathing is so loud in my head I can't think straight. I inhale the warm scent of his cologne, closing my eyes to find my train of thought again. He sets the container on the counter in front of me and steps back. My voice is breathless as I say, "Thank you." I pause, collecting myself. "Were you done eating?"

He nods, tapping his cup against his chin. My skin tingles as I move to the table and place the few remaining slices of pizza into the container.

With leisurely, steady footsteps, he follows me.

"Sorry," I tell him, looking up as I remember the conversation that was interrupted by the knocking on the door. "Were you going to tell me something earlier?"

He smiles with his lips pressed together. "Nah, I can't remember. Not a big deal." I can't read his expression, can't tell the difference between sadness and frustration, perhaps because there's a mix of both.

I'm not naïve. I understand this will never be easy between the two of us—seeing each other date—but I also know that no matter how difficult it is, it's necessary. I don't particularly see Mark as an option, but he's sweet. Shyness isn't always a negative. There were plenty of good things about him in school. Top of the class, decent athlete, well liked. If I'm going to exist in town, it won't hurt to get out of these four walls and reconnect with people other than my brother and Garrett.

With the leftovers from dinner put away in the refrigerator and the pizza box thrown away, I tell him, "Thanks again for going with me today. I don't remember if I said that, but I appreciate everything." I take a step backward, feeling awkward when he just nods again, still not saying a word. "And now I'll get out of your hair and give you a break."

His brows draw down, confused. "You were never a bother, Tessa. Don't act like spending time with you is a chore."

"Still. I know you probably had other things planned before I came into town with my flat tire. I'm just... I just want to say thank you for helping me, like you always do."

He twists his lips into a wry grin. "What are friends for?"

"Right." I take a hesitant breath, then step backward and away from him, heading for my room to get ready. Inside, I turn to my closet, sorting through the clothes I brought with me.

"You're really going to go with him?" Garrett's voice comes from just outside the door. When I turn, it's mostly open, but he hasn't entered.

"I think so, yeah." I hesitate. "He's nice."

"Sure. He's nice." He's definitely irritated, but he has

no right to be. We aren't together. That was his decision. "And you like him?"

"I don't really know him. Just from the few times he was around with you guys."

"I mean, is this really the best time to be going out with anyone? With so much else going on?"

I stop going through my clothes, turning to face him with my hands on my hips. "Why don't you just say what you really want to say, Garrett? Do you not want me to go with him?"

He runs a hand over the top of his head. "I didn't say that."

"Do you know something about him I should know? Is he a bad guy?"

"No." He scowls. "No. He's...whatever. I'm just trying to make sure you're ready for this. You just got back into town. You don't owe him a date because he was nice to you."

"I'm well aware of that."

"And you still want to go?"

Now, stubbornness gets the best of me. "Yeah, I do. Unless you can think of a reason I shouldn't."

His hands go up, and he takes a step back. "Nothing important, no. Have fun with your *favorite* cookies."

With that, he disappears into the hall, and I hear his bedroom door shut seconds later, leaving me alone with my spiraling thoughts.

CHAPTER TWENTY-SIX

GARRETT — PRESENT DAY

Fuck this.

It's ten o'clock at night. *Where the fuck is she?* I feel like a worried parent, pacing in front of the door, watching for headlights on the road. She should be here by now.

Not that she had a curfew. She's a grown adult, and I can't control her. Maybe she won't come home at all. Maybe she'll stay over at his place.

And that would be fine.

Cool liquid pours over my hand, and I look down to see that I've crushed the cup I'm drinking out of. It's one of those flimsy silicone ones Will brought home from a trip, convinced it's going to save the world by eliminating plastic or something.

I curse and shake the liquid from my hand, storming into the kitchen to get a towel and soap to clean the mess from my hand and the floor.

The bag of cookies from Overflow is sitting on the table, and I consider trashing it. How pathetic am I, really? Stupid, fucking Mark Summers and his pretty-boy smile. Who cares if she doesn't like the cookies he bought her? Not my problem. Why didn't she correct him? Everyone knows she hates Joanie's cookies. She always said they were too dry. I mean, she's wrong, but whatever.

And why the fuck do I care?

Tessa Becker is not my responsibility. She's not even my date.

She's not mine.

I grab the bag of cookies, walk over to the trash can, and step on the lever, dangling them over the bag. Then I groan and take them back to the counter. Even when I'm furious with her, I still want to make her happy.

What is that about?

I tell myself it's not a big deal. That Will would've done the same thing. He would've let her go on the date with a guy who doesn't know her *at-fucking-all* because *free will* or some shit. And then he would've gotten dressed when he was dog-tired, driven twenty-seven minutes across town and back just to get these stupid, fucking cookies and bring them home to her. When she didn't ask. When she probably doesn't even want them. Just to *maybe* see her smile.

He definitely would have.

Probably.

I think.

Otherwise, it's just pathetic.

I storm out of the room, scrubbing up my mess in a vengeful haze until my fingers hurt, and the floor is probably cleaner than it's ever been. *This girl makes me lose my mind.* Nothing new there. I return to my pacing, every flash of light as a car drives past making my heart lurch. I should've never let her leave. I should've fought it somehow. There's a killer on the loose, for goodness' sake.

Maybe.

Sort of.

God. I scrub my face with my hands. *Snap out of it. She's a grown woman. She can make decisions on her own.*

Still, I can't help feeling protective over her for numerous reasons. Then again, I was getting ready to tell her about the stolen jewelry if the knock on the door hadn't interrupted us, so maybe this is a better way to end the evening. Maybe I'll just go to bed and pretend this entire night never happened.

Once I tell her, I have no idea how she'll react. Maybe she'll never talk to us again. Maybe she'll turn us in to the police.

These past several years without talking to her other than an occasional holiday or birthday text have been enough to drive me crazy. The few times she's visited—knowing she was just down the street at Frannie's, with Will, and I couldn't do anything about it—

were nothing short of torture. Now that I have her back, I'm not sure I could handle putting myself through it again.

Still, she deserves the truth. As much of it as I understand.

I check the clock again. I should really text her. Just to, you know, make sure she's okay. Ask if I should leave the door unlocked.

Did she bring her keys? Nope. They're in the bowl next to the door.

So, logical question, *Are you coming home? Should I leave the door unlocked, you know, since you don't have keys?*

She can't fault me for asking. Any reasonable person would.

I catch a glimpse of myself in the mirror, and I'm pretty sure it's the exact image you'd find next to "stress" in the dictionary. My hair is frazzled from running my hands through it, eyes red from rubbing them. My back looks as if I've never bent it a day in my life, shoulders stick straight and stiff.

I could just go to the restaurant. Just show up at Joanie's and pretend I didn't realize where they were going. If I don't hear back from her quickly, maybe that's what I'll do. *For her safety.*

I won't interrupt. Maybe I'll just watch. Make sure she's safe.

A light catches my eye outside, and this time the

vehicle turns down our street and slows in front of our house.

My heart jumps in my chest, apparently participating in some sort of triathlon I wasn't made aware of with the way it's racing. My entire body floods with a mix of relief and new concern—*did she have a nice time? Will she be a little wine drunk, lips red from being kissed?* I swallow, bile climbing in my throat as my thoughts descend the stairs of my own personal hell.

Will she be seeing him again? Tomorrow, maybe?

Then, worst of all: *Did he touch her?*

Did she want him to?

Did she sleep with him?

My blood boils at the thought, and by the time he walks her up to the door, I'm practically balancing on a razor blade, I'm so on edge. I can't breathe right as I watch him lean in for a kiss.

I'm going to die right here, right now.

Time of death, 11:13 p.m.

At the last second, she turns her head slightly, and from what I can tell, the kiss lands just next to her mouth.

I have just swallowed the sun whole, and it's now living inside me, warming me from the inside, shining light on the entire room. I sit on the couch, then turn to adjust my legs, attempting to look more casual. I lie down, then sit up, resting against the arm.

When she walks in, I'm standing again, body stiff as a board.

She doubletakes, jolts, and claps a hand to her chest. *"Jesus.* Sorry. You scared me." She shuts the door with another look my way. "I didn't expect you to still be awake."

"You thought I would go to bed without knowing you were safe?"

"I was fine," she assures me. Then, more gently, she adds, "I'm sorry if I worried you."

"Worried me." I scoff. "Of course I worried about you. You were the one just saying there might be a killer on the loose."

"I know that. What am I supposed to do? Hide away and refuse to live my life because of it?"

I inhale through my nose. She's right. More than that, she doesn't deserve this frustration. Even through my anger, I know she did nothing wrong. "Did you at least have a nice time?"

"Yes," she says, but her voice betrays her. She didn't have a nice time, but only a jerk would celebrate that. *Right?* "It was really nice, actually."

Yeah, I bet. She has no idea I saw the way she brushed him off at the door. "Great. I'm glad. I'm going to bed." I move around her and toward the hall, then into my bedroom and shut the door. I drop down on the bed, huffing a breath.

She's going to make me lose my mind.

This woman is going to make me lose my damn mind.

I can hear her moving around in her room and

know she's probably undressing, probably recounting the night. Thinking of him. Maybe I misread that inter-action at the door. I was far enough away, maybe she actually did kiss him back. My throat is too dry.

When I hear a buzzing from next door, my entire body goes on alert. Every hair on my neck stands on end as I hold my breath and listen.

Yes, there's definitely a steady hum coming from the other side of the wall. *Buzzzzzzzzzzzzzzzzzzzzzzzzzzzzzzzzzzzzzzzzzzzzzzzz.*

Oh god. Is she...

My chest is tight. Is this what a heart attack feels like? Images of Tessa in bed, hand slipping under the covers, toy putting the pressure right where she needs it flood my mind.

Heat climbs my neck. I should give her privacy. Turn on my TV so I can't hear anything. Better yet, I should go and take a cold shower and get my shit together.

*Or...*I could offer my assistance.

Just that thought has me on fire, my skin ablaze with thoughts of her. I move toward the wall instinc-tively, pressing my fingers against it.

This is so wrong.

Buzzzzzzzzzzzzzzzzzzzzzzzzzzzz.

"No, fuck this," I growl, pressing off of the wall and out of the room. I should burst in, demand to watch. Demand to join in. But I'm not an animal, despite my current feral state. I bang on the door and the buzzing stops. Caught red-handed. "Tessa, open the door."

Within seconds, the door opens, and she stands in front of me, fully clothed in baby-blue silk pajamas—a matching shirt and shorts. Her lips are dripping with white foam, and in her hand, she holds a toothbrush.

An electric toothbrush.

Fuck me.

The balloon inside my chest deflates rapidly, as if it's been popped with a needle.

"What?" she asks, mouth full.

I close my eyes, pressing my finger to the space between my brows. *What is wrong with me?*

When I open my eyes, she turns away, walking back to her bathroom to spit out the toothpaste and rinse her mouth. I step farther into her room, watching in the mirror as she dries her lips. She didn't shut the door, so I'm not breaking any rules here.

She turns back around, leaning against the bathroom counter. "Um, hi there. You look ready to pass out. You're sweating. Are you okay?"

Without warning to either of us, I cross the room, both hands going to either side of her face as my lips crush hers. She's stiff in my arms for two seconds, and I worry I've overstepped, but then, she's mine.

I feel her melt against me with an exhale of breath. I claim her mouth with mine, scraping my teeth along her lips. A little whimper escapes her, and I lift her up, setting her on the counter and pressing myself between her legs, letting her feel what she does to me.

Her hands are in my hair, nails scratching my scalp as I drag kisses across her cheeks to that space behind her ear that drives her mad. I move along her collarbone and up her neck, kissing and licking every inch of her I can.

She pulls me back to her mouth, and it's like I'm home. I never want to stop this. My hands find the buttons on her shirt, and I tear them open with reckless abandon, my entire body a pulsing flame. With her shirt open and only her black bra between us, I drop my mouth to her chest, pressing my lips into the space between her breasts. I nip at the tender skin there, and she rolls her pelvis forward, grinding against me. She's practically lying down at this point as I tower over her.

"Please, Garrett," she whispers, head tilted back, eyes closed.

I step back, stopping.

She blinks slowly, legs spread, shirt dropped off her shoulders, body on display for me and me only. Her chest rises and falls with heavy, erratic breaths as she studies me. "W-what…are you doing?"

I'm out of breath, too, as I say, "Does he make you feel like this?"

She puts a hand to her chest, trying to catch her breath. "What?" Her legs slowly slide together as she sits up straighter.

"Because if he made you feel…an *ounce* of what I

just made you feel, you should go for it. If not…what are we even doing?" With that, and against everything in me begging me to stay, to continue what we were just doing, I walk away from her.

It's only the second hardest time I've had to do so.

CHAPTER TWENTY-SEVEN

TESSA — AGE 17

We pull up in front of Mark Summers's house—
Garrett, Will, Cory, Britney, and I—when the party is
already in full swing. It's just past ten, and the house is
packed with people. Mark's house is on a dead-end
road on the outskirts of town, so it's the perfect place
for a party when his parents go away for work.

I don't remember what they do, now that I'm
thinking of it, but it's something in finance or enter-
tainment. Most importantly, it requires them to be
away often.

The house is a two-story, brick colonial with black
shutters. Light streams out from six of the eight identical windows, which give glimpses into the packed
party inside.

Will steps from the driver's side of the car, scanning
the house. "I've gotta go find Cassidy. Catch you guys
in a bit."

He jogs ahead, slipping in the front door before we reach the steps. Once there, we all split up. Britney zips across the living room and leaps onto the back of the guy she's currently seeing, a senior named Evan that I don't know all that well.

Cory finds a group of guys, who welcome him with loud shouting of his name and several of those weird handshake-hug things that boys our age seem to do.

Garrett takes my hand and leads me to the table to get drinks. He gestures to the variety of options. "Are you drinking tonight, or no?"

He knows I'm not big on alcohol, but I've had it a few times. Still, the party tonight feels too over-whelming for me to be comfortable with anything that amplifies that. "No, thanks. Just soda, please."

"Yep. Sure." He grabs a root beer—my favorite—without having to ask and cracks it open for me before opening a Dr. Pepper for himself.

"You can drink, though, if you want."

"I know." He nods. "I'm okay. Your brother and Cassidy seem to be getting along well."

"It's weird, right?" I agree, wrinkling my nose as we move away from the table. "I've never seen him date anyone for this long. I'm not sure I've ever really seen him date at all."

"Well, I think they started hanging out around my birthday, so yeah, it may as well be a decade for him."

I laugh. "She's fine, though. I mean, he could be with someone worse. I don't mind her."

He shrugs, taking another drink. "Hey, I wanted to talk to you about something. Can we go somewhere quieter?"

"Is this you trying to seduce me?" I tease, running my fingers up his shirt.

"Always." Taking my hand, he pulls me toward the back of the house and out onto the porch, which is surprisingly quiet. Farther out in the yard, there's a fire pit, though it's already too warm this spring for it to be lit.

He leans against the porch railing. "So, I think my parents are considering leaving."

His words catch me off guard. "Leaving? Like going out of town?"

"Yeah, but, um, permanently."

"Wait, what? You're moving?" Why does he sound so calm? How can he possibly say this to me with a straight face?

"No. Well, er, I'll be going off to college after graduation, and I think they're planning to wait until then so I don't have to enroll in a new school for just a few months, but yeah. If they leave, it'll mean I might not be around as much for holidays and stuff."

The news is a devastating blow. "So what are you saying?"

Finally catching the look on my face, his unreadable expression morphs into one of sorrow. "Don't be upset. I'm, this isn't, I mean, I wasn't trying to make this a big thing. It's still not a done deal, but they've been talking about it more and more. I'll still come visit as much as I can, and now that you have a car, you can come visit me too, but I just wanted you to hear it from me before Will mentioned it."

"Will already knows?"

Guilt weighs on his features. "He's my best friend. I'm telling you both."

I want to point out that he told Will first, but it's not fair. I don't want this relationship to cause issues for any of us, but I'm just wondering when I'll stop feeling like the third wheel. More and more, I'm forced to remember Will had him first. "So when will you know for sure?"

"I don't know, really. But I'll tell you as soon as I do. I just wanted to give you a heads-up because…it seems like they're pretty serious about leaving."

"Is it because of me? Do they not like us together?" My dry eyes burn with impending tears. "Have they said something about my mom?"

"What?" He balks. "No. *No.* They love you. And your mom. You know that. It has nothing to do with you guys. It's just, well, all the deaths happening have them spooked. Especially as Jenny gets closer and closer to Emily and Amber's age, and the police still haven't caught whoever's doing this." He rolls his eyes. "I don't know if there's even a suspect right now. They just want to get away in case it is a serial killer, and I can't say I blame them." He turns his head to look at me. "Do you think your mom would ever consider the same?"

I think on it for a moment, but the answer is obvious. "I can't imagine a world where she leaves this place. She grew up here. She has friends here. The church. Pastor Charles and Mrs. Mabel have really helped us out lately. Her whole world is here. You know how she is. She's settled."

"Yeah, I get all that, but I mean, come on. Someone is also murdering girls and their moms here," he points out. "I hate the idea of leaving for college, and you having no one here to protect you. It's the only reason I'd ever consider staying." With another sip of his drink, he's talking to himself more than me. "I could take a year off, and then we could apply to colleges together. If my parents do leave, I could ask your mom about staying in Will's old room after he moves out. I'm sure he wouldn't mind."

"Wait, no. You can't put off college for me. That would be so unfair. You've been looking forward to this for years. It's why you joined so many clubs. You've already gotten scholarships lined up."

"College will still be there. Maybe some of the scholarships, too." He sounds angry, but I know he's not. He hates that this is coming as much as I do, but right now I can't be selfish. Even if I really, really want to be. "Nothing is as important as keeping you safe."

"Have you met my mother?" I ask, forcing a laugh.

"That woman is a pitbull. No one will mess with me as long as she's around." Pressing my fingers to his chest, I walk them up step by step with each new word. "Not. Even. You."

He raises his brows with a challenge and wraps an arm around my back, tugging me against his body and pressing a kiss to my lips. "You're not wrong," he whispers, his hand tightening on my back in a way that warms me to my core.

"We'll be okay," I promise him. "We can talk on the phone every night. Text when we can. I'll come visit you on the weekends, and we'll figure out holidays. It's just one year. With fall, spring, and summer break, it'll feel like no time at all." Tears prick my eyes. "And then we can go wherever we want. *Do* whatever we want."

He kisses my lips again, heat sweeping through me as his tongue brushes mine. When he pulls back, it's with a look of regret. "Will you at least ask her? Just talk to her about it?"

"Yeah, sure, I'll ask, but I really don't think it will matter. You know how Mom gets. Stubborn as can be."

"Oh, I know." He chuckles. "Where do you think you got it from?"

I swat his chest. "Watch it."

He opens his mouth to respond but pulls me into a kiss instead. I close my eyes, lifting my hand to cup his face. He makes my heart race and my entire body flutter. My butterflies for him are everywhere.

"Ahhhhhhhhhhhhhhhhhhhhh!"

Ice spikes through me. My thoughts fragment. *A scream. That was a scream. It was coming from inside the house. Run. Help.*

Garrett looks at me, and it's clear we both understand. "That was Will."

CHAPTER TWENTY-EIGHT

GARRETT — AGE 18

I keep Tessa close as we rush through the packed house, the party devolving into pure chaos before our very eyes. Half of our classmates are running toward the sound, while the other half darts away from it. Everywhere I look, people are scrambling either to find out the source of the chaos or to escape it.

Someone shoves past me. Someone else trips and falls coming down the stairs up ahead.

"Will!" I shout, trying to hear him, but it's impossible to hear anything in this place. The house is deafening with footsteps and shouted directions, people looking for the ones they came with, and everyone scrambling and fighting to make their way around.

I keep a tight hold on Tessa's hand. It's the only thing that matters aside from finding Will. I have to get them both out of here.

"Move!"

"Watch it!"

"What was that?"

"Have you seen Sarah?"

"Dude! Did you hear that?"

"What the fuck?"

When I finally lay eyes on Will, he's standing next to the open basement door with a horrified look on his face, eyes wide and wild as if he's seen a ghost. His hands are up close to his chest, clutching something either invisible or unseen from where I stand across the room.

The basement door is open, and people are slowly making their way down, while others are fighting for a way up with equally haunted faces.

In the basement, more people are screaming. Justin Davis comes up the stairs with his phone pressed to his ear, a finger pressed to the other. "We need an ambulance."

Tessa and I make terrified eye contact for a split second, more determined than before as we zigzag our way through the crowd to reach Will. When we do, I drop her hand to step in front of him. "Will. Man. What's going on? What happened? Are you okay?"

His eyes drop to mine, and he shakes his head. "No. No, I'm not. It's... It's Cassidy." His skin is pale. Ghost-like. He looks as if he's going to pass out.

"What did she do?" Tessa demands, voice sharp.

"She's dead." He glances toward the basement.

"What?" A dismissive laugh dies on her lips. "No. What are you talking about?"

Will covers his face with his hands, sobbing. "She's dead."

I look at Tessa, whose expression displays a fraction of the disbelief and terror I feel. She doesn't want to believe it, and neither do I. "Stay with him."

She wraps her arms around her brother, a blank stare on her face, as I dart away from them and make my way down the stairs with the crowd, determined to prove Will wrong.

This has to be a misunderstanding. It can't be that someone else has died. It just can't.

There are fifty-four people in our graduating class. Half of them are girls. Three of those girls can't be dead in a matter of months. It's impossible. It's stupid.

Serial killers are supposed to be smart, aren't they? Why would they make their operation as obvious as this? Why would they target our town?

When I reach the bottom of the stairs, there's a crowd already gathered around. The air is electric with a palpable sort of panic. I squeeze my way through, nudging people out of the way to get close.

When I do, I find Cory sitting on the ground next to Cassidy's body, both of them absolutely soaked with blood.

CHAPTER TWENTY-NINE

TESSA — PRESENT DAY

I'm still sitting on the bathroom counter, still half drunk on his kiss, when he backs away.

"Because if he made you feel an ounce of what I just made you feel, you should go for it. If not...what are we even doing?" He shakes his head, stepping back farther from me as if I'm a ghost who's haunting him. Maybe I am. Goodness knows he's haunted me.

How could I ever tell him that, though?

More importantly, how can he not see it?

He shuts my bedroom door then, and moments later I hear his own door shut. With a puff of air, I begin buttoning my shirt. My entire body is pure flame, pulsing with little waves of electricity as I replay what just happened.

Did it just happen? Somehow, it feels like a dream I've had a few times now. The one where he comes back. The one where he never left. The one where we finally make it work.

With my shirt buttoned, I look myself over in the mirror. My hair is coming out of my ponytail, and my cheeks and neck are flushed pink. Evidence of what he does to me is everywhere, and I can't ignore it, even if I wanted to.

Which I don't.

I cross the room quickly, not bothering to knock on his door as I barge inside. He's standing next to the bed, and I can't tell if he was coming toward the door or staring at it the same way he's been staring at me all this time.

Like he despises me and is starving for me in equal measure.

"What the hell was that?" I demand, waving my hand back in the direction of my room.

He curses, looking down. "I shouldn't have done that."

"Why?" I demand. "You regret kissing me?"

"It's not about regret. We agreed back then that this couldn't work. You've held up your end of the deal, and I need to hold up mine. I just... It's not easy."

"Not easy because you want me or because you don't want someone else to have me?"

He jerks his head back, face pinched. "Excuse me?"

I jab a finger in the air at him, mad now. "Back then, when you finally went after me, it was because

Brendan was interested. And then once you had me, you lost interest—"

"Oh, you know that is not what happened—"

"And now Mark wants me, and suddenly you're kissing me again. After all this time. You can't tell me that's a coincidence."

"Of course it's not a coincidence," he groans, hands on either side of his head. "Because it makes me fucking insane with jealousy to see you with anyone else. Not because I don't want you. Not because I have ever, for a single second, not wanted you. Because I have, Tessa. Jesus Christ, I have wanted you every second of every day for as long as I can remember." He shouts the words like he's losing grip, hands out to his sides in the air. "How can you not see that?"

"Maybe because you walked away!"

"I went to college."

"You ended things before you left!" Fury storms through my veins. Troops heading into battle. "Don't act like that's the reason we didn't work."

"It is! Long distance was too hard, but I offered to wait. I offered to stay here with you!"

"What? So we could resent each other in six months? I wasn't stupid. You needed to go to college. I just didn't expect you to run off and forget about me."

"What the hell are you talking about?" he demands. "I never forgot. That is not what happened. Don't twist the story."

"You never called. You didn't text. When I tried to

call you—when you actually answered my calls—you always acted like you were too busy. Like I was a burden. So I stopped trying."

"Because it was too hard. Don't you get that, Tessa?" he says my name with a whispered breath, exasperated. "All I thought about when you weren't with me was you. When you visited after your graduation, that was the first time I'd felt alive since the moment I left. If I didn't call or text you enough, it's because it literally tore me apart to hear your voice and know I couldn't be with you then. I was so excited for you to visit, and if I ever acted like it wasn't all that I wanted—that every single phone call wasn't what kept me breathing —it was just because I didn't want you to see how hard it was for me to be away from you. I didn't want you to know I was hurting. I didn't want *that* to be your burden."

I stop short at the revelation, his pained eyes telling me it's the truth. "Why didn't you tell me that?"

"Because I was a teenage kid who had no idea how to handle his feelings, let alone explain them to you. Because I didn't want to scare you off. And because…" He reaches out his hand, but stops short of touching me. "Because I was in love with you and terrified you didn't feel the same way."

"You were in love with me?" I demand. "Since when? You should've told me."

"I was going to tell you. I was. But then…" His head suddenly seems to hold the weight of the world as he sinks down onto the bed. "There's so much that happened back then. So much, and it just all felt so heavy. You were here, and you were happy, and I couldn't tell you I loved you without telling you everything else. And that killed me. It kills me to think you ever felt like I didn't want you." Pinching the bridge of his nose between his fingers, he releases a heavy breath. "Or that I only wanted you because someone else did."

"I told Mark I couldn't see him anymore," I whisper, divulging the truth I'd planned to keep to myself a while longer.

He stands and steps toward me. "You did?"

"Of course I did," I say, breathless. "He's a nice guy. A really nice guy, but..." I meet his eyes, trying to say so much with just a few words. "He's not you."

CHAPTER THIRTY

GARRETT — PRESENT DAY

"Do you still want me?" My voice is shaky, but it's nothing compared to the vibrations I feel inside my body. Every part of me is in tune with her. I can't think of anything except for the words she just uttered—*he's not you*—and the fact that she's in my bedroom right now, staring at me in a way she hasn't stared at me in years.

"I've always wanted you. I never stopped—"

I don't even let her finish the sentence. I can't. I need her. I grab her, cupping her face. I try to be gentle, to savor, to worship, but it's impossible when I have her here after I've dreamed of this—a second chance— since the day she left.

I press my lips to hers, claiming her mouth over and over again. She is mine. She's always been mine, and I've always been hers. I can't wait any longer. I lay her on the bed and run my tongue down her chest while I unbutton her shirt again, kissing each new inch of exposed flesh. She smells sweet, like coconut, and tastes like heaven. I've missed her taste, her scent. I've missed her.

I close my eyes, pressing the moment into my brain so I'll never forget it.

"You have no idea how bad I want you," I whisper, refusing to take my lips from her skin. She sits up, pulling her bra over her head before grabbing my shirt and tearing it off me.

Neither of us can stand to wait another second when all we've done is wait for years. Everything was slow motion, but now the race is back on. *Full speed ahead.*

I want to remember every second of this, save it in my mind so I can replay it later. "Are you sure about this?" I whisper, needing confirmation. I couldn't live with it if she regrets it in the morning.

In answer, she pulls my mouth to hers and kisses me deeper. "So sure. I need you."

I nip at her jaw, then her neck and shoulder, pressing gentle kisses after each bite. I make my way across her skin, marking her and soothing her in quick succession.

I'm feral when I reach her chest, reveling in the fact that this is real. It's no longer in my dreams. And god knows I've had plenty of dreams just like this.

I flatten my tongue, tracing it up and over her breast, slowing when I reach her nipple before sucking it into my mouth. Her back arches, and she releases a guttural moan from deep in her chest.

"Mm-hmm. I remember what you like, my good girl."

She strokes the back of my head, mouth open in answer, pure longing on her face. "Garrett..."

I pull her into my mouth again, holding eye contact this time. I want to see her fall apart for me. *And oh, she does.* My girl responds immediately, arching her back higher, pressing up off the mattress. I smile against her, swirling my tongue across her nipple as my hand moves to take care of the other one.

She drives me mad, making sounds I've only heard in my dreams for so long, cries that can only come from those lips, moans that haunt me.

I pull back, and she stills, watching me as I slowly trail kisses along her ribs. I kiss each little hollow, inhaling deeply as I go, burying my face in her skin. I can't get enough of her.

I could die happy like this, in her arms. I drag my mouth down her bare stomach, scraping her skin with my beard. Tomorrow, when she gets dressed, she won't be able to unsee the proof that we were together tonight. That she was mine. That I'm still the only one who can make her feel this good.

When I reach her shorts, I tug them down. She lifts

her hips to help me as I ease them over her hips and off her legs.

Starting at her knees, I nip and kiss my way up her thighs, her cries growing more impatient with each one. She loves to see me like this—wanting her, needing her more than air—and I'm happy to make it happen.

"Please…" she begs again.

I hum. "You know I love hearing you beg for it. What do you want, my good girl?"

"Touch me."

I run a finger up her calf. "Touch you…here?"

She pins me with a glare, and I slide my finger up, teasing her inner thigh. "Here, then?"

"Garrett." She huffs.

I slowly brush my fingers up until I'm nearly where she wants me, going completely still. Goose bumps form under my fingers. "Is this where you want me?"

She props up on her elbows with a devilish grin. "Touch me before I do it myself."

At once, I slip my fingers inside her, curling them up and working slow circles with my thumb. "Is this where you want me, baby?"

She falls back with a gasp, unable to speak.

"Yeah, you like that?"

She purrs her delight as I work my fingers inside her, and when I feel her start to tighten already, I dip my head down, replacing my fingers with my mouth.

She bucks and takes hold of my head, pinning me against her. "Yes. Please. Don't stop."

She's more vocal now than I remember, and my body responds to it with fire on fire. I push against her, adjusting to get on my knees, hooking her legs over my shoulders as I push her closer and closer to the edge.

When I feel her start to shake, she tenses and stills, not ready for this to be over. I chuckle against her skin. "Going to make me work for it, huh, baby?"

She should know better. It only takes ten seconds to get what I want, coaxing the release out of her like a triumphant warrior returning from battle. When I finally hear her cry out, I smile, but I don't let up. Her body goes rigid. Then, seconds later, she's utterly languid in my arms. When she lets out a long breath, I ease her back down on the bed.

I press another kiss to her sensitive skin, then drop to my knees on the ground at the bedside, digging a condom out of my drawer.

She sits up, and I pull her down to the ground onto my lap. She kisses me gently at first, then with more fire. "You're so fucking sexy," I whisper in her ear, kissing just under the lobe.

With wide, doe-like eyes, she crawls down my body, dropping to her hands and knees in front of me and taking me in her hands. She bites her bottom lip, giving me a coy little smile.

Slowly, oh so fucking slowly, she wraps her lips

around me, and I swear to god I see stars. This woman is a goddess. A temptress.

She's heaven and sin all wrapped into one, and she's mine.

My whole fucking world.

I close my eyes, throwing my head back as her tongue slides down my length. "Fuck yes." She moves faster, apparently spurred on by my praise. "That's my girl."

I'm not going to last long if we keep this up. I grab her hair, then her face, pulling her up to meet my mouth, devouring her with a new sense of urgency as I grab the condom, tear it open, and sheathe myself. She eases onto my lap again. This time, we work together to guide her down on top of me.

"You good?"

She nods, moving slowly until I'm completely inside her, and then, *fuck.* This is heaven. I've died and gone to heaven, and I couldn't be happier about it.

I'd die a million times if it always feels this good.

We rock together in perfect unison, our skin slick with sweat. I hold her against me and pump into her, then slow down when she takes control, kissing my lips as she rides me. We tease and tempt each other, going right to the edge but refusing to go over. We're both stubborn like that, I guess, which is what makes it so electric between us.

I don't want to stop.

I never want to stop.

And finally, when the molten metal fills my veins, all thoughts cease. We go over the edge of the cliff in a chorus of cries and moans and "yeses," and she's smiling at me in that way she always has. I know then, all at once, nothing has changed, yet somehow, everything has changed.

CHAPTER THIRTY-ONE

TESSA — AGE 17

I cross the hall and knock on Will's door, putting lip gloss on as I go. When he doesn't answer right away, I knock again. "Will? Are you in there? I need to borrow your extra charger. Mine's at Britney's."

Again, there's no answer.

"I'm coming in. Hope you're not doing anything weird." I turn the knob and step inside his bedroom only to find it empty. "Cool. Talking to myself over here." I make my way to the nightstand and tug it open, digging through a wad of tangled cords until I find the right one. Once I do, I move to shut the drawer, but something stops me. "What the..." I stick my hand into the drawer and freeze when I realize what I'm looking at.

"What are you doing?" My brother's angry voice makes me jump. He's in the doorway, drying his hands on his shirt. His eyes lock on the drawer, and we both know he knows what I've found. "Get out of there!" he shouts, rushing toward me to slam it shut. I barely pull my hand out in time to avoid it being smashed.

"Why do you have pictures of random girls from school in your nightstand?"

They aren't naked pictures, either. Those would be equally disgusting, but a little less weird, maybe? I don't know. These are just photos of them being normal. Random, even. They look like the selfies you could easily find on someone's MySpace, Tumblr, and Facebook profiles.

I jerk the drawer open again and retrieve the stack before he can stop me. An unsettling feeling takes root in the pit of my stomach as I flip through them. There are only three photos here, and as I realize that, it steals my breath.

Cassidy Cole. Emily Gray. Amber Allen. In that order. If you reverse it, it's the order in which they died.

I wave the stack of pictures at him, trying to understand. "What are these?" I need him to explain it to me in a way that makes sense. A way that would make me certain he's not a creep or a weirdo. Or worse.

"None of your business." He snatches them back. "I just have them, okay?"

"Do I want to know why?"

"You aren't gonna, no matter what you want," he grunts. "I don't go through your stuff."

"I needed to borrow your charger."

He waves it away. "You got it, now go."

"Will, what's going on? What is that about?" I don't budge. "You're freaking me out. Is it some sort of weird porn thing?"

He scowls. "Don't be disgusting."

"Why else would you have them? Give them here." I try to take them back, but he raises them above his head. I grab hold of his arm and tug down, but he's stronger than me and his arm hardly budges.

"Forget it. Get out of here!"

"No! I'm not going to have the weirdo stalker brother. Give those to me." Without looking at me, he keeps the photos high above my reach. I jab a finger at him. "Seriously, the girls who died? Do you have any idea how bad that makes you look? What will people say if they find out—"

"You're not going to say a word," he warns, his voice cutting. It's his turn to jab his finger at me, nearly touching my nose. "Do you understand? Not a word to anyone!"

"What's going on?" Momma asks, appearing in the doorway with her jacket still on. I didn't hear her get home from her monthly Christian women's meeting at church.

"*Nothing,*" Will says, with what my mom would call 'a tone.' When she raises a brow, he backtracks quickly. "Sorry. Nothing. We were just goofing off."

Mom's eyes fall to me, but I don't know what to say. I don't want Will to get into trouble when I have no idea what's going on. Besides, we've never been ones to rat each other out, and I won't start now.

"We're fine."

She nods. "Good. Now wash up. I brought home sandwiches from Domenico's." Looking around the room, she asks, "Is Garrett not here?"

"No," we answer at once.

She clicks her tongue. "Oh, well, I brought him something just in case. We'll put it in the fridge."

Once she's gone, I turn back to Will. "Promise me you aren't doing anything wrong with those."

"Like what?" he asks, his upper lip curled.

I can't bear to ask the question that's on my mind. "Like I said, those girls are dead, Will. It doesn't look good."

"What are you saying? Are you asking if I hurt them?" He steps away, clutching the pictures and shoving them back in his nightstand. "You really think I'd be capable of killing someone?"

"No. I just... I'm scared, you know? Cory was arrested, but they let him go because his prints weren't on the weapon. I know they're saying they found other stuff at his house now, but until he's arrested again, we don't know the truth. Someone else at that party might have killed Cassidy. You were with her. If it was an accident or something—"

"How long have you been waiting to ask me that, Tessa?" he cries.

"I just..."

225

"Get out. If you think I'm capable of any of this, I guess that says a lot about us, doesn't it?"

"Stop. I want to help—"

"Out!" he whisper-shouts, pointing toward the door.

With my head down, I leave with the charger and a sick feeling bubbling in my gut.

CHAPTER THIRTY-TWO

GARRETT — AGE 18

It's chilly for an April morning when I reach the ball court at the park and find Brendan, Mark, and Justin standing around. It doesn't take long for me to realize Will isn't there.

"Hey!" I call, startling them. They're huddled in a circle looking at something near the far corner of the court.

"Hey." Mark looks over his shoulder. "Did you hear about Cory? I guess they found some stuff at his house that could connect him to the other murders. Apparently his dad lost his job over it."

"He wasn't arrested," I remind them. It's the same conversation I've been having all week at school. "He was brought in for questioning, but they haven't proven anything yet."

"Yeah, but whatever they found at his house must

be bad," Brendan says. "My dad says he thinks they'll have arrested him by the end of next week."

"My parents were talking about it, too. I guess they're pulling him out of school because of it. Or because someone keeps spray painting his locker," Mark adds with a bit of a chuckle.

"Or stealing his clothes in gym," Justin says.

"I heard someone beat the shit out of him yesterday." Brendan sucks his teeth, shaking his head as if this is all just water cooler gossip and not our friend's life we're talking about.

I can't believe this is what it's come to. "Yeah, I heard that, too. Pretty shitty if you ask me."

Brendan's shoulders are tense as they all turn to face me. "What'd you say?"

"I mean, come on. We don't even know that Cory did anything wrong. Like you said, the police let him go." When no one says anything, I add, "Guys, we know Cory. Do you really think he would kill someone?" I've seen it happening at school, the way everyone turned on him when he came back. The way they've made his days hell. I should've done more to stand up for him, and now I'm ashamed to say I didn't, but cheering because his dad lost his job or he's having to be pulled out of school just feels sick.

"Whatever," Brendan says. "He was caught red-handed in the basement with her, knife and all. Who else could've done it? The boogeyman?" He wiggles his fingers in the air, taunting me.

"Maybe you hadn't heard his prints weren't on the knife," I argue, knowing they heard, and they just don't care. "Plus the basement door that leads outside was left open. Whoever killed Cassidy could've bolted out into the yard when they heard him coming down the stairs. Cory said he went down and found her, tried to resuscitate her or whatever. There's no proof he did anything wrong and that's why they let him go." Frustration spirals in my chest when he scoffs and rolls his eyes.

"That basement door leads to the woods, idiot. Unless you're suggesting Bigfoot came along and killed her, there's no chance anyone would've made it to the driveway covered in blood without being seen. The woods go nowhere."

I clench my jaw. He's not wrong. Tessa and I were some of the only people outside and we never saw or heard anything until we heard Will scream. The sound was clear for us because the exterior door to the basement was open when he went down there and saw Cassidy's body. I like to think we would've heard if someone had gone running, but then again, we were... preoccupied. It haunts me to wonder if we might've been the only chance of catching the killer, and we missed them.

"Look," Brendan goes on, "I'm just glad they finally caught someone. It's been more than six months since Amber and her mom died. Meanwhile, Tommy Ward's running around with his thumb up his ass like he

229

doesn't know which way is left or right and can't figure out why the sheriff's badge is on his chest. We needed answers, and now we have them. Thank God Cory's such an epic fuck-up, or the police would still be wandering around chasing their tails."

I flinch at the harsh words, though I know it's just regurgitated nonsense most of the town is saying. Nothing about his statement is original. Parents and kids alike are celebrating that we finally have our killer, just waiting for the holes in the case to be filled in so an actual arrest can be made.

"Wow. So much for loyalty." I wave a hand at them, starting to walk away. "I'm done here."

"Loyalty?" Brendan shouts, stopping me in my tracks. "What about your loyalty to Emily? Everyone knows the two of you were hooking up. Guess you don't care now that he killed her."

I storm back across the court, voice trembling with radiating fury. "If Cory killed someone—and that's a big *if*—I hope he gets what he deserves. But right now we don't know that he did it, and we definitely don't know that he had anything to do with the other deaths. The stuff everyone's saying they found at his house could just be rumors. You sure are quick to condemn a friend we've all known since kindergarten." I cock my head to the side, something occurring to me for the first time. Why is he so eager to get everyone to believe Cory's guilty? "Maybe you're the one who has something to hide."

He steps forward so we're chest to chest. "Maybe you're just mad because you know I could take your girl if I still wanted her," he sneers.

"Ha!" I laugh, throwing my head back. "You couldn't take my order at a Wendy's, bro, let alone my girl."

"Wanna bet?"

"I'd pay money to see you try."

"Maybe I will."

"Okay, guys, chill out." Mark steps in, shoving his way in between us, hands on each of our chests to keep us back. "This is stupid. Let's just play some ball, okay? That's why we're all here."

We both nod, and I look around. "Well, not all of us. Where's Will, anyway? Anyone heard from him?" He's been weird lately. Distant and quiet. He hasn't wanted to hang out as much. I know a lot of it has to do with Cassidy, but I can't stop worrying it's also about Tessa and me. Things have changed with our dynamic, where she used to be the third wheel with the three of us, and now I'm finding it difficult to keep it all balanced and not make either of them feel that way.

I'm not sure it's working.

"Haven't heard from him." Brendan unlocks his phone, and as he does, I get a glimpse of the image on the screen. It has to be the one they were all huddled around looking at before. Quickly, he swipes it away and opens his messages.

My blood runs cold at first, then red hot. "What the fuck was that on your screen?"

He pales when he realizes what I've seen. "Nothing. Mind your business."

I know what I saw. A nude photo of a girl on his phone. My stomach churns as I realize the last girl he spent any time with was Tessa. Did she send him…

I'm going to be sick.

"Was that Tessa?" I demand, wondering now if there was some credibility to his earlier threat.

Brendan's lips curl up into a cruel smile. "You really are obsessed with the fact that I had her first, aren't you?"

"It's not her," Mark says quickly, putting a hand on my shoulder.

"Then who?" I don't believe them.

Suddenly, they all look guilty.

"I said don't worry about—"

"*Goddamn it! Who?!*" I shout. My voice echoes through the quiet park.

Every single head points to the ground before Brendan coughs, clears his throat, and finally says, "It's, look, it's from before, obviously, but it's, it's Cassidy, okay?"

CHAPTER THIRTY-THREE

TESSA — PRESENT DAY

We're lying in bed later as the sun begins to peek through the blinds, when the worry sets in. I don't know what any of this means or what I even want it to mean.

Garrett and I have always had this weird push-and-pull relationship, but when tested, we weren't able to make it work. What if that hasn't changed? What if I'm reading too much into this, and he doesn't want it to change?

Putting all that aside, I'm supposed to be going back home soon—a home that is nearly four hours away. The fear of long distance was such a problem for us once, it caused the end of our relationship before it ever really began. So will that mean I'll have to come back here after I worked so hard to build a life alone away from this place? It's not like I have anything special in the city. I do freelance web design, so I can do that from anywhere, but it was scary going out into the world when all I've ever known is this place and these people. To return to it—to my friends and Will and Mom—feels like giving a piece of that up. As much as it might seem like a soft place to land, it's also saying goodbye to the work and bravery that went into starting over in a place where I can't ask my neighbor to borrow their car when mine's in the shop or where the police officer who pulled me over hasn't known me since I was in the womb.

The people here don't understand that part of me, but Garrett and Will do. They left, too. I wonder if they had the same reservations about coming home.

All of these thoughts are swirling in my head, making me dizzy with worry, when his voice cuts through it all.

I hadn't even realized he was awake.

"I need to tell you something."

My muscles tense. Those words feel worse somehow than 'we need to talk,' which shattered me the first time, and I'm not sure I'd survive a second.

Slowly, I turn my head to look at him. His dark hair framed by the white pillow looks ethereal and innocent, so peaceful it hurts. "Okay."

He rolls onto his side, squeezing his eyes shut. "I wanted to tell you before any of this happened, and I'm so sorry I didn't. I was going to tell you last night at dinner, and then everything happened, and I was so swept up in it—"

"Are you married?" I squeak out the only possible thought I can imagine would make him look this worried.

He balks. "What? No."

"Then what? A child? Do you have a kid?"

His brows draw together. "Woman, you bungee jump to conclusions. Don't you think Will would've mentioned that?"

"He didn't tell me you lived here."

He opens his mouth, pauses, then says, "Fair point."

"Are you engaged? Or...moving? Are you leaving?"

He puts a hand on my arm. "Take a breath, and I'll tell you."

I release a slow breath on command.

His eyes search mine, looking for answers I surely don't have. Finally, he speaks, and what he says sends spirals of shock through my body.

"Britney didn't steal Cassidy's jewelry back then. And neither did Cory."

"What are you talking about?"

He braces himself, not meeting my eyes for a long pause. When he finally does, there's a pain on his face I don't understand. "Will is the one who stole it. And... and I helped him."

I can't fathom a world where this is anything other than a cruel joke, but as I study his face, trying desperately to find a hint of the laughter I know must be there, I come up empty. "What are you talking about?"

"When Will was dating her, he came up with this... plan. It was just about the Hollywood stuff. The necklace and bracelet from whoever. He thought it was harmless, I guess. I mean, we didn't hurt her. We wouldn't have. But then...she *was* hurt. And we got scared. The missing jewelry...it never had anything to do with her murder. But then we couldn't tell anyone that, or we knew we'd be implicated in everything. It all just happened so close together and..." As he trails off, he's staring hard at nothing at all. Lost in this impossible memory. "But now that they're trying to blame Britney, I just...I can't look you in the eye without telling you the truth."

Fog fills my brain over his confession, muffling and blurring everything he just told me, trying to unscramble it, force it to somehow make sense. But the truth is, it can't. What he has just told me is impossible. "I...I don't understand. How...*how*?"

"I don't know all the details. Honestly, I don't. There was a day when Will knew they wouldn't be home, so we told your mom he was staying over at my house. Then we drove over to Cassidy's in the middle of the night. I stayed in the car to keep watch while he broke in. He knew where her mom kept the jewelry, and he used your mom's key to their house to get in. And we just, I don't know, we just took it, and that was it."

"That was it?" I cry. "You stole two priceless pieces

of jewelry, not to mention implicated my mom in the crime and cost her so much—her dignity, her clients, her livelihood, her reputation—and *that was it*? But *why*? Why would he even do that? What did he do with it? Was he planning to use the money for college or something? He had grant money and scholarships." I should stand up and change, but I'm frozen in place.

"I don't know," he admits. "I don't know why he wanted it. I thought maybe you guys were having financial issues, and neither of you wanted to talk to me about it. I know how hard it was with just your mom, and this was right after everyone had started firing her. At the time, I didn't understand what was going on with that, but Will said people were just nervous. Battening down the hatches or whatever. Still, I knew it was hard and he wouldn't take or borrow any money from me, even when I tried. Cassidy's family was rich, you know? They didn't need the money. I guess I framed it as some sort of *Robin Hood* scenario in my head to ease my guilty conscience. I thought I was helping him help himself in the way he felt like he needed to. I thought it was a stupid ego thing, but I didn't ask questions. I didn't need to know. Will has never asked me for anything that wasn't important, and so I helped him. We didn't speak about it afterward. I couldn't. I know it's wrong and unforgivable. I'm just so sorry."

I sit up in bed, massaging my temples as if I'm

trying to make space for this new reality in my head. "You and Will stole Cassidy's necklace and bracelet?"

"Yes."

"On the day she died?"

"No. A few days before. It was bad timing, but that's all it was, I swear."

I close my eyes. Things *were* hard then, probably even harder than Mom allowed us to see. But why was Will shouldering that alone? It wasn't his place. And why would he ever think something like this would make it okay? *Stealing?* Mom would never have allowed it. "He must've pawned them. That's why they found the bracelet earlier and then the necklace now." I chew my lip in thought. "Britney must've gotten the necklace recently, but she would've recognized it, right? Unless Justin bought it for her as a gift, but again that doesn't make any sense. If they found it at a pawn shop, there would be records, right? The police will be able to track it down." Which might mean they'll trace it back to Will. I don't say that part out loud, but we seem to realize it at the same time.

Garrett swallows. "If he pawned it, it would've had to be far away from here. Everyone in town was on the lookout for that jewelry. No one would've bought it from him."

"Maybe he waited until you were away in college, but that still doesn't explain how Britney got it." I pull my legs up to my chest, bouncing my chin on my knees as I try to piece it all together. "It also doesn't explain the other robberies. There was the coin collection from Amber's and the china from Emily's. Was that Will, too?"

"If it was, he never told me about it."

I rest my forehead on my knees, clicking my tongue as my mind struggles to make sense of this mess. "There has to be something else. It's too much of a coincidence."

"I don't know. Maybe someone saw us steal the jewelry and wanted to frame us."

"But then why didn't they? Nothing ever came out to connect you two to Cassidy. It was always Cory." Anger flashes in me. "And my mom." Without warning, the memory of the photos in Will's nightstand come racing back.

"What is it?" Garrett reads my expression.

"Right after Cassidy was killed, I found these pictures in Will's nightstand of the girls who had died, including Cassidy. When I asked him about them, he got really mad, and that was when we went through that whole period where we weren't speaking. When you…"

He gives the world's smallest nod. "Broke up with you, yeah."

"Was it because of the pictures? Did you know about them?"

"I told you. It was because I was going away, and Will was dealing with some stuff, and it was all too much—"

"You keep saying that, but you're really saying nothing."

"I'm not. It's the truth."

"How would I even know what the truth is? After all, you've clearly gotten good at lying to me over the years." Anger swells in me suddenly. *How could they do this? How could they lie? What else have they done?*

"That's not fair. It wasn't really my secret, and it killed me to keep it from you. I was the one who decided to tell you now because of Britney."

"Well, how noble of you." I charge out of bed, whipping the covers off and wrapping them around myself as I stalk across the room.

"Tessa, wait—"

"No, you wait!" I shout back, stopping in my tracks. I whip around and point a trembling finger at him. "You lied to me for years. My brother lied to me for years. And my mom went through hell for it. And for all I know, you're still lying."

"I'm sorry," he says softly. "I'm sorry I lied. I'm sorry we hurt you. I'm sorry Frannie was ever in the middle of it."

I turn to face the door, catching his eye in the mirror on the wall. "You should've told me last night. Before we..."

"I know. I'm sorry I didn't."

"There's nothing else to say right now." I pull open the bedroom door and shut myself in my room, dropping down on the bed. My entire reality has shifted, and I don't know how to right it.

Why would they lie to me? How can I ever trust either of them again? What other lies might there be? More than that, more than anything else, there's a single question pulsing in my mind: *Why did Will steal the jewelry in the first place?*

CHAPTER THIRTY-FOUR

GARRETT — PRESENT DAY

Once again, I'm torn between my best friend and the woman I love. Will would never be okay with me telling Tessa about the jewelry or any of the rest of it, but I had to.

I'm sick of lying to her. I'm sick of other people's drama being the thing that keeps my heart broken. I could handle it when I thought it was just me. When I thought she was happy.

But I've seen how unhappy she is. I've seen how she lights up when we're together, how she must wonder, how she must hate me for everything I've done—most of which she still doesn't have an explanation for.

Will is on his way home right now, and when he gets here, I'm going to ask that he tell her everything. I'm going to demand it in fact. And if he won't, I will.

I love him. He's a best friend and a brother to me. I would and *have* gone to lengths to protect him beyond what I could previously fathom. I've stood by his side and chosen him time and time again, but enough is enough.

Out of bed, I dress quickly and find Tessa sitting in the living room on the couch, leaning forward over her knees, hands folded together atop her legs. She's staring into space, processing, and I'll give her as much time as she needs to do just that.

"You have cookies from Overflow." Her matter-of-fact tone slices through me. She's hurting, and it's my fault.

The cookies. I'd completely forgotten about them. It feels so stupid now. "Um, yeah. I had some things to do in town yesterday evening, and they sounded good."

She rests her chin on her fists. "You didn't get them for me, then?"

I consider lying even more than I already have about the errands, but something stops me. "What do you think?"

Her face softens slightly as she finally turns her head to look at me. "It's very sweet of you."

"You deserve to have someone who does nice things for you. And who remembers which restaurants you like."

"And that someone should be you?" She's still not moving, so I don't either.

"It should be whoever you want it to be, but...I'd like to put my name in the running, yeah." The joke falls flat, but she smiles, even if it's sad and a little lost.

"For what it's worth, I *am* sorry," I tell her. "It doesn't matter that I am. It doesn't fix anything, but I wanted you to know anyway. I'm sorry I couldn't tell you back then. I'm sorry I couldn't be honest. I really am trying to work on that."

She turns her head to look at me, a very clear picture of anger and sorrow painted across her face. "Just be honest with me. Is that the reason we broke up? The jewelry?"

"I swear to you it isn't."

She stands now, her eyes a bit glazed as if she's looking *through*, rather than *at*, me. "That night of your graduation party when we…"

She doesn't need to say the words aloud for me to know what she means. That blush on her cheeks reveals all of her thoughts.

"Yeah."

"You hinted that there was a reason you broke up with me that you couldn't talk about."

I run my tongue along my teeth. "Yes, there is."

"What is it?"

"It's complicated."

She sighs, starting to walk away, but I catch her arm. "Wait, please. I will explain everything. I swear I will."

"When?"

"Today. As soon as Will gets here."

"Why?" she demands, hands out to her sides. "What does any of this have to do with my brother?"

"It's just…not really my secret to tell."

"You broke up with me over Will." Her tone is pointed. "What? Because he asked you to?"

"No." The answer is quick and sharp and honest. Will never wanted us to break up. In truth, I'm not totally sure he realizes when we did. He was so buried in the rest of it. "No. But he needed me."

"And you had to choose?"

"It's not that simple."

"Of course. Why would it be?" Again, she starts to walk away, but she stops and spins back. "That night… you were drunk, and we…"

Suddenly, she's so shy.

"Yes," I say, saving her. "I remember."

"Was it because you were drunk or because you still wanted me?"

I roll my neck, pleading with her. "I wasn't that drunk, Tessa. I wanted you then as much as I've ever wanted you, as much as I want you now. I never knew how to stop." *Even when I wished I did.*

Slowly, she nods. Then, before I'm ready, she's out the door, and this time I can't think of a single thing to say that might change her mind.

CHAPTER THIRTY-FIVE

TESSA — AGE 17

> Are you coming over today?

The text I sent Garrett is still sitting on my phone from this morning, unanswered. It's not like him to ignore me for so long. I want to ask him about the photos Will has. Surely there's some explanation, but Will won't give it to me if so.

He won't speak to me at all, actually. He wouldn't look at me this morning in church, and we sat on the pew with Mom in between us. Will and I don't fight. Even when we were younger, we didn't have the typical squabbles most siblings do. After Dad died and Mom had to take on extra jobs to keep us afloat, it was always just the two of us. We were each other's parents, best friends, and confidants all rolled into one. We didn't have time for petty arguments.

It's why his friends are mine, and mine are his.

We've always spent time together because we wanted to. Which is why now, sitting across the hall from him, knowing he's angry with me, is uncomfortable.

It's as bad as the one non-speaking fight I've ever had with Britney was.

If I tell Garrett about Will's photos, will that make it even worse? More than anything, I just want to understand, but maybe this is one of those things a sister just can't.

Like when we were younger and Will used to tease me about the posters of *NSYNC that adorned my walls.

But this isn't the same thing. If the photos hadn't been of Cassidy, Amber, and Emily, I'd accept that, but those three throw a wrench into everything. Maybe he had them before and forgot to throw them away.

Maybe it's much less sinister than I imagine. I can't see Will hurting anyone, so maybe it's just some weird guy thing. If I want to stay sane, I have to believe that's the case.

With a sigh and shreds of a plan taped together, I cross the hall and knock on his door gently, hoping he can hear the apology in the soft thuds.

"Will? It's me. Can we talk?" I wait for a while, then add, "Please?"

I get no answer except for the volume on his TV being turned up. This isn't like him. I'm starting to worry now.

"Will, please," I shout over the TV.

When I get no response, I twist the knob and push the door open slowly, giving him plenty of opportunity to shout or slam the door shut. When he doesn't, I step inside.

He's curled up in a ball on his bed, his back to me, a hooded sweatshirt on with the hood pulled up over his head. I grab the remote from his side and turn the TV off. Quickly, he rolls over, glaring at me for a second. Then, just as fast, he turns back toward the wall.

I pat his calf. "Look, I'm sorry, okay? You have to know I wasn't trying to snoop. Why would I do that? *When* have I ever done that? I was just looking for a charger. I know you're not a bad person. I know you didn't hurt Cassidy or anyone else for that matter." I pause, but he doesn't acknowledge me or move in any way. "I hate fighting with you. Talk to me, please."

"Go away," he grumbles.

"Why?" I try to roll him over, but he fights me. "You're scaring me. Seriously. What is going on?"

"Nothing," he snaps. "I just don't want to talk to you. We aren't friends, okay? You're my annoying little sister. That's it. I have to put up with you, but it doesn't mean I want to. Maybe it's time you deal with the fact that I don't tell you everything. Actually, now that I think about it, maybe it's time we stopped telling each other anything at all."

I reel back as if I've been slapped, tears welling in my eyes. "I don't understand what I've done that's so wrong. We *are* friends. I tell you everything."

"Yeah, well, maybe I don't want to hear about your stupid friends and your stupid boyfriend anymore. Did you ever think of that?"

I hear the hurt in his voice even if I don't understand it. "Is this about Garrett?"

"No." He scoffs. "I'm just over it, Tessa. Leave me alone."

"Over what? Maybe you should talk to someone. If not me, maybe Pastor Charles or Mr. Taylor at school. I know the school counselor is supposed to be cheesy, but he's really—"

"Leave me alone!" he bellows, rolling over on the bed and lunging at me. My heart skips a beat, but he stops himself, almost like he's afraid of his own outburst. The anger disappears from his face, and he turns away, burrowing his face farther into the mattress, defeated. "I don't want to talk to anyone in this stupid, fucking town."

I've heard my brother curse a few times in my life, but never at me. Never like this. The person I'm staring at is unrecognizable. "Is this about Cassidy? I know how bad you must be hurting and how much you cared about her—"

He jumps from the bed, storming across the room. "Get the fuck out of my room, Tessa, before I do something I can't take back."

I flinch. "What did you just say?"

"Just go." There's a flicker in his eyes that scares me. Something dark and dangerous and impossible to reconcile with the brother I've known for the past seventeen years of my life. That man feels miles away now, impossible to reach.

"Why are you being like this?"

"Tessa!" he barks.

"What's going on?" Garrett is there standing in the hallway, and I have no idea how much he's heard or what he must think of us. I'm just so relieved to see him.

I run to him, throwing my arms around his waist, and sink into the peace he brings me. "I'm so glad you're here."

His arms come around me, but it's brief and distant. He pulls back just as quickly. "I'm going to talk to your brother, okay?"

"Okay." I back up as he disappears into the room and shuts the door in my face. He didn't realize how close I was, probably, but if anyone can solve this and get Will back to normal, it's Garrett.

Still, that doesn't stop the tears from streaming down my cheeks. What is happening to my brother?

CHAPTER THIRTY-SIX

GARRETT — AGE 18

I'm shaking with adrenaline as I shut the door to separate Tessa from this situation. I don't want her to see me in my current state. Coming in the house and hearing Will screaming at her sent every nerve in my body into a spiral. It took several minutes for me to be able to walk in here and look at him without wanting to beat the shit out of him for daring to even raise his voice at her.

When I speak, my tone is a roll of thunder in the midst of a storm. "What was that?"

Will tugs the hood around his head, flopping down on his bed without looking at me. "I told you not to come over this weekend."

"Yeah, well, I didn't listen. Why are you yelling at your sister?"

"Why do you care?" he snaps.

I fold my arms across my chest and stare at him,

trying to understand but also not willing to keep entertaining this pity party.

Groaning when he notices I'm not going to keep arguing, he adds, "She's in my business. I need time. Space. Or has everyone forgotten my girlfriend just died?"

It's been a little over a week, which isn't long, sure, but they also hadn't been together that long. I'm sure he's sad about her death, I'm just not convinced this is about her. At least not completely. "Is that all this is about? Or is it about the jewelry? Do you know they think whoever stole her things is the one who killed her mom? They were missing days before the party, but no one noticed. What did you do with them? You can't pawn them now. If they trace it back to—"

Will grabs the remote and turns the TV up, likely so Tessa won't eavesdrop, though I heard her door shut earlier.

"Shut up about that, will you? Do you want me to get caught?"

"Of course not, but you can't just pretend this isn't happening. Have you thought about going to the police to tell them the truth? What if they figure out it was you? If you come clean about it now and tell them—"

His eyes go dark, gaze sharp. "They won't find out anything unless you tell them. My prints and DNA are in that house because we were dating. End of story. They have nothing else on me."

"What did you do with them?" I ask again.

"They're both gone. Don't worry about it."

"Gone like you sold or pawned them? Because that'll be possible to trace, probably easily."

"No. I threw them out. No one will find them. They're long gone."

I swallow. "What is going on with you? Why did you steal the stuff in the first place? It's not like you. I didn't ask before, but I think I deserve to know now. And why are you acting like this? Why are you shutting out the people who are just trying to help?"

He ignores my first question. "I don't want anyone's help. I'm fine."

"Are you? Because you reek like you haven't showered. You haven't come down to play basketball. You're yelling at your sister. Ignoring me. That's not you."

"Maybe you don't know me."

"Is it because of Brendan and Cassidy?" My words cut through the room like a hot knife on ice.

"What did you just say to me?" He stands and takes a step toward me.

I don't budge. "Did you find out?"

His face is unrecognizable. "Did I find out what?"

I swallow. "I was at the park earlier, and Brendan had a picture of her. He said... Well, he told me they'd been messing around. They're neighbors, I guess, and it's always been a thing. If I found out Tessa was messing around with someone else—"

"This is not about you!" he shouts, his warm, rank breath hitting my face. "It's not about my stupid sister.

253

It's not about Cassidy or fucking Brendan Taylor, okay? It's my shit, and I'll figure it out. I do not need you or anyone else, so go."

I press my lips together. "They're saying Cory's dad lost his job. Did you hear that?" I study him, looking for a hint that he knows what's going on. "Do you know who did this? Does it have anything to do with why you're acting so weird?"

"Oh, now *you* think I'm a murderer too, hmm?" Returning to his bed, he drops down and rolls over on the mattress away from me.

"No. I don't. But I think you're acting strange because you feel guilty. Or maybe because you know who did it. And if you do, and you let our friend go down for it, I don't think you'll ever forgive yourself."

Slowly, he turns over to face me, his expression still an angry pout, but at least I'm getting calm eye contact again. Less I-want-to-kill-you eye contact, anyway. "You have no idea what you're talking about."

"So tell me. Tell me what's going on so I can help you."

For a second, I think he's contemplating it, but then he says, "You wouldn't understand. Please just go."

"Try me."

He looks at the door, then back at me. "I can't tell you, man. Please just, just leave."

I sit down next to him on the bed, staring at him long and hard. "Since when don't we tell each other everything? What's the point of brothers?"

He swallows, looking down. "Fine. You really want to know?"

"Yes. I really do."

"Don't say I didn't warn you."

And then...he tells me everything.

That night I'm lying in bed staring at the text message I've typed out to send Tessa. She deserves more than this.

Better.

But this is what I can give her. It's *all* I can give her.

> We need to talk. I'm sorry about this, but with me going away to college next month, I think it's best if we break this off before either of us gets too attached. I don't want to hurt you now or ever. I hope someday you can understand.

I squeeze my eyes shut, cursing myself. Then I press send and turn off my phone.

CHAPTER THIRTY-SEVEN

TESSA — AGE 17

"I don't even want to go to this stupid party," I whine to Britney, who is sitting on the floor applying another coat of lipstick. She loves to mix the colors until she gets the perfect one. Tonight she's doing a pale mauve and a rich, dark red to get a muted, deep red. I could never pull something like that off, but Britney couldn't find a color that looks bad on her if she tried. "Why don't we just go to the movies instead? *Dark Shadows* is supposed to be good."

"It's your brother's graduation-slash-moving-away-from-this-dump-truck-of-a-town party." She stares at me pointedly, rubbing her lips together. She puckers, pleased with her appearance, and turns around. "Just because Garrett is a weird little man-baby all of the sudden doesn't mean you're not going to eventually regret missing this."

I chew on my lip. She's right. I know she's right, and still, I hate this. I don't want to go.

"I know you and Will are in kind of a weird place since Cassidy died, and I wish I had better advice there, but what I can tell you is that if you don't go to celebrate with him tonight before he leaves, you're going to be angry with yourself in the future when you guys work things out. And I'd be willing to bet the same goes for Garrett."

"Garrett dumped me via text six weeks ago and has been completely ignoring me since. How can you possibly think we'll ever be okay again?"

"Because you love him. And look, far be it from me to defend a man, but I think he loves you, too." She stands up and moves over to the bed where I'm sitting, tucking a piece of hair behind my ear. "I won't pretend to understand how guys' minds work, but I do know what it looks like when they're into you, and that boy is in L-O-V-E. I don't know why he broke up with you. Probably because he's an idiot, but maybe he truly thinks he's being kinder to you by not making you do the long-distance thing. Either way"—she leans in conspiratorially—"the best way to get even? Show up looking like your hot self and let him know what he's missing." She kisses my cheek, leaving a perfect, red impression on my skin. I drop my jaw and glare at her.

"You're suggesting I make him jealous?"

"With a capital J." She winks.

When we arrive at the party, Britney has worked her magic on me. My dark hair has been curled into loose waves, my makeup is just a bit edgier than I'd do myself, and I'm wearing one of her minidresses.

Our first stop is the drink table, where Britney pours us two shots of vodka. Vodka is always her go-to because she says it doesn't give you bad breath. "Okay, one shot for courage." She passes me a glass and we tap them together. I don't even think about the million reasons this might be a bad idea. I just swallow it.

The fire burns my throat, and I suck in a deep breath as she takes the glass back, nodding and smiling. "Attagirl. One more." She refills the glass.

"What's this one for?" I ask, my throat still burning.

"For luck." I squeeze my eyes shut and down the next shot, coughing as I swallow it. She pats me on the back like a proud momma. "Now, let's go get you *over* him and *under* someone else."

I swallow again, trying to catch my breath as she places the shot glasses down and moves us through the party with expert precision. "The first step," she reminds me, "is to find someone near him, but not in his direct line of sight, and flirt. Hard. Dance with him. Whatever."

"I'm not only here to make him jealous," I remind her feebly, but my eyes are already scanning the space for Garrett. It's hard—harder than I've wanted to admit. I've lost a best friend and the boy I fell for in one fell swoop, and I still don't understand why.

"Duh. You're here to dance with your best girl." She bumps my hip. "Seriously, you're going to feel so much better after tonight, I promise. He doesn't get to make you hide away. These are your friends, too."

I hug her with one arm, and a gust of wind rushes under my dress, reminding me how short it is.

"Oh. *Him.*" She points to a guy I don't recognize across the room while I'm distracted by tugging my dress down. He's standing at the head of a table where they've set up beer pong, chatting with two other guys.

"Who is that?"

She turns to me, eyes wide. "Do you remember Connor Wade? He graduated two years ago."

I squint at him. Everyone knows Connor, who was easily the most popular person in his grade. Last I heard, he joined a band and moved to Nashville. "Doesn't he work with that country singer? What's his name?"

"Clayton Beckett," she says with a nod. "Yeah. He's his guitar player. They're getting ready to go on their first tour. I can't believe he's here."

I grin at her. "Are you sure *you* don't want him? Is that drool?" I pretend to wipe under her lip, and she swats my hand away with a scowl.

"Don't be silly. Tonight's about you, and this is just a sacrifice I'll have to make." She raises her brows playfully as she says this.

"Connor will not be interested in me." I sigh. "He's twenty. He's probably just here because his mom teaches Sunday school with mine. I'm sure she told him to come say goodbye to Will before he leaves."

"Girl." She looks me up and down. "You're so hot tonight, I'd do you." She bumps my hip. "And I'm ninety-six percent straight. Now, come on. I'll introduce you." She grabs my hand and drags me across the room and directly up to Connor, who looks over from his conversation, slowly losing his train of thought.

"Um, hi."

"Connor," Britney says, ever the unashamed, unafraid diplomat. "Do you remember—"

"Tessa Becker." He nods, cutting her off. His voice is warmer than I remembered, friendlier. "Of course I do. Good to see you. Your mom still brings me a pumpkin pie every time I'm in town."

I smile, thinking about Mom. "I didn't know that." It doesn't surprise me, though. She does so much that I don't see. "I also didn't know you'd be here. Welcome home."

"I was in town for a quick visit before we head out on tour." He shrugs. "Not sure if you've heard, but I'm going on tour with Clayton Beckett."

"I—"

Britney cuts me off before I can confirm that I knew. "No way!" she exclaims. "We hadn't heard." She beams at me broadly. "Why don't you and Connor go somewhere where you can talk, like the kitchen maybe, and he can tell you all about it?"

"Oh, I don't—"

"I'm happy to," he says. "It'll be good to catch up." When I look over, I notice his eyes lingering on my body before they bounce back up to my eyes. When Garrett looked at me, it made me feel flushed. With Connor, I just feel leered at.

"I...uh..." In the kitchen, Garrett is leaning against the fridge. He's surrounded by his friends, my brother included, but he's clearly not part of the conversation that's happening. Instead, he's staring at me.

Glaring, really.

I stare around him as if I'd been just scanning the room and actually hadn't seen him at all, then step closer to Connor and smile. "Sounds great."

"Cool." He puts a hand on my shoulder as Britney steps back and lets us pass. "Did you graduate this year?"

"Next," I remind him. "My brother graduated this year."

"Right. I guess I always thought you two were twins or something." He takes a sip of his beer. "I have to say, you really grew up." His eyes are on my breasts again. "I mean really."

I force myself to smile. "Thanks." At least he's hot, even if he is obnoxious. Stopping in the doorway, I lean against the frame. "So tell me more about the tour. That must be so exciting."

"Yeah, Clayton's a good guy. Killer musician, too. We've got sixteen cities lined up, but we'll probably have more before it's over." He bobs his head. "You like our music?"

I've only heard Clayton's single that they overplay on the radio, and I thought it was too simple for my taste, but I smile and lie. "Love it. It's so crazy I know a celebrity."

He feigns humility. "Oh, well, I'm just glad to be doing what I love." Stepping closer, he has me boxed in as his hand comes to my shoulder, playing with the strap on my dress. "You know, I could probably arrange for you to meet him if you want."

I can feel Garrett's eyes on me, burning into me, and it spurs me on. I put a hand on Connor's chest, eyes wide. "You really think so?"

He nods, running his tongue over his lip. "Oh, sure. We're real good friends, too. I could maybe get you some backstage passes once we're out on the road."

"That would be amazing."

He runs a finger over my cheek. "I can't believe it's been so long since we've hung out." We've never hung out, unless you count Sunday school, but I don't argue. "Hey, I'm having trouble hearing you in here. Do you want to step outside?"

"Um, sure." I risk a glance at where Garrett should be only to find he's not there. I deflate in an instant. Maybe he really doesn't care.

Before I can think about whether to amend my

answer, Connor pulls me out of the kitchen and onto the back porch. It's dark out here, with no streetlights or neighbors for miles. Quiet too. I can hear the steady thrum of music coming from inside the house, but it's softened. I take in a deep breath.

"It's finally starting to warm up. You know, I'm thinking of going to college in Nashville. Do you like it there?"

"Oh, it's amazing. Beautiful city, beautiful music." He chuckles deep in his throat, then steps closer, brushing hair back from my face. "Beautiful women. But this place has that going for it, too."

I swallow, heat climbing my neck. Suddenly, the darkness is suffocating. Is he really, truly hitting on me right now? Am I okay with it?

He nudges me backward against the side of the house, boxing me in, and I try my best to enjoy the attention. Garrett doesn't want me, and I need to move on.

Connor is here, he's gorgeous and successful, he's a good guy if a bit annoying. There's no reason I shouldn't let him kiss me.

Which is exactly what he's about to do.

His lips find mine as I think the words, almost as if I willed it to happen. He tastes of beer and something bitter like cigarettes. His hands are rough—calloused and cold—and they go to my neck, not my face like Garrett's always do.

I pull away from him, angry with myself. I can't do

this. I can't compare everything and everyone to Garrett.

"Hey, sorry. Something wrong? Did I misread this?" Connor pulls back in an instant, both hands off of me.

"No, I'm sorry, I—"

"Hey, it's okay. Do you want to go back inside?"

He's so kind and *so* hot I'm only realizing now how badly I need kind and hot. Someone with no strings attached. Someone who doesn't even live here. I couldn't ask for anything better.

If I go back into that party, I'm just going to want to leave. I'll go home and pout while Garrett is here having fun. *Not* missing me.

I don't have to love Connor. This can just be fun. Britney is always having fun with guys, and she never gets her heart broken. I can do this.

"No," I say firmly. The alcohol in my belly warms me, giving me courage. Britney was right about needing it to get through this. "No." I step up on my tiptoes, kissing him again. His kiss is fine. Nothing spectacular or mind blowing, but maybe this is normal. Maybe you're not supposed to end up with the guy whose kisses blow your mind because it hurts too much when you lose him.

Fine is enough. *Fine* is great.

I kiss him harder, faster, but he eases back, slowing our kisses down. Doesn't he see I don't want slow? I want fast. I want him to kiss me like I'm his first breath of oxygen after he nearly drowned. Like it's my kiss solely that's keeping him alive.

His hand slides down my side, grazing my breast, and I wrap a leg around him, pulling him closer. He's being so gentle with me, and I hate it.

His hands wrap around me, cupping my ass, and I rock my hips forward, forcing away all thought. He presses closer to me, his hardness resting against my stomach.

Someone clears their throat in the darkness, and we jump apart like two kids being caught by their angry parents. As my eyes connect with Garrett's outline in the moonlight, as the faintest scent of him hits my nose on the wind, my heart seizes.

"Sorry, man, *ocupado*," Connor teases, cupping my shoulder.

Garrett doesn't move. He doesn't even look at him. Doesn't acknowledge his presence. He's only looking at me.

"Can you give us a minute?" I ask.

Connor waits for Garrett to answer, not realizing I'm looking at him.

Finally, Garrett glances his way. "She's talking to you."

Connor's smile falls as he looks down at me. "Oh. Shit. Um, yeah, sorry. Okay. Well, I'll, uh, be inside when you're done." He kisses my lips again, but only briefly. "You're okay?"

"Yeah. I'm fine." I'm not fine. I'm pretty sure I'm having a heart attack. Is this real? Is he really here?

With that, Connor makes his way back inside, leaving us alone in the moonlight. As the door shuts, Garrett crosses the porch, his footsteps so slow it's painful. When he reaches the railing, he leans against it. Several excruciating seconds later, his eyes flick up to meet mine, and my heart rams itself into my ribcage like a feral animal caught in a trap.

It's as if it screams, 'Mine,' at the mere sight of him.

As if it doesn't know the devastating news yet. As if the rest of my body can't bring itself to tell it.

Good. Better it doesn't know, really.

"Didn't realize musicians were your thing." His voice is, at once, a balm and a strip of sandpaper scraped across my bare skin. I've missed him, yet I hate him. My emotions war inside me, and all I can do is stand here and stare at him, trying not to cry.

"Didn't realize it was any of your business."

He blinks. "How much have you had to drink?"

"A few drinks. I'm not drunk."

His lips twitch, but otherwise his face is steady and unreadable. "Do you like him?"

"Why do you care, Garrett?"

"I'm curious."

"You broke up with me. Then you ghosted me. I'm allowed to move on. To date other people. To kiss other people. To sleep with other people."

He flinches at each word. Then, a slow nod. "If that's what you want."

It's not what I want. What I want is to have him back. What I want is to understand why he left in the first place. "It's all that I want."

"Connor?"

"Connor," I confirm, though I'd half forgotten his name before Garrett reminded me.

"You like it when he touches you?"

Something deep inside me twinges. "Y-yes." I can't hide the shake of my voice.

His lips press together, and he stares at me. His chest rising and falling is the only sign that he's still alive.

He lifts his foot, taking a steady, agonizing step toward me. Then another. Then another. He doesn't say a word until he's right in front of me, so close I can feel the heat of his skin. He rests an arm on the wall above my head, leaning in until we're nearly forehead to forehead.

"You like when he kisses you?"

"Mm-hmm."

"Yeah?" He lifts his free hand to my chin, tilting it up to face him. "How does he kiss you, Little Bit? Is it soft and gentle?" He presses his lips to mine, barely a breath of a kiss, and I don't have time to react because I'm in such shock. I wish I'd savored it more. My lips search for his in the air, but he's too far away. "Or does he kiss you the way you like? Does he kiss you like he hates you?" His mouth claims mine in a fiery passion, equal parts flame and fury. He nips at my lips, sucks on my tongue. He kisses like he's trying to kill me, like he wants my every last breath for his own. No one's kiss has ever been as all-consuming as Garrett's is. When he stops, I'm out of breath and panting, embarrassed by how easily I crumbled.

He doesn't back up or give me space to think, just stays right in front of me as if the kiss never happened. "I asked you a question."

"He...it's fine. It's enough."

"Enough?" He scoffs. His hand trails down the front of me, over my breast. My nipple responds to his touch, hardening at the brush of contact. Slowly, his fingers tease their way down my stomach. He doesn't say a word, just stares at me. My mouth is open, waiting, begging for him to do something. Anything. I should be embarrassed. I should tell him to stop, but I can't. I won't.

I inhale as his fingers reach my thigh and brush the hem of my dress. Entire countries are discovered, founded, established, and involved in wars within the time it takes his fingers to skate up my thigh and brush against my panties. He nips my lips. "You deserve more than *enough*." His fingers brush across the fabric slowly, oh so slowly, and then, when I'm ready to combust, his fingers meet skin.

I cry out before he's had time to do a single thing, so shocked and turned on and disgusted with myself I can't do anything but close my eyes and enjoy the sensation.

His face slides against the side of mine until his mouth is next to my ear. "Look at me." His fingers stop and my eyes rip open.

He pulls back to his original position, face just in front of mine. "Don't you dare close your eyes and think about someone else when I'm the one who makes you feel this way. Do you hear me?" His fingers begin moving inside me again, waves of sensation coursing through my muscles. "I'm the only one who makes you feel this way, aren't I, baby?"

I whimper. It's all the answer I can give as my legs shake, threatening to give out. The gentle massage of his thumb sends currents of desire through every part of me, and I drop my head back, eyes closed.

He stops. Pulls his hand away.

"No," I beg. My eyes are back on him in a second. With a look of pure fire, he drags his middle finger over my bottom lip, and I can taste myself on his skin.

The world is silenced by the beating of my heart as I watch him lift the same finger to his own mouth and draw an identical line across his bottom lip. A wicked smile flickers across his face as a shaky breath escapes my throat.

His eyes don't leave mine as his tongue replaces his finger, licking away every trace of me from his lip. Drinking me in as if I'm his favorite flavor.

Heat hot enough to solder metal is the only thing that exists in the space between us.

"Don't look away again." A tugging sensation sweeps through my core as our eyes dance between each other's, so much unspoken there. His hand returns to work as his lips find mine. His kiss is bruising. He kisses me like he's been trapped in a desert, and I'm the first water he's seen in weeks. Like he wants every last ounce of me for himself. He kisses me like I might save him.

Angrily, his fingers work faster, curling inside me as I fall apart. I'm close, but I'm afraid if I tell him that, he'll stop. I fight to keep my eyes open, eyes on him.

Molten lava spreads through me, making my body heavy as I feel my muscles tensing. I'm right there.

I—

"Garrett—"

I cry out as he drops to his knees, pulls my panties to the side, and brings me over the edge with his mouth working me in a raw act of possession. My body is fire and ice and warm honey and a million glowing stars. There are no thoughts or feelings or anything other than…

YES.

Our surroundings disappear, going fuzzy at the edges, and pure euphoria claims me as its own.

As the world begins to take shape again, and I realize where we are and *who* we are and how royally bad of an idea this was, I adjust my dress and underwear, staring at him as he stands up. I want to ask what this was supposed to be, why he would do this, but I'm afraid of the answer.

The longer I let what happened sink in, the more I worry it was a goodbye.

He's leaving, and I'm staying, and there's nothing I can do about it.

He swipes his mouth with his thumb, his eyes burning holes in me. Maybe he's had enough to drink that he'll regret this when he sobers up. Does he already regret us? I think that would be enough to destroy me.

"You deserve more than fine, Tessa. You deserve everything. Do not settle for someone who isn't enough just to piss me off."

"I wasn't—"

"You were." His jaw twitches in the moonlight, his face cast in shadows. "You forget how well I know you. Which is very well. I'm not worth you making a mistake you can't take back."

I fold my arms across my chest. "So sleeping with someone who isn't you would be a mistake?"

"Sleeping with someone you don't care about because of me would be a mistake," he says plainly. "I'm not worth that."

"How can you say that?" Now, I can't fight the tears. "How can you kiss me? How can you do what you just did with me and not care?"

"I never said I don't care. Of course I care. Jesus, I

care more than I could ever—" He cuts himself off, looking away, then finally finishes with, "More than you know."

"You left, remember? Not me. Don't judge me for the way I heal my heart. I need to move on. You promised you wouldn't hurt me. You promised you were mine. And then you just ghosted me." I'm sobbing without realizing it as he pulls me into his chest, holding my head against him.

"I am yours," he promises, his voice cracking as he touches my hand to his chest, right above his heart. "Of course I'm yours. Can't you see how badly I hate watching you with anyone else? Can't you see I'm miserable?"

I pull back, taking his face in my hands. "Then what is the problem? We will figure it out. As long as we're together, we can figure anything out."

He takes my hands from his face, kissing the knuckles, then my palm. "It's not that simple. I'm sorry. I wish that it was." Another kiss to my palm. "You have no idea how much I wish it was."

"It can be."

"No." His voice is firm then, and he steps back, dropping my hands. "No. I will always be yours. But right now, you just can't be mine."

He steps back again. Then, with a final look my way, he disappears inside.

CHAPTER THIRTY-EIGHT

GARRETT — AGE 19

"Congrats, graduate." Will pulls Tessa into a hug in the living room of our apartment.

With the exception of her recent graduation ceremony, where I only caught glimpses of her from across the school's gymnasium, it's been nearly six months since I saw her briefly last Christmas, and it's every bit as hard as I've imagined. She looks good. Grown up in a way that feels impossible in such a small window of time. Her hair is shorter now, just above her shoulders. She's never had it this short, but I like it. It suits her.

"Thanks." She smiles awkwardly, then looks at me. There's a moment where it's clear we're both trying to decide how to move forward. Do we hug? Shake? High-five? Wave?

We're friends. We've texted and spoken on the phone occasionally, once her hatred cooled to a mild dislike. Mostly just to say Merry Christmas, happy birthday, or for her to check in on Will. Since my parents decided to move away, Will and I have spent our breaks and holidays there with them, only going to visit Frannie and Tessa for a few hours the day after Christmas.

It's too hard to see her. To be in the same room and feel the electricity that radiates from her and not be able to touch her. I'm not a strong enough man.

We're walking a fine line, where I had to do the most devastating thing I've ever done, and then I had to stand by my decision.

But now, everything is different, and I want to tell her why. Finally, I can explain myself.

I'm lost in my own thoughts when she sinks against my chest with a hug. On instinct, I gather her in my arms, holding her snugly against me. It's as if this is the first time my lungs have been able to take a full breath.

She is, at once, familiar and changed. Her perfume is new, spicier than the florals she wore before, but there's still the lingering scent of coconut in her hair. It's painfully comforting having her in my arms again, a jarring reminder of all I've lost.

"Hey, stranger." Having her against me makes everything better. I've never experienced anything like this.

It's been a whole year, and I'm no less gone for this girl.

"Hey." I clear my throat. "It's, um, good to see you."

Before I'm ready, she steps back, dropping her arms away from me. "Yeah." She smiles. "Sorry I missed you guys at the graduation. Britney was throwing a party at the lake house, so we left right after the ceremony. Mom told me you stopped by."

"It's okay," Will tells her. "We just came in for the day, so we couldn't stay or anything."

Even on his own, Will hasn't gone back to his mom's house more than two or three times since graduation. Everyone assumes it's because of the awkwardness between Tessa and me, and Will and I have let it be assumed. Until now, it was easier. Even when it killed me.

"So what are the plans for tonight?" Tessa asks as if this is just like old times. In so many ways, that's exactly how it feels. "What are my Nashville mustdos?"

Will grins and cups his hands around his mouth, speaking in a booming, game-show-host voice. "Well, little lady, I'm glad you asked. We're taking you to Broadway so you get the full Nashville tourist experience. There, you will be guaranteed to see the following: a shit ton of drunk bridesmaids, swarms of equally drunk men wearing cowboy boots for the very first time, awesome musicians, not-so-awesome musicians, and not a single *actual* Nashvillian, excluding the workers." The booming voice fades away, and he chuckles to himself. "Seriously, we avoid it like the plague."

"Sounds perfect." An infectious smile curves on her

lips. "I'm going to take a shower and change, and then we'll go."

Will watches her walk away with a tender look on his face. Their relationship is better now, but still not what it was. He explained away his behavior, blaming it on a bout of depression after Cassidy's death. It's not a total lie. Will *was* depressed, just not wholly about that.

I've waited for this day for over a year now, and I still don't know whether tonight will make everything better or worse. When I hear the shower kick on, I clear my throat.

"Listen, I want to tell her everything tonight. I know we said we'd decide when the time was right, but she's graduated now. We got the results back. It's time. I can't wait any longer."

He folds his arms across his chest. "I've been thinking about that a lot too, actually."

"Yeah?"

He scratches his eyebrow with a sigh I feel in my bones. "I don't think we should tell her at all. Think about it. She doesn't have to find out. No one is better off for knowing about this. Just let her be happy. It's the last thing we can give her. The best thing."

"What? No." My voice is strained. Panicked. "That was never the deal. We agreed—"

"And I changed my mind. You saw what it did to me when I found out. We can protect her from this."

"No, we can't. We have done everything, *all of this*"

—I wave a hand through the air—"to protect her, but we're done now. You want her to be happy? This is the way. That's exactly why I want to tell her. It's the only way to explain what we did. The only way to make her understand why I broke things off. I want to make her happy. I…" Chills line my skin. "Will, I love her. I can't lie to her and pretend I don't anymore. She's it for me."

Will is sympathetic, but not convinced. "If you love her, you'll find a way to be together without causing her unnecessary pain." He pats my shoulder. "She'll forgive you without needing to be destroyed by this. Just talk to her."

My jaw goes tight. I can't believe he's doing this. "Telling her the truth was always the way out. Always. We talked about this. How can you ask me to keep lying to her? I have a good reason for what I did, and I deserve to be able to tell her that. Especially after everything else I did for you."

His eyes darken with pain, and I regret my words immediately. "None of that was for me. I never asked you to break up with her. I didn't want your help." He shakes his head, his expression grim.

"I know, but you needed me, whether you'll admit it or not."

He rubs a hand across his forehead, head bowed. "Look, you're my brother. If you hadn't pulled me out of that darkness back then, I'm scared to think about what would've happened to me." He pauses, his eyes lingering on the hallway. "But if you tell her the truth, you'll be putting her in there. Are you really ready to do that again? Because if I could live my life not knowing, I think I'd be better off."

I swallow. Is he right? Is wanting to tell Tessa the truth about everything back then selfish?

"Fine. I'll figure something else out."

He gives me a long look, like he wants to say something else. Maybe to apologize, but eventually he just says, "I know you will."

The music is too loud. The beer is too expensive. The people are too obnoxious. Everywhere you look, there are rhinestones and tassels, boots and cowboy hats.

"I feel like I'm in a John Wayne movie," I mutter to Will.

Of course, he can't hear me because Luke Bryan is currently asking a country girl to shake it for him at a volume loud enough to be heard by said country girl's ancestors. I hate Broadway with a passion, but when I look at Tessa, she's swaying in place, completely and utterly happy, and the rest of it fades away.

Nothing else exists for me when it comes to her. She's everything...and I'm terrified.

I messed it all up before, and I know there's a good chance she'll never forgive me. That she's moved on, and I missed my chance, but I also know I'll hate myself forever if I don't ask.

We stay until last call, and I know I'm getting old because it feels like we've been gone for three days, not three hours, when we make it back to the apartment.

Will gives me a knowing look as Tessa asks if she's sleeping on the couch.

"No," I say quickly. "You can have my bed. I'll take the couch."

She looks at me, her eyes glassy, cheeks red. She's buzzed at this point, but with a burger in her belly, she's no longer drunk enough that she doesn't understand the reality of why that might be a bad idea. "Are you sure? The couch is more than fine for me."

"Totally sure. Your brother hasn't washed his sheets since we moved in, and I sleep on the couch most nights anyway, so this makes the most sense."

Behind her, Will makes a face that says, 'Oh yeah, sure,' and I roll my eyes to tell him to buzz off. He yawns loudly. "Welp, I'm going to hit the hay, put some headphones on, and crash. Did you have fun tonight?"

"Headphones? Did this Broadway trip sell you on country music after all?" She laughs but quickly moves on. "It was the best." She throws her arms around her brother, and he rubs her back. "Thanks for taking me."

"You're welcome, and I hope you're just being nice and honestly hated it because we are never going back."

She tries to suppress a giggle. "Oh. I've gotta get my bag out of your room before you go to bed."

"I've got it," I interject, stepping around them and down the hall. In Will's room, I grab her lilac duffel bag and carry it back to mine, placing it on the end of the bed.

Tonight's the night. This is my chance to finally tell her the truth—or at least, the part of the truth Will won't hate me for. I have no idea what I'm going to do, but this is it.

I release a long, slow breath. When I turn around, she's there, though I hadn't heard her come in. Warmth hits my cheeks.

"Oh. Hey."

"Thanks for getting that." She moves around me, dragging a finger across her bag. The air is charged with crackling anticipation, like those candies that pop on your tongue, and I wonder if she feels it, too.

"Oh, sure. No problem." I run a hand against the back of my neck. "Um, I'm really glad you came tonight."

She bobs her head, studying the ground like she might take a test on it later. "Yeah, me too. It was nice to get away. Thanks for"—she gestures toward the bed, not meeting my eyes—"this, by the way. You really didn't have to—"

"Oh, sure. Seriously. It's the least I could do."

"So how are you liking—"

"Did you decide what you're—" I say at the same time, and we both stop, laugh, and wait. I gesture toward her.

"How are you liking Nashville?" she finishes.

"It's nice. Definitely different." The conversation is heavy and stilted, and I need to just say what I came to say before she gets tired. "Hey, listen—"

"Could I ask you somethin—"

Again, we laugh.

"You first this time," she says, gesturing to me.

"Right. Well, I guess I just wanted to say..." I stop, looking around. Suddenly, I'm sweating.

"I really missed you," she bursts out, stopping me short with the world's best interruption. Her eyes soften, and she leans her head to the side.

"You did?" I stare at her like if I blink, she might disappear and force me to wake up.

"You know how much I missed you." She gives me a laugh filled with nerves.

"No," I tell her definitively. "No, I didn't." I step forward as if finally giving in to the magnetic pull I feel between us, and at the same time, she steps toward me.

We collide somewhere in the middle. Both our hands go up so we're clutching each other's shirts, grasping and tugging like we can't have a spare inch of air between us. Her lips are on mine in a second, and the world is brighter, the air easier to breathe.

I trace my tongue across the fullness of her lips. My mouth hasn't forgotten her. She's there, in every memory, every moment.

All at once, the tension eases in me, and I feel her shoulders loosen as she sinks into the kiss. It's punishing and angry. Drugging. She pulls her shirt over her head, and I tug mine off just as quickly.

"Are you sure about this?" I ask, my lips already back on hers with savage intensity.

She nods against my mouth. "Shut up."

I laugh as we fumble to the bed, like we never missed a step. My lips reclaim hers, demanding more. I want to take my time with her. We've done everything but this, and I want to do it right, but at the same time, I've been waiting too long to hold her again. To have her again.

I kiss a path down her soft stomach, but she sits up before I reach my target.

"I need to taste you," I beg, searing a path with my hand down her stomach and onto her thigh.

She pushes me onto my back with a devilish gleam in her eyes. "Me first." Her lips come down on my bare chest, and the world careens on its axis. I lie back as her tongue draws a line down my body to my pants.

We work together to pull them off, and then her mouth is on me, pure and explosive. My eyes roll back in my head as her fingers burn into my thighs.

I lurch forward, pinning her down and finally getting my mouth on her. She cries out, hands on my head, and the fire in my veins spreads to my heart.

When I have her nearly there, she rolls us over and slips back down to take me in her mouth again, as hungry for me as I am for her. We're back and forth, warring over who can have their tongue on the other for longer, fighting for control, refusing to relent.

Her tongue swirls around me, and my body trembles with pleasure. "You like that?" She pulls away just long enough to ask before doing it again.

I'm going to lose my mind over this girl. There's never been anyone so perfect for anyone else.

"I like *you*," I mutter, holding her head in place as I pump into her mouth once, then twice. Her eyes lock with mine, wide and trusting, and liquid fire hits me all at once. I freeze, holding her completely still until I've regained control. I won't lose this war.

She giggles as I slip back between her legs, running my tongue against her. The laughter dies away soon enough, and then she's moaning, grasping my hair, and calling my name. I feel her tighten around my fingers and smile with pride. It's been so long since I heard that, and right now, it might as well be a fucking lullaby.

As she comes down, I crawl up the length of her body, painting her with kisses. I settle myself between her legs and lean across her toward my nightstand, pulling a condom out of the drawer.

I tear it open, watching her watch me, her eyes suddenly less confident. "Are we okay?"

She swallows, nodding, and rests her hand on her chest, still catching her breath. "Yeah. Of course."

"We don't have to…"

"No." She takes my hand, lacing her fingers through mine. "No, I want to."

My heart squeezes as I pull her hand to my lips, pressing a gentle kiss to her knuckles. I hope, with that simple kiss, I'm telling her everything I want to.

I love you.

You're it for me.

I'm going to fix this.

I slide the condom on and position the tip at her entrance. My hands shake as I guide myself inside. This is different and new for us. We've never…

Heaven.

Pure, white-hot, brilliant, exploding stars and a million suns, heaven.

Jesus.

Fuck.

I grip on to her hips, looking down at the world's most perfect view. "You good?"

"I'm perfect." She smiles up at me with a dreamy expression.

"I'll say." *She's so fucking beautiful.* Slowly, I work myself into her, building up the heat we had just moments ago. I want so much more. I want everything, but for now, all I can do is move just like this.

Anything else, and this ends, and for now, I'd sooner die than make this end.

When we're done, we change into pajamas, brush our teeth, and find our way back to bed. I stand in the space between the door and the bed, but before I can say anything, she pats the place next to her. "Stay."

That is probably the best word I've ever heard.

My chest feels as tense as the fists at my side and the muscles in my back as I slip into bed next to her. I have no idea where this leaves us, and I want to be clear about my intentions. I roll toward her, and she eases into my arms, her breath warm against my bare chest.

"I can't believe tonight happened," I tell her, breathing against her hair.

"I know. It was... Somehow, it was just what I needed."

I press a soft kiss to her head with a smile I feel in my toes. "Happy to help."

She hums and kisses my chest in return. "I mean it. I think I've been holding out for some closure with us, you know?"

That word—*closure*—is an ice bath dunking I hadn't been expecting. I lean away from her slightly. "What?"

"Yeah. You know, I'm really happy now. It was so hard at first." She holds me tighter. "I missed you, and I was broken, but...I get it now. I understand why you broke it off, and...I think it was the right thing to do. It doesn't mean we won't always care for each other, but I think it's obvious our friendship is the best part of what we have, you know? And this part was pretty nice, too." I feel her cheek pull into a smile against my chest, hear it in her voice. How can she smile while she says this? Can't she hear my heart cracking just below her ear? "So, I guess what I'm saying is, this was some sort of closure that maybe we both needed."

I don't respond. I can't. I'm not even sure I'm breathing.

"Anyway, Will probably told you I was accepted to a school in Chicago, and I'll be moving there soon. So this was...just exactly what I needed, you know? I can move on now and not be hung up on you. It was the perfect goodbye, so thank you."

"Um, yeah..."

"I'm happy," she says softly. "And...and you're happy too, right?"

I clear my throat, blinking away tears. "Yeah. I'm... so happy." Ten seconds ago, it wasn't a lie. I missed my chance. I was going to tell her. I should've told her before we slept together, but then she kissed me, and all thoughts ceased.

When she's in my arms, no other parts of the world exist, and because of that, because I'm so intoxicated by her, my window has closed, and I'll never know if telling her the truth might've healed us or simply hurt us more.

I'll never know if she'll forgive me for a crime she still doesn't understand.

Will's words from earlier replay in my head, barely audible over the splintering in my chest. *Let her be*

286

happy. Then I hear her words from just a moment ago. *I'm really happy now.*

I've been the source of so much unhappiness for her, and I clearly misread tonight completely, but how can I tell her anything now when it might just make everything worse?

I can't be selfish. I blink back tears, kissing her hair. "Good night, Tessa."

I guess this is goodbye.

CHAPTER THIRTY-NINE

TESSA — PRESENT DAY

I go to see Mom alone next. With my car back, I just want a chance to see her on my own. Even if she can't comfort me like she used to, there's still something comforting about being in her presence. I just want to sit with her.

Not to mention the fact that I need an excuse to be away from Garrett. I'm not mad at him necessarily. Disappointed, obviously, but what do I have to be mad at him about anyway? It's Will who did something wrong. Will who broke the law and lied to me, even if Garrett aided and abetted.

But he lied to me, too. Garrett, whom I've trusted all my life *with* my life, has been lying. About this and who knows what else.

Somehow, that feels like the biggest betrayal.

The nursing home is busy today with everyone getting ready for Christmas. The lobby has a big

Christmas tree in the center of the room, and there's just something warmer about the place.

When I reach Mom's room, a nurse is just leaving. "Well, hey there." She gives me a wide grin.

"Hi. I'm Francis's daughter, Tessa."

"Oh!" Her eyes light up. "You are in luck! Come here." She waves me over to Mom's bed, and I'm surprised to find her watching us. Her eyes move from the nurse to me and back. "We're having an excellent day. She even seems to be regaining some of her finger strength." She taps Mom's fingers, then puts her hand under Mom's, and slowly I watch Mom tap the same pattern.

Tap.

Tap.

Tap. Tap.

"She just finished with physical therapy, so I'm not sure how much longer she'll be awake, but what a treat." She looks at Mom then. "Ms. Frannie, did you see Tessa? She's here!"

Mom's eyes flash to me again.

"Hey, Momma." I sink down beside her on the bed, taking her hand. "Look at you. You look so pretty today." I brush her hair aside. Behind me, the nurse sneaks out the door after whispering a heads-up that she'll be right down the hall if we need anything.

"Will's coming home today, so hopefully he'll get to see you tomorrow. He didn't make it back for Britney's funeral, but—"

Tap.

Tap.

Tap.

Mom taps my hand furiously.

"What is it, Momma?" I watch her carefully, trying to understand. "You want to see Will?" She's still, her eyes holding mine, wide and almost fearful. "Are you hurting?" I look at the machines next to her bed, but aside from the oxygen tank, I have no idea what I'm looking at to know if something is wrong. "Should I get the nurse? Blink for me, remember? Blink twice for yes, once for no."

Her watery eyes squeeze shut with force. A very clear blink. No.

"No, you don't need the nurse?"

Blink. No.

"Then what is it?" I move closer. "Is it about Will?"

Blink. No.

"Um…" I think back, trying to remember what I said before she started tapping my hand. A terrible thought thunders into my mind. "Is it about Britney?"

Blink. Blink. Yes.

Tap. Tap. Tap.

My blood runs ice cold. "What is it, Mom? Do you know something about Britney? Do you know what happened to her?"

Blink. No.

I sigh. "I don't understand. Are you just…sad?"

She doesn't blink, doesn't say anything.

"It's very sad. We're going to miss her."

Tap. Tap. Tap.

"Oh! Wait!" I remember the laminated sheet of letters Nurse Emma showed me and jump up from my chair, rushing across the room to get it from the drawer in the kitchen. When I return, I show it to Mom.

Blink. Blink. Yes.

"Yes. You remember this? We're going to use it to tell me what you're trying to say, okay?" An idea occurs to me. "Do you think you could point to the letters?" I lay the paper on her lap and place her hand on it gently, waiting.

She glares at me, and I swear she almost looks annoyed.

"Okay, okay." I take the paper back and slowly move my finger across each letter. "Tap when I get to something. Oh, actually, wait!" I stand and cross the room again, searching for the notebook I just saw in the drawer with the laminated page. I tear out a piece of paper and pull the pencil from its rings before returning to the bed.

Slowly, I run my fingers across the letters, waiting and watching Mom closely. Just when I'm beginning to worry she's losing the movement, she taps her finger.

T

I write it down on the paper. "Good job, Momma. T. Okay. T what?" I start back at the beginning of the alphabet. This time, when I land on E, she taps her finger. "Okay, T-E." Again and again we go as I spell out the words she's trying so desperately to tell me.

T
E
L
L
W
I
L
L
S
H
E
K
N
E
W

When I have that part figured out, I read it again. "She knew? Knew what?" I run my fingers across the letters, but she doesn't tap her finger a single time. Slowly, I do it again. "Come on, Momma. What did Britney know?"

If she's tired, she shows no signs of it. Her eyes are still open and watching me, but she's refusing to tap. That's the whole message. I spin the paper back around, rereading the note.

"But this makes no sense. What did she know?"

She stares at me.

"Did someone hurt Britney?"

Still, nothing.

"Fine. Something else, then. Um, oh! Do you know who wrote the note I showed you the other day? The one that said, 'Murderer?' Do you remember what I'm talking about?"

Blink. Blink. Yes.

"You do? Do you know who wrote it?"

Blink. Blink. Yes.

I look down at the paper, planning to start a new note, when suddenly it clicks. *This is the same paper.* Did the person use this particular notebook paper to write the note because it was here? Or were they, too, trying to get Mom to give them a message? Maybe they were even the one who brought the notebook in the first place.

Carefully, I scratch the pencil across the page, shading it lightly in hope there will be a message there, indented in the paper. I hold my breath, looking for a single letter to appear, but there's nothing.

I rush back over to the notebook in the drawer, skimming through the blank pages in search of a sign or a clue about who it might've belonged to, but there's nothing. Refusing to give up, I sit by Mom again with the sheet of letters.

"Who wrote the note, Mom?" I scan the letters again, and when I reach the T, she taps her finger.

T.

Already, I'm thinking of every person I know whose name starts with T.

E.

Terrence Fisher, the owner of the local hardware store? Teresa Hazelwood, my third grade teacher?

L.

T-E-L

L.

W.

I groan, patting the paper. "Yes, I get it. Tell Will. I will tell Will, I promise. But give me something else, please. Who wrote the note?" I scan the page again.

T.

E.

L.

Forget it. "Okay." I sigh. "Okay, Momma. I will. I'll tell him." I squeeze her hand, pressing a kiss to her skin before I stand up and put the paper back, frustration rattling me. When I return, Mom's eyes are closed, and whether or not she's asleep, she's apparently done with today's visit.

CHAPTER FORTY

GARRETT — PRESENT DAY

When I hear a car pull up outside a few hours later, I assume Tessa's back from wherever she went. It took everything in me not to follow her, to keep her safe, to beg her to forgive me, but I didn't. She needed space, and I can't blame her for that.

I read something once about how you're supposed to sleep with your head pointed in a certain direction for better health. South, I think. Maybe east. It had something to do with Earth's magnetic poles and the iron in our body. When you sleep in the wrong direction, the iron in your blood pulls toward the opposite pole, causing a heap of problems, if the study is to be believed. I don't know. It's probably complete crap, but the message stuck with me because it's the closest thing I've ever heard to describing the way I feel about Tessa.

Like everything in me—my blood and cells—are drawn to her. They push against my skin to be closer to her, as if we were magnets. When I'm not with her, I'm on edge. My axis is off-kilter. I buzz with an uncomfortable energy that can only be calmed when she's around. She's a part of me, in my very tissue and running through my veins. I need her like I need oxygen, and right now I'm terrified my supply is about to be cut off again.

When the front door opens, I'm waiting in the living room as Will enters. He drops his bags down on the floor and gives me a look I can't quite read.

"I didn't think you'd get back until tonight."

"Advantage of driving, I guess. I didn't have to wait for a flight." He scans the room. "Where is she?"

"Out." I jut my chin toward the door.

"Don't like the sound of that."

"I told her about the jewelry."

"*What?* You swore—"

"I know." I cut him off, not in the mood. "I know I swore, and I have lied to her and kept your secret for you for years. But I can't anymore, man. I'm sorry. You need to tell her everything once and for all, or I'm going to."

He looks away, a muscle in his cheek twitching as he grits his teeth. "It's only going to hurt her."

"She deserves to know," I argue. "I mean it. No more lies."

A sound at the door draws our attention as it is pushed open. Tessa's gaze falls between us as she takes in the scene, then her arms go wide as she runs to her brother. "Will." She hugs him tightly, then pulls back. "Now that that's out of the way..." She slaps his chest. "You lied to me." Her tone is playful, but she's furious.

"I know." He groans, rubbing his chest where she hit him, though we all know it didn't hurt. He spends far too much time in the gym for that little slap to have done anything.

"Why?" she demands. She explores both our faces with her gaze. "Someone had better start talking. Now."

"Can't we have dinner first?" he asks lightly, clearly teasing...but not teasing.

"No." She shakes her head, crossing her arms. "Also, I have a message for you. And I'm not sure which bridge we need to cross first."

"A message?" His face goes serious. "What kind of message?"

"One from Mom."

His body tenses with the news. "She's awake? And talking?"

"It's complicated." She bares her teeth. "I'll show you when we visit her."

"Well, what was the message?"

Running her tongue along her teeth, she meets her brother's eyes. "She wanted me to tell you that *Britney knew.*"

I clock the exact moment Will processes the news, as his back goes pin straight. He makes a face at me, so serious I know it's all about to spill over. No more lies. No more secrets. This is it.

"She wouldn't tell me *what* she knew, but she kept saying to tell you that she knew." Her eyes dart between the two of us. "Do you know what that means?"

He sighs and runs a hand over his face. This is the moment that has been looming for years now, and finally, it's here. No more secrets. No more lies. "Yeah. We should sit down."

"Will, just tell me. I don't need to—"

"You're going to want to listen to him," I tell her, gesturing across the room.

"You know?" she demands, her tone sharp.

"I wish I didn't, trust me."

Sensing the seriousness of whatever is happening, she crosses the room without a word and sits down. "Now, will someone please tell me what's going on?"

Will takes a seat next to her, but I linger in the doorway, feeling so out of place yet not willing to leave her. I have no idea if she wants me here, but until she tells me to leave, I'm staying.

He opens his mouth, closes it again, pinches his lips between his fingers, adjusts on the couch, and leans forward over his knees, wringing his hands together in his lap. His nervous tell has always been the same as hers.

"Will, say something," she groans. "Jesus Christ."

He puffs a frustrated breath. "Well, actually, it sort of involves him."

"Who?" Her brows draw down as I roll my eyes. *Jesus.*

298

"Just tell her," I urge him, growing exasperated.

Will's head dips down again before he looks at her, squaring his shoulders, and here it goes. "It's about Pastor Charles. And whatever you're thinking, I promise you it's so much worse."

CHAPTER FORTY-ONE

TESSA — PRESENT DAY

"It's about Pastor Charles. And whatever you're thinking, I promise you it's so much worse."

His words repeat in my head, utterly impossible. I laugh, angry that he's still joking with me after all that we've experienced. I know he's not, I guess, if I really think about the look on his face, but it's impossible. "You're lying."

"I'm not." His voice is forceful.

"Pastor Charles is… I mean, come on, he's *Pastor Charles*. What could he possibly have done?"

Will scratches his forehead. "Uh, everything?"

"I don't understand." I stand, folding my arms across my chest as I pace. It's so impossible it's laughable. Except no one is laughing. "Why are you saying this?"

"I don't even know where to start." He releases a heavy breath and rests a hand on his head. "Um, well, he's the reason I stole the jewelry, for one thing. He asked me to."

My jaw goes stiff. "Of course. Oh, Will. He was testing you. Don't you see that? He was testing you to see if you would sin, and you did."

"No." His head shakes in denial. "That's what I thought at first, too. But he was serious. He said...he said it wasn't right that Cassidy's family had something in their house, just sitting there, worth all that money when it could pay to feed hungry families in our town for a year. When it could pay off a house. When it could turn the lights on for the families who'd had theirs shut off."

I can tell he's hurting. I just can't make sense of any of this. "So what? He asked you to steal the jewelry, and you just...did? Without even questioning it?" Even as he says it, I understand how it could be true. Pastor Charles is a leader in our community. He's someone we trust. From the time we were infants, he's been a figurehead in our lives. If he told me to go stand in traffic, I'd probably do it. We've been taught not to question authority, but especially not when that authority is God or His messengers. If he did this, if what Will's saying is true, there has to be a good reason.

"No, not at first. I wanted to ask Mom about it, to see what she thought, but he told me sometimes men of God have to do bad things for the greater good. Like God flooding the earth to save it. I was helping, he told me. Not only the church and community, but Cassidy's family. He said it was a sin for them to hoard their wealth, that they were being held prisoner by it, and once it was gone, they'd be free."

I sit down next to him again, putting a hand on his knee. He looks so distraught, even now, I have no choice but to believe him.

"He gave me this stack of pictures of girls who needed to be punished. The pictures you found in my nightstand. That's why I freaked out so badly. Cassidy's picture had the necklace and bracelet in the display case in the background. He used the picture to show me what I was supposed to take, then gave me the photos of Emily and Amber, too. He told me to keep them together because he might need me to go on another *mission* for him in the future. So I snuck over there and took the jewelry, and I gave them to Pastor Charles. He thanked me and told me God would reward me for what I'd done. But then...Cassidy died a few days later, and suddenly everything went crazy. I was so scared I'd be caught, and they'd think I had something to do with her death."

"But you didn't?" I confirm. At this point, I have to confirm everything.

"I didn't. I swear to you I didn't. I never found her at the party until someone told me they'd seen her in the basement. When I got down there, she was already..." He covers his eyes, sniffling as he tries to regain composure. "And then Cory was there, and he was blamed, which took the pressure off of me, but it ate at me. At least it did until then they found every-thing else at his house a few days later: the china, the missing bracelet, and the coin collection. And I thought maybe he'd stolen the bracelet from the church or something, but also maybe he really had done all the rest of it. If he'd stolen the other missing stuff—the china and the coin collection—and killed Cassidy too, it wasn't so hard to believe he'd also killed the others. And if that was true, what was it going to hurt for him to go down for the jewelry if he'd done so much worse?"

I draw my brows together, confused. "So you think Cory actually *did* kill all those people?"

"I did," he admits. "At first. But then later I found out it was Pastor Charles who claimed to have found the stuff in Cory's room. He said he went to Cory's house to pray for him with his family and that was when he saw the bag of stolen stuff. Cory's family said they'd never seen it before, but it was their word against Pastor Charles, and of course, he was believed. I just...when I heard that, something didn't feel right. So I talked to Mom. I told her everything. What I'd done. What he'd done. I just kind of exploded and told her every last detail."

"And what did she say? She must've been furious."

He looks away for a long while, like he's thinking hard, his face solemn. "She was. But, Tessa, it wasn't just about that. It..." He licks his lips, looking down.

303

"What is it? What can be harder to tell me than all of this?"

"Pastor Charles isn't just our pastor." He swallows and smooths his hand over his mouth, looking up as he says, "He's also our dad."

The words slam into my chest and shatter me. It's the biggest lie of the day. I stand up, physically rejecting the statement. "No. Stop it."

"Yes." He stands up, too, following me, speaking faster. "Yes. Think about it. Think about how weird Mom always was with Pastor Charles. One minute she loved him, the next she was angry with him. One week we couldn't miss church, and then we'd go an entire month with her visiting the church in Elmdale or Walter Hill."

"That doesn't prove anything. We have pictures of Dad."

"We have pictures of a man with a baby," he says, taking my hands. I'm trembling, as if the idea is trying to force its way into my head. "A man with two babies. We don't have pictures of Mom and Dad. And we don't have pictures of Mom, Dad, and us."

"One of them always had to take the picture." I rattle off the excuse we've been given all our lives.

"Or it was a lie," he says, his voice as soft as his eyes. "Mom lied to protect us. Because he asked her to."

"He's married."

Will nods. "Mom was working as the church's

secretary when the affair started. It lasted three years. After you were born, he cut it off."

"Mom would never—"

"She did." His voice is firm, then he adds, more softly, "She did, Tessa. I'm so sorry."

"This is impossible." And yet, I see it. I feel it in the way I've seen Mom look at him, sometimes with disdain, sometimes with love, just like Will said. I see it in the way she gave us stories about our father that never quite added up. Or the way she never wanted to speak about him unless we pushed.

We trusted her.

Just like she trusted him.

Just like Will trusted him.

"So what?" I ask, pacing once more. "What else did Mom say?"

"She..." He looks at Garrett, and my heart sinks. "She told me there were others. Other people Pastor Charles had affairs with. Other kids he fathered."

Tears sting my eyes because I know what's coming next. I'm going to be sick as I stare at Garrett, who appears equally ill. "You?"

He drops his head, looking at the ground. "No," he says eventually, and my entire body goes numb.

"Did you say no?"

"Not me. Not my mom. But when I broke it off, it's because I couldn't be sure. I couldn't ask my mom because I thought she might lie to me about it, and I couldn't tell you what I suspected and sit in some weird limbo. But I also couldn't keep seeing you, getting more attached and letting you get more attached, until I knew for certain. Eventually, I did a paternity test without my parents' knowledge and found out my dad is definitely my father."

"But why didn't you tell me once you knew?"

Garrett looks at Will, who clears his throat. "Because we found out something worse than all of this."

"How can anything be worse than this?"

"He was behind it all," Garrett says.

"All?" I press.

Will's heartbreak is evident on his face. He hates telling me this. "He asked other boys in church to steal things, too. I wasn't the only one. Told them similar things—that wealth was a sin. That the women deserved it. Dalton Steele stole Ella Gray's china. Mark Summers stole the coin collection from Amber Allen. He had us each steal something, and then, a few days after it was done, he killed the women and girls."

My knees are weak, and I'm falling to the floor, but Garrett catches me. I didn't even realize he was so close. He holds me tightly to him as we sink down onto the couch. "Easy does it."

"You're lying. Please tell me you're lying. How could you possibly know this? You know how ridiculous rumors can get here."

"It's not a rumor." His face is etched with pain. "He knew he could make it look like a robbery gone wrong, and no one would ever piece it together because none of us would ever admit what we'd done. Until we did. Until he framed Cory, and I started to wonder how he would've had all those pieces and what that would mean. Mark was the first one I figured out because I knew he was close with Amber. He would've been an easy choice. From there, we figured out Dalton, and the three of us compared stories. It's not okay what we did, but it was sick the way he'd manipulated us. The things he said, the way he played with our minds, it really messed me up."

"Why didn't you tell me?" I demand. "Why wouldn't you warn me? You left me here, in danger. You left me here, and you knew what he was. *Who* he was."

"I tried," Will says. "I begged Mom to leave, but she wouldn't. She said she had to stay, to try and stop him. To take him down from the inside somehow. If I had told you, if you ever let it slip, if you even *looked* at Pastor Charles in a way that made him think you knew, you would've been in danger. You could've been killed. I had to go. I had to act normal, but I couldn't be around Mom. I was mad at her then, for staying here, but also for lying to us about our dad. For taking us to church when she knew the darkest part of this town was standing at the pulpit telling us how to be good." His upper lip curls. "She knew, and she could've done something—"

"She did," I argue. "You said she did."

"Not enough." He's bitter. Angry.

"But once I left, someone should've told me."

"I was going to," Garrett says, drawing my attention to him. His eyes lock with mine with a sort of unexpected fear. "I was going to tell you everything the night you came to visit us after graduation. I knew then that you weren't my sister. I knew you would be safe if you left, if you came with us, even, but...you were happy." His eyes flick to Will. "You were getting out. I didn't want to..." He pauses. "I remember how dark it got for Will during that time, after he found out. When you told me you were happy, I was terrified to ruin that."

"You were going to tell me?" That truth, that memory, that night—they sit squarely in my chest like a ball of light. What would I have done with that news then? How would I have handled it? How will I handle it now?

"I didn't want to hurt you any more than I already had," he says.

"Fine, you thought you couldn't tell me. But why didn't you go to the sheriff once you knew?" That's the part that doesn't make sense for me. "And why come back here?"

Will speaks up. "We came back to protect Mom. But the killings had stopped. We thought he got spooked, but we couldn't leave her here alone. As for the sheriff, we had no proof, just our word and the things we'd pieced together. It all fits. Besides, even with proof, we were afraid if he found out, he'd turn the town against us. He'd frame us for the murders, somehow. And, more than that, we were afraid for you. We were afraid that if he'd killed six times already, he might kill again. What if some of the kids who died were his, you know? What if he was taking them out, getting rid of evidence? You just needed to make it one more year and get out."

"Except he couldn't have killed all six of them. He wasn't at the party when Cassidy died. Someone would've seen him."

Will runs his tongue over his teeth. "That's the piece we can't figure out. Maybe he was working with someone else, or maybe he found a way to do it himself. I wish I knew. All I was worried about after that was keeping you safe. Keeping myself away from you so I didn't accidentally slip up. If you knew the truth, there was a chance he'd kill you too, and I couldn't risk it. I begged Mom to take you and leave, but she wouldn't. I was doing all I could do to keep you safe."

"But why? Why wouldn't she leave?"

"Because she was protecting the other kids. Mom said the only thing standing in a bad man's way is a good one. She said the darkness goes where light refuses to be. Had she left, he would've won. Evil would've won. Darkness. If she ran away to protect herself—and you—it left everyone else at risk, and she couldn't live with that on her conscience. After I told her what was going on, Mom made sure Pastor Charles never had a private meeting with boys at the church. If she couldn't stop it, she came in often to interrupt or made excuses to be in the room. She started to warn the other moms, too. They were all talking. A whole whisper network. She was waiting for proof to have him arrested, but it never came."

The weight of everything I'm learning is exhausting. My life has been a lie. My mom lied to me. My brother lied to me. Garrett lied to me. Pastor Charles lied to me. Every pillar in my life feels a little less steady. And then there's Britney. "So what does any of this have to do with Britney?"

Will chews his lip. "That's the other question I don't have a straight answer to. If Mom said Britney knew, I'm assuming she means she found out about Pastor Charles before she was killed, which would help prove our theory that he was killing people, but we need to be sure." He nods, standing up. "I know this is a lot to process, but we need to go see Mom."

"I'm not going anywhere," I say firmly, shaking my head.

Both men eye me. "What are you talking about?" Will demands. "This is important."

"You have just told me my entire life is a literal lie. Everything. Everyone." I can't bear to look at either of them. It all just burns from the inside out, like I'm imploding right in front of them. They lied to me. They kept me in the dark. In danger. And everyone around me knew about it. I think about the way Pastor Charles comforted me at Britney's funeral, how Garrett stood right there and watched it happen, how he said nothing. Did nothing. He could've warned me. He could've done *something*.

"I need to see Mom," Will says, his voice low, firm, and still questioning. "Come with me. Please." He reaches for my arm, but I jerk away.

"No. I need a minute, okay? I just need..." I touch my chest, sucking in a ragged breath.

"We'll wait," Garrett says firmly. "We can wait."

"I need to go. I need to talk to—"

Will starts to argue, but Garrett cuts him off. "Then you go. I'll stay with her."

"No," I cry. "No." I look up at him finally, glowering. "You go too. Both of you. Go and give me space."

"You shouldn't be alone right now," he says, reaching for me.

Again, I jerk away, stepping back. "I don't want to talk to you right now. Either of you. I understand you had your reasons, and I even almost understand them, but you have to understand what it feels like in my head right now."

"I do," Will says. "Because I was there."

"And you were mad at Mom for putting you there, right? For lying to you?" I pin him with a glare, driving the point home.

Understanding washes over his face, and finally, he nods. "I never wanted you to find out."

"And somehow, that stings worse." I run a hand over

311

my mouth. "Please just go. Both of you. Go and visit Mom and find out what you can, and then, when you come back, we can talk with clear heads. Right now, I don't want to… I can't do this."

The men exchange glances, a full conversation passing between them without uttering a word, then they nod.

"Are you sure?" Garrett asks.

I nod without looking at him, my arms crossed.

"We won't be gone long, okay?" Will says, taking a hesitant step backward. "Promise me you'll be here when we get back."

I lick my dry lips. "I'm not going anywhere today." I let the last word linger in the air, a warning and promise that after today, there are no guarantees.

When they're gone, I sink onto the couch, elbows resting on my knees as I process everything I've just learned. The necklace. Mom. Will. Pastor Charles. My dad. Everything.

Everything.

Everything.

Everything.

It was all a lie. I was kept here in the shadows, lied to and manipulated and sheltered to protect me from a man I trusted. A man who was the most fatherlike figure in my life. *But he is my father.*

He's my…

I stand and grab the bowl where our keys go from

the coffee table, throwing it across the room with a feral scream. How could they do this to me?

Who else knows? Who are the other children? My... siblings?

Could Britney have been my sister?

So many questions race through my mind. This news chopped my world into pieces with a cleaver, fracturing parts of myself, my beliefs about life and goodness and community.

Everything is ruined. Everything is over.

Even if they had a good reason, how do we ever come back from this? How could I ever trust them again?

A knock on the door interrupts my thoughts, and I look up to see they've only been gone twenty minutes. It's not nearly long enough.

I cross the room quickly, whipping open the door. "What do you—"

Except it's not Will. And it's not Garrett.

Pastor Charles stands in front of me, his blond hair pressed down around the sides as if he's been wearing a ball cap. "Tessa." My name leaves his mouth with a heavy breath. "I was looking for Will."

CHAPTER FORTY-TWO

GARRETT — PRESENT DAY

The ride to the nursing home is made mostly in silence. I still don't know what's going on in Tessa's head. I know when Will first told me, when he was going through his own battle with it, I needed a while to process. It not only meant that so much about my life was a lie, and that my family might also be a lie, but that there was a good chance Tessa and I could never be together again.

Will needed me more than Tessa, as much as I hated it. He was in a darker place than we'd realized, and he was processing it alone. As much as Frannie tried to help, he pushed her away. I was the only one who could break through the wall he'd put up. I had to focus on him, on getting him better and getting him out of there. And I did it.

I hate every day I was away from Tessa, but I will never regret saving my best friend.

Still, in this moment, I'm furious with him.

"We should've told her back then," I say as we pull into the parking lot of Oak Meadows.

"We don't know that it would've been better." Will doesn't look at me as he unbuckles.

I turn to face him. "She would've had a chance to talk to your mom about it then. To learn more of the truth than we can ever give her. We aren't the right people to help her deal with this, man. She needs Frannie, and she's…" I wave a hand in the direction of the facility, out of breath and out of words. With a shake of my head, I push open my door. "Let's just go."

He's not going to agree with me. He'll always think he was protecting her, but he may have just cost me everything. I finally had my chance with her again, and now we may have just fucked it all up.

I should've told her.

I chose Will over Tessa once, but that night, I should've been braver. I should've chosen her, fought for her—damn what Will said.

When we reach Frannie's room and push the door open, I stop short at the sight of someone sitting in a chair next to her bed. Her blonde head turns to face us, and it takes several seconds for me to process who it is.

Mostly because my family doesn't attend Pastor Charles's church.

"Mrs. Mabel?" Will asks. I slip a hand into my pocket, trying to think. Why would she be here? What are the odds?

Pastor Charles's wife, Mabel, turns to face us completely, her expression serious. "Will, hello." She stands.

There aren't supposed to be visitors in this room. Tessa was right not to trust this place.

"What are you doing here?" Will asks, moving in front of me.

Mabel's hands go up. "I come in peace, I promise." Her voice is soft, and my bet is she's lying, just like her husband. She casts a look back at Frannie. "I visit your mother often."

"Why?" That's Will again, asking the question we both need answered.

"Francis is someone I consider a very dear friend." She looks sad, not secretive. "Please know I pray for her every day."

"Forgive us if that brings little comfort," Will mutters.

Mabel eyes him with a kindness I don't expect. "Your mother was kind to me when she didn't have to be. When she probably shouldn't have been."

"What are you talking about?" Will asks.

"I shouldn't say more. It's her story to tell, and I truly hope someday she'll be able to." She picks up her bag from the back of the chair. "I'm sorry if I intruded. I'll just go." Her heels click across the floor, but before she reaches us, Will cuts her off.

"Does it have anything to do with what your husband did? Who he is to us?"

Mabel goes still. "What do you mean?"

"I think you know exactly what I mean," he says.

Mabel looks at Will, then at me. "You know?"

"Guys—" I try to stop him from saying anything—we don't know that we can trust her—but Will's already speaking.

"We know what he is and what he's done. We know that he hurt Britney. And so many others."

Mabel looks down, and I know she's going to deny it. Or worse, attack us. Pull a gun from that bag and kill us all. But when her head lifts back up, there are tears in her blue eyes. "Your mom is the one who told me. About the affairs. The kids. Being a good, little preacher's wife, it meant I couldn't work. My job was to stand by my husband's side. To look pretty. To smile. To be scrutinized without complaint." She sniffles, wiping under her nose. "Little did I know, my husband was taking advantage of so many in the congregation, convincing them he loved them, that God had told him he was meant to be with them." Her voice goes dry and painful as she says that last part. Her cool eyes flick to Will. "He liked to do that. To convince you that whatever bad thing he was doing was God's will. I know you know something about that."

Will doesn't confirm it, but he doesn't deny it either.

"For years, I prayed for understanding. To understand why I was meant to endure such pain. Why I had to stand there and smile and shake the hands of every woman who'd—" She cuts herself off. "To look at the faces of every child who carried my husband's chin or his dimples or his eyes. Eventually, I confronted him. I wanted us to pray about it. To seek counseling, but do you know what he told me? He told me God had told him it was his job to fill this town with Godly children. Like Noah. He had to rebuild a town that was failing. To drive out the darkness and sin."

The Noah comment reminds me eerily of what he said to Will, about the ark and the flood. I'm not religious, but I've heard enough about it from everyone in this town to get the picture.

"I let it go *for years.*" She sniffles again, drying her silent tears as quickly as they fall. "And then when your mom told me what he'd done to you, Will, and what she suspected, I started looking for proof. Mostly, I wanted to prove her wrong. I'd done everything right. I'd been a good woman. A good wife. I didn't believe God would test me like that. Punish me like that. Everything changed when Mr. Allen confided in me that Amber had been pregnant before she was killed. The father of the baby…" She pauses, collecting herself. "The father was a boy whose mother I know had an affair with my husband, just like Jill had. He and Amber were likely both my husband's children. If that baby had been born, every one of Charles's secrets could've been exposed."

She drops her head forward. "If I'd had any proof, I have to believe I would've gone to the police, but I didn't. Instead, I started paying more attention, and I learned more than I ever wanted to. When Amber told her mom about the pregnancy, Jill confided in my husband. That was when the plan was set in motion, I think. He's smart, you know. Get the boy to steal the thing, convince everyone it was a robbery. He even gave them all these packets of photos of the victims. Added a new picture each time he planned the next one. He told me it was so he could easily frame any one of them, if he needed to. But what he didn't count on was friendship. You see, Amber had told Emily and Cassidy about her pregnancy before she died. They suspected the baby's father had done it, so they'd told their mothers. The baby's father, unfortunately, was Sheriff Ward's son. So they felt they couldn't tell him, and the next best person to tell was, they thought, their pastor."

She sniffles again. "They trusted him and he killed them, too. All to cover up his sins. And when his plan for Cassidy and her mother was interrupted because Cassidy had snuck out to a party, he followed her there and saw the plan through." She's eerily quiet for a long time. "My husband framed Cory Thomas because he worried the police were starting to put things together. He didn't know what rumors had made it where, and he knew he needed someone to frame in order for it to all be over. But there was no way to prove it. Even when I confronted him, and he eventually admitted it, he said—and I knew he was right—no one would ever believe me. It would be his word against mine, and we both knew who people would trust."

Will takes a step toward Frannie's bed, checking on her. "My mom told Tessa that Britney knew about Pastor Charles before she died." His eyes flit across Mabel's face, examining her. "Did he kill her, too?"

Mabel licks her lips, looking away. "Britney and I used to overlap with our visits on occasion. Never on purpose, but it was a happy coincidence when it happened. She once mentioned to Frannie that Charles should come up and say a prayer over her, but Frannie became agitated. Her heart rate accelerated, and the nurses had to sedate her. The next time I came back and Britney was here, she had a sheet of paper torn out, trying to get Frannie to spell a word."

"Murderer." I fill in the blank as it clicks in my mind before Mabel gets the chance. "Frannie was warning Britney about him."

Mabel rubs a hand over her arm. "Britney was having an affair with Charles. It seems he never really stopped what he was doing, he just found the next generation."

It's a gut punch, and I see that written all over Will's face.

"I told her everything, and she gave me that piece of truth. She was...she was pregnant. Justin had a vasectomy after Tilly was born, so it could only be..." She pauses, collecting herself. "It seems my husband was expecting yet another baby. She must've confronted

Charles. I only know that she didn't come back to visit, and I didn't see her again until the day we got the call that she'd died." She chokes back a sudden sob. "He didn't even have the decency to act shocked."

I cross the room toward Frannie, feeling suddenly protective of her. I will never agree with her staying in this town despite knowing so much. I will never be able to understand it, but this woman was a second mother to me. She is just one person, one tiny woman, who looks so fragile in this state it's as if she could shatter with a touch, and yet she didn't back down. She fought and she tried to stand up to a man she once loved and respected. A man she should've been able to trust.

Behind me, Mabel clears her throat again. When I turn around, she's still talking to Will. "He held onto the necklace because it was the most expensive piece, and the bracelet was enough to frame Cory by itself, but I guess he finally found someone worthy of his favorite toy. The final piece of his twisted puzzle." She shakes her head. "Whatever Britney said to him, it made him so angry that just killing her, just taking her away from her daughters for the rest of their lives, didn't seem like punishment enough."

"I'm going to turn myself in," Will says, his voice somber. "I'm going to talk to Sheriff Ward and tell him everything."

"No," Mabel says sharply.

"I've been quiet long enough because I thought it

was over. I thought he was done, but with Britney, too... Tessa is—do you know how badly my sister is hurting because of him? And I could've prevented it. I could've stopped him."

"You couldn't have." She's eerily calm. "He's smart, Will. Smart and powerful, and that is a dangerous combination. If you had tried to stop him, if you had told anyone what you did back then, what you knew, he would've killed you, make no mistake about it." Her eyes go distant, clearly thinking about something, and when they find focus again, she nods. "Which is why it has to be me. I came here to tell your mother goodbye. To tell her I'm finally going to end this, as I should've done years ago."

"What are you talking about?" Will asks before I get the chance to.

"I'm going to Sheriff Ward myself. I'm going to tell him everything. Everything I've learned throughout the years. The way he wielded his power, the way he's used people's trust and respect for his position to control and manipulate and harm the people of this town. I will tell him about the thefts—though I see no reason to bring any of you boys into it, as Charles was the real culprit—and the murders. The six back then and Britney now."

"He couldn't have killed Cassidy," I say, finding my voice. "I know what you said earlier, but someone would've seen him if he was at the party that night. He wasn't there."

Mabel looks down, wrapping her arms around herself. "My husband learned how to hide in plain sight years ago. He knew who would keep his secrets, who would turn a blind eye. If he'd asked anyone in town not to mention that they saw him, if he told them he was there to help counsel a child who needed someone to talk to, do you think they wouldn't? People saw him that night. Kids. Your friends, I'm sure. But Charles knows how to lie, how to trick, how to pull strings. Even if they saw him, they would never believe he was capable of what happened. Even if they saw him with the knife with their own eyes." She shivers, swiping her hands over her arms. "My husband has tried to play God with this town, and I allowed it until that night. When he came home with blood on his clothes, that's when I learned the truth about everything."

"Why didn't you tell?" Will demands.

"For all the reasons I've told you. I wouldn't have been believed. I had no proof, just my word against his. He promised me we'd go to counseling then. He tried to frame Cory, and I, at least, was able to pull strings and whisper in enough ears to make sure that didn't happen. All these years, I've lived with a man who I've believed is my direct line to God, but when I look in his eyes, all I see is darkness. How do you reckon with that? Watching him smiling in public, kissing babies, holding hands of families as they lay their loved ones to rest. Watching people turn to him in their darkest hours, all the while knowing what he's capable of and being helpless to stop it. I was trapped in a prison I chose while he got sneakier and craftier."

"So what's changed?" I ask, staring her down. I want to believe her, but for all we know, she's lying about everything. For all we know, they're working together.

"Britney," she says. "It has taken me days to accept that coming forward will shatter her family, that they will be one more casualty in my husband's path, but if we can prove the child she was carrying is Charles's, it might be enough to dim the light in people's eyes when they look at him. Once that shiny façade has dulled, I think I can convince the sheriff of my story. Either way, I have to try. I can't let him hurt anyone else. If there was any other way… Believe me, I have wrestled with my demons over this. I do not want to leave my husband. I made a vow to him, but he's caused enough harm to this community." She narrows her eyes at Will. "Will you forgive me for this?"

"I thought you weren't going to tell them I was involved."

Mabel takes a step toward him. "Not that. I only meant…he's your blood, you know. Those kinds of wounds run deep."

"He's not my family. Mom, Tessa, and Garrett are my family. Britney was our family. If I could've stopped him years ago, I would have."

Mabel pulls a tube of ChapStick from her purse and swipes it on her lips with shaking hands, staring straight ahead in thought. She clicks the lid back on and drops it in her bag before turning her attention back to Will. "I'm very sorry you were ever involved in this." Her eyes travel toward Frannie. "And your mother. You didn't deserve it."

Will's face is stony, but his voice softens as he says, "Sounds like you didn't either."

She squares her shoulders and nods, tears in her eyes. "It's going to be okay, boys. A wise woman once told me the only thing standing in a bad man's way is a good one."

Will glances at his mom, his voice cracking when he speaks. "The darkness goes where light refuses to be."

"So let's go be the light, shall we?" A single tear streams down Mabel's porcelain cheek.

Across the room, Will digs his hand into his pocket and pulls out his phone. He glances at the screen, then at me. "It's Mark."

My chest goes icy.

"Hello?" He presses the phone to his ear, staring out the window. "Wait, wait, wait, wait, wait. Slow down, man. What are you talking about?" His eyes find mine, and he swallows. "Tessa's at home. Fuck. How fast can you get there?"

I'm already moving past Mabel and out the door. I don't need to hear any more. I don't need to know anything else. I will run the entire way back to Will's house if that's what it takes.

When he catches up with me in the parking lot, we

fling ourselves into the car, and he whips out of the spot, gunning it.

"What's happening?" I demand, gripping the handle above my head for dear life.

"Charles went to see Mark, but he wouldn't let him in. He said he asked him about the coin collection, like he was trying to set him up. He thinks he was recording him."

My throat is tight, and I lean forward, like I can will us to go faster with just my mind. "He knows Mabel's going to turn him in."

Will grips the steering wheel so tightly his fingers are white. "Based on what we know, I think so. And he didn't get what he wanted with Mark. Another scapegoat."

"Which means he's going to find you next," I confirm what I've already pieced together. "Which means he's going to find Tessa."

CHAPTER FORTY-THREE

TESSA — PRESENT DAY

"Will isn't here right now." My hands tremble, and I grip the door to steady them, hoping he won't notice. Will's words ring in my ears, the warning about looking at Pastor Charles in a way that might clue him in to the fact that I know his secret. If he knows, he could kill me.

It's a terrifying realization, considering this is the man I spent most of my life convinced could read my mind in the pew from where he stood at the pulpit.

Pastor Charles steps forward, like he's preparing to come inside, but I stand my ground, so he's suddenly right in my face, nearly touching me. He pushes his small, wire-rimmed glasses back on top of his head. *I used to think he was so handsome, but he's my dad.* The dad that I've dreamed of knowing, grieved my entire life, was always right here. I can kind of see it now in Will's blond hair and the wrinkle in the space between his eyes. I can't help mentally cataloging all of my friends and classmates now, looking for the similarities.

This is so messed up.

I force the thoughts away.

"Would you mind if I waited for him? Mrs. Krueger said she saw him coming into town this morning. A day earlier than usual, in fact. You must be relieved to get some extra time with him." He makes no effort to step back, just keeps staring at me, his green eyes drilling into mine.

My phone is in my back pocket. If I could get to it without him seeing, I could call 911, but it's too big a risk. My heart pounds in my ears as I stare him down. "He went to visit Mom at Oak Meadows. You could probably find him there." I hate that I'm sending him anywhere near them, but if I can get him out of here, I will call Will and warn him.

Pastor Charles clears his throat and takes a half step back finally. "Is everything okay, Tessa?"

My heart is a spinning top that has fallen over. Every breath is shaky. "Of course." Then I add, "Um, I just, I'm not feeling well. I really shouldn't have company."

"Nonsense," he says. "The Lord only gives us what's meant for us, sickness included. You shouldn't be alone if you're ill. Will should know better." His hand goes to my forehead, his smooth palm brushing my skin, and I feel sick. *My father should've done this. If you were any father to me, you would've done this.* The heavy scent of his cologne fills my nostrils as he clicks his tongue and lowers his hand. "You don't feel warm. Have you been running a fever?"

"I took medicine earlier. Dr. Jacobs said it's a virus."

He looks over my head. "I should stay until Will is back."

"That's okay. I'd really rather—"

"Your mother wouldn't want you to be alone." He pushes the door open abruptly, moving past me, and his mention of my mother sends me into a spiral.

With his back to me, I pull out my phone, hand shaking.

"It's a tragedy what happened to Britney, you know," Pastor Charles says. When I look up, he's staring at me, and the look in his eyes chills me to my bones. "I know the two of you were very close."

I nod, my voice completely absent from my throat. I fight to find it. "It's been really hard on everyone."

"When anyone in our community suffers, we all do." His voice carries the same weight it does every Sunday morning. I should be able to trust him. I hate this universe we've slipped into. Where the good people are suddenly bad, and the ones you thought you could trust, you suddenly can't. Perhaps if I can buy time, talk to him about Britney, Will and Garrett will arrive home.

That's the only way out of this. I have to be smart.

"I, um, I was wondering if you know anything about Britney's death." His eyes widen, and I quickly add, "I mean, any more than what they've said in the paper. I'm struggling with the idea that she was in such a dark place, you know? I just thought...maybe she would have told you if she was struggling with something. Maybe the rest of us didn't see it."

He nods, pulling the glasses the rest of the way off of his head and tucking them into his shirt pocket. "She did confide in me that she and her husband were struggling with the news that she was expecting again."

That news shocks me to my core. "She was pregnant?" I wonder if Kristy knows this. Why wouldn't she have mentioned it?

"She was. And her husband wasn't happy."

I swallow, because I already know her husband isn't able to have kids anymore. She told me when he had his vasectomy right after their second daughter was born. I guess he might've had it reversed later, though that seems unlikely, especially if he was unhappy about the pregnancy. Britney always said she wanted two girls, and that was exactly what she got.

But if the baby's not Justin's, what does that mean? For all I know, he could be lying, but why?

If they do a paternity test on the baby, there's no doubt they'll find out the baby wasn't his. But I suspect Pastor Charles doesn't know that Justin had a vasectomy. I remember what Kristy said about the police suspecting Britney had been having an affair.

"I can't believe he was mad." I pretend to think out loud. "Why didn't she tell me about the baby?"

He folds his hands, massaging his thumbs over the skin of his knuckles. "We can't begin to judge our brothers and sisters on their journeys. The Bible says a good man's heart pumps God's word like blood through his veins, Miss Becker. We're all tempted in life. We all fail our Father. But what's in our veins matters—both the sin and God's word. I believe Britney Davis had the Lord in her heart. She won't be answering for any more sins than you or I will. All we can do is pray for 'em. Right now, what Britney's family needs more than anything is for us to pray for 'em real hard."

Even as he says the thoughtful, gentle words, there's something almost bitter in his tone. Something borderline vindictive. Am I imagining it?

I swallow, forcing away a theory growing in my mind. *It's ridiculous. Impossible.* Britney would never have cheated on Justin. Not with Pastor Charles, a man old enough to be our... *The man who is my father.* If it's true, if there's some sick dimension where it's true, Britney was carrying my half-sibling. I can't breathe.

"Yes. Of course." I start to move past him. "Lots of prayers. I, um, I'm going to make something to drink. Can I get you tea or coffee? I think there's some lemonade in there."

"You sit," Pastor Charles says, the command radiating through me. "Let me help. I should be the one getting you something, since you're under the weather and all." He smirks. "Name your poison."

His words creep across my skin like a spider. *Now's my chance to call for help.* "A glass of tea would be great. There are cups in the cabinet by the fridge."

He turns to walk away, but stops before he reaches the threshold. "How's your mother, by the way? I keep meaning to stop by and visit her, but I haven't had the chance to. I think Mabel probably visits enough for the two of us." He laughs under his breath.

Something about the question sends chills down my spine. I think about my mom then, about her going to work every day under the thumb of this man. About how badly he must've hurt her and how he wielded his power over everyone in this town, including her, all my life.

I also think about her accident and how the doctors have never been able to determine whether she had the stroke before she fell down the stairs or if the fall down the stairs caused the stroke. Something tickles in the back of my brain. "Oh, you hadn't heard? She's alert now. Talking and everything."

He visibly pales. "What?"

"Yeah. That's why Will came home early and why he's there now visiting. I just got back. She was able to say a few words last night and this morning. They'll still need to do physical therapy for her to walk again, but the doctors can't believe it. I guess prayer works after all."

He nods, patting the pocket where his glasses are

with trembling hands, as if he might've lost them. "The Lord works in mysterious ways."

A new idea occurs to me. A flicker of possibility in this upside down world we find ourselves in today. "Yeah, it's strange. The doctor said her memory is still a little fuzzy, but she remembers a man who visited her the day of her accident."

His eyes narrow. "A man?"

Suddenly, he's eerily still.

"Did you know of any man she'd been seeing? I know how close you two are. I just thought she might've told you."

"As a matter of fact…" He pauses, taking a moment to breathe. His hand goes to his stomach as he looks away. "Oh, your mother wouldn't like me to tell you this, and the Lord doesn't like a gossip, but she did confess to me that she'd been seeing someone new. You know how we get to talking while we work. Sometimes the truth just slips out."

"Oh?"

"I'm afraid he's a married man." He nods. Very solemn. Very serious. As if his mask has been ripped off all at once, I see the liar within. The darkness. I see everything he's been hiding, and I know how easily he could've manipulated Mom, Will, and everyone else in this town.

I fidget in place. "Are you sure? That doesn't sound like her."

"Now, I don't want you to think badly of her. We all

make our choices, and no sin is worse than another, but it's true. She was seeing Anthony Davis. Britney's father-in-law."

I gasp, drawing my brows down in a good little act. "What? *No.*"

"Yes, yes. I'm afraid so. In fact, we should probably go to the police, don't you think? In case he did something untoward to cause her accident. I don't want to believe it, but if she's saying there was a man with her that day, well, I've never known your mother to be a liar. Of course, she could be confused. But if not, if Anthony wanted to keep his secret, well, I don't want to accuse him, but you never know what people will do." He leans his head to the side with a sympathetic look. "You're sick, though. You shouldn't have to deal with this. Your mom has been very loyal to me." His hand goes to his chest. "I consider her family. Let me visit with her, then I'll talk to Anthony. And then, once we have all the information, we can go to the police together if we decide it's necessary." The sincerity on his face makes me nauseous. I can see right through it, but I can so easily see how I once might not have.

"Are you sure?"

"Very sure." He nods again, hurrying past me and across the room toward the door. With his back to me, I glance down at my phone still in my hand, preparing to call the police and then Will as soon as I get the chance. When I look up, he's standing in place, watching me. "I think I should take that, Tessa."

My heart drops, and I swear it's a feeling as painful as if it hit every rib on the way down. "My phone?"

"The Lord doesn't like a gossip. The Bible says if your hand causes you to sin, you should cut it off and throw it away. Let me remove the temptation for you. At least until we have all the facts. I know how tempting it will be to tell someone what I've confided in you."

"I don't think I can give you my phone, Pastor Charles. Will might need me. Or Kristy. I won't call anyone, though. You have my word. I would never want Mom's reputation to be ruined by rumors."

He nods slowly, his jaw moving side to side as he releases a slow breath through his nose. "How about a compromise?" His lips twist into what should be a smile but looks more like a grimace. "Why don't you lock it away in the china cabinet?" He points to Mom's old china cabinet sitting against the wall in the hallway. It's mostly empty now, but I can remember when it was full of her collectible dolls.

"Why would I do that?" I press. *Come on, Will. Where are you?* It could still be hours before they come home. I'm on my own here. Completely and utterly alone.

"We could lock it up, and I'll take the key, and then when I see Will at Oak Meadows, I'll explain everything and give it to him. By this afternoon, you'll be free to have your phone again no problem."

"I don't think I'm okay with that," I say. I can't bring myself to look him in the eye, and I hate myself for it.

"Tessa, I'm afraid I'm going to have to insist." He holds a hand out, gesturing toward the hallway. "It's for your own good."

His voice, the chilly tone it has taken on, sends a shard of ice through my core. I nod and turn around. I don't have a choice. He's going to make me do it. Once he leaves, I'll use a voice command to call Will. I'll shout through the glass. It'll be okay.

Slowly, I make my way across the room toward the hall with Pastor Charles just behind me. I can practically feel him breathing on my neck. We reach the china cabinet, and I look up, lifting my hand to open the door.

In the reflection in the glass, I catch a glimpse of Pastor Charles behind me, his face hard, and the words spill out of me before I can stop them. "Did you hurt my mom?"

His face doesn't change. "I'm sorry." I see it coming seconds too late. The green wooden lamp that's usually on the end table beside the couch is in his hand, and he lifts it up.

He swings, and strikes my skull with all his might.

Crack. With the impact, my head is thrown forward.

My forehead slams into the metal, ornate knob on the china cabinet.

I pull back, dizzy, and pain explodes in the back of my head as the lamp connects with my skull again.

I tumble forward, my head a raging kaleidoscope of reds and blues and yellows and stars. Black splotches fill my vision, making it impossible to see what he's doing. I try to sit up, but my head is filled with sandbags.

I drop back down just as another blow slams into me. The scream that leaves my mouth is animal-like. It doesn't sound human. It doesn't sound like me.

Me.

Me.

Me.

The word is funny. Sort of squishy and round.

Around and around and around we go.

The world spins round, and I'm right there with it. My head is warm, throbbing, and nothing makes sense.

Sense.

Sentence.

Sequentence. Is that a word?

Tessa.

It's my name, I think, but I can't be sure where it came from.

I can't even be sure it's my name.

In the distance, a door slams, and there are footsteps.

Feet.

Feet.

Impossible feet.

Everything hurts, and the words slip away from me like the name of a song I can't place. The sounds fade. It's scary, in a safe way. Like it should be scary, but it's not. It's a cloud. A pillow. And I'm sinking into it.

Someone touches me, and I'm on my back, but I can't focus on that. I can't focus on anything. My head is a boulder, sinking down, down, down.

My hearing goes first so I'm floating in nothingness, then my vision fades completely to black, and I'm gone.

CHAPTER FORTY-FOUR

GARRETT — PRESENT DAY

I'm not ready to say goodbye.

"She's going to wake up," Will says. He's sitting next to Tessa's bed, looking at her, but he's talking to me. It's about the eighty-fifth time he's said it today. It's as if he thinks he can speak it into existence.

Science doesn't work that way. We've lost enough people by now to know that. If it did, Frannie would be back to normal. She'd be getting her happy ending, too.

We shouldn't have left her. We should've told her the truth before. If Tessa dies right now, it's our fault. It's my fault. I will never forgive myself.

I called Sheriff Ward on the way to the house, and Mark headed over too, but we were the ones who made it first. Will damn near killed us on the way, but all that mattered was making it to her in time. I don't take chances when it comes to her safety, everything else be damned. Call me obsessed. I don't care.

Mark was there next, with Sheriff Ward just behind us.

"She's going to be so mad about the bandage." His hand goes to the thick, white gauze around her head. "She always said white wasn't her color." He starts to laugh, but he chokes on his laughter, and it quickly turns into a sob. His hand goes over his mouth as he clasps his sister's hand. "She has to wake up."

Other than that, he doesn't say much, just stares at her, but he hasn't left her bedside since we got here nearly three days ago. Neither of us have.

His cheeks are sallow, the whites of his eyes bloodshot. I imagine I look the same. We need sleep and food and something to drink besides hospital coffee, but we're both too stubborn to leave the room to go get it.

She should be awake by now. That's what the doctors keep telling us. She's unconscious from the blows to the head when he attacked her. She was out before I got to her. I'll never forget the way she looked, lying there, face down. I thought she was dead. I was pretty sure I died, too. I collapsed next to her, a ringing sound in my ears as I turned her over and screamed—begged her to wake up to come back. Mark and Will managed to disarm Charles and hold him down while we waited for the sheriff, but it was by sheer dumb luck. He was disoriented, distracted, and it was two against one.

She has a skull fracture, and had minor brain bleeding, but the doctors fixed her. They told us they fixed her. She's coming back to us.

I'm not ready to say goodbye. She has to come back.

I pace at the end of her bed, watching her eyes for signs of movement.

Will holds her hand and strokes the top of it with his other. "How soon are we going to tell her everything else?" He's trying not to cry as he asks. "About Britney. And Mabel going to the police."

I dry my eyes. "The second she wakes up," I tell him. "No more secrets."

"She's going to take all the credit," he tries to joke through his tears again.

I can't think enough to joke, but I know it's what he needs right now. *He might be all I have left of this family. My family.* "She'll never let us live it down. It'll be the Smash Bros winning streak of 2004 all over again."

Pastor Charles's downfall can't be credited to just one person, though. Not Tessa, though I'll let her claim credit as long as she wants. Not us. Not even Mabel. Over the course of the past three days, we learned that Britney called the police about Pastor Charles the day before she died to let them know about Ms. Frannie's warning. She also confessed to her sister, Kristy, about the affair with the pastor, so a petition for a paternity test had already been ordered with her autopsy.

Sheriff Ward had been putting all of the pieces together, going back years to get it all lined up, so Mabel coming forward meant he was able to put all the final pieces of the puzzle in place.

The man we all trusted, the man supposed to help

this town, is sitting in the county jail right now, and most of the town couldn't be happier. He'll post bail, probably, and there will be people in this town who side with him or believe him, but I'm not going to worry about any of that unless I have to. It doesn't matter. *He* doesn't matter. The truth is out there—the real truth.

Cory's and Britney's names have officially been cleared of speculation. Mabel is picking up the pieces of her broken life. Things are safer here for the first time in years.

Now, we just need Tessa to wake up. To open those pretty eyes.

We tried. We tried to get there to save her, but it wasn't enough. I pulled him away from her with every ounce of strength I had. I protected her until the sheriff got there. And I'd do it again. I'd trade places with her if I could.

I'm not a hero. I'm a coward too scared to lose the woman he loves.

Nothing is good without her. Tears sting my eyes, and I walk away, pouring another cup of this terrible coffee and downing it quickly.

"She's going to wake up," he says, but I'm not so sure he's talking to me. "It's not going to be like Mom."

I sit down in the chair and close my eyes, hoping with everything in me that he's right.

When I wake, Will is still asleep in his chair, his head thrown back, snores echoing through the room. I stand up slowly, trying not to wake him, and sit on the bed next to Tessa.

Slipping my hand into hers, I keep my voice low and plead with her, "Hey, beautiful." I press a kiss to her fingertips and smooth her hair down. "Look, you have to wake up now, okay? I'm, um, I'm not ready to say goodbye. Do you hear me?" My voice cracks, and I drop my head. "You can hate me. You can be pissed at me. You can never forgive me. It's okay. It'll all be okay, but you have to wake up. You do, okay? You do because I love you. And I refuse to live without you. Do you hear me? I love you so much it hurts. And I hate that we ever spent one day apart, but if you'll just wake up, I'm going to make it up to you. I promise. We keep our promises, right? Come on, baby. Just open your eyes. I told you everything. We finally get our second chance, and you don't get to leave me. Not like this. He doesn't get to win, Tessa. Do you hear me? That man took you from me once. I refuse to let him take you again. I will spend the rest of my life groveling, begging for another chance, if you just open your eyes." I press her hand to my heart. "I need you, Little Bit. Open your eyes. I need you to come back and make me laugh and drive me mad and...and love me in a way that no one else can." I lean forward onto her chest, splintering in two as silent sobs tear through me. I can't lose her. I refuse to lose her.

And yet, I'm starting to feel her slipping away.

CHAPTER FORTY-FIVE

TESSA — PRESENT DAY

Something heavy sits on my chest, making it hard to take a breath. When I open my eyes, something bright shines in them. I wince, squeezing them shut. The world is so bright, and my head is full of concrete. I can't...focus. Can't...

I'm drifting again, floating.

In the distance, someone is talking. A TV maybe, but just one voice.

A man's voice.

His voice.

"Not like this. He doesn't get to win, Tessa. Do you hear me? That man took you from me once. I refuse to let him take you again. I love you too much for this to be it. You have to wake up."

Garrett. My heart swells at the thought of him, warms as if touched by sunshine. Eyes still closed, I reach for him. His head is lying on me, and I run my fingers through his hair. He tenses under my touch, and after a few moments, I hear him whisper, "She doesn't get to go like this. I can't lose her, man. I'm not letting her go. This can't be it for her."

He thinks I'm Will. I open my mouth, clawing to find my voice, though the muscles don't seem to want to work. My throat is dry and scratchy, like it's filled with sand. I can't seem to swallow. I clear my throat, forcing air out in the form of words. "It's…not."

His body goes still against me—completely frozen— then, slowly, the weight is lifted from my stomach. I force my eyes open again, needing to see his face.

"Tessa?" His voice is hesitant, like he doesn't believe it.

How long have I been out?

The light burns my eyes, but I can't close them because there he is. "Oh my god." The words come out of his mouth on a choked sob. He clutches my face, pressing a kiss to my head, my cheeks, my nose, my lips. "Oh my god. Oh my god. Oh my god. You're awake. Can you hear me? Are you okay? Oh my god. Will!"

Sleep fights for me, clawing me back to its depths, but then my brother is in my face, and they're both laughing and hugging and squeezing my hands.

"She's okay. She's okay," Garrett repeats over and over, like he needs to hear it to believe it himself.

"We should get the doctor," Will says, though neither of them move.

"Are you okay?" Garrett croaks. "Are you hurting?"

"Do you remember what happened?" Will sits down on the edge of my bed, and Garrett takes the spot on the opposite side.

The memories come in flashes. Mom. Garrett. Will. Pastor Charles. It's all there. The truth and the lies, the heartbreak and the secrets. Britney is gone. Mom still isn't better. Garrett loves me.

My eyes flick to him, a bit more of what he said moments ago coming back to me. "You love me." It's not a question. I don't have to wonder anymore. It's just a fact. A safe space to land. Mad and sad and hurt as I am, he is my soft place to land. My light in the darkness.

He kisses my hand. "I'll spend the rest of my life proving it to you."

Will pretends to roll his eyes, then looks at me again. "Did you happen to forget all the stuff about being mad at me?"

I fight to suppress my smile. Of course I haven't forgotten, but none of it matters anymore. I don't need to know how it's going to work out to know that it will. I have the two men I need in my life—my two best friends—and the rest will come with time.

The guys spend the next few minutes taking turns filling me in on everything I missed: That Pastor Charles is being held in jail for attacking me. That Mom and Mabel have been conspiring against him together for years. That Britney was sleeping with

Pastor Charles. That he killed her to protect that secret, as well as his others. That Sheriff Ward believes us. That Mabel has told Sheriff Ward she's willing to testify and say Charles acted alone, leaving the boys out of the investigation into the stolen goods. That they've just been waiting for me to wake up, to come home to them.

"I think that's everything," Garrett says, tracing a line down my finger. "It's a lot to take in."

It is, but it's what I needed to hear. "The victims in this are getting their justice. We did that."

He places a hand on my stomach, and Fourth of July sparklers ignite under my skin. "I'm so sorry we left you alone."

Alone. I remember that feeling with Pastor Charles at the house. How I was so completely alone. I never want to feel that way again. "But you saved me."

"Hey, I get some credit for that, too," Will cuts in with a smirk.

"Thank you, both." I dust away a tear.

Will looks between us with a soft smile, then stands and runs his hands over his knees, sighing. "Alright, well, I'm going to let the doctor know she's awake. Then I'm going home to shower. I'll bring you a change of clothes from home, assuming you aren't leaving her side."

Garrett nods. "Thanks."

"You'll be okay?" He's looking at me as he asks.

"I think I'll manage. Will you do me a favor, though?"

"Anything."

"Call Mom and tell her what happened. Let her know he's going to go down for everything and that I'll visit as soon as I can. She can hear us. It's important she hears that."

"I'd been planning to go tell her," he says, "but I didn't want to leave you."

"She needs to know now. She doesn't deserve to wait another day living with the fear of him. She needs to know the light won this time." Tears prick my eyes.

"I'll tell her." Will kisses the top of my head, then points at Garrett with a warning glance. "Take care of her."

"You know I will."

"I know."

Something unspoken passes between them, a moment of eye contact that I don't understand, before Will leaves the room. When he does, Garrett rests his chin on his fists. "God, I really thought I was going to lose you."

"I still had plenty of yelling at you left to do. What can I say?"

He laughs under his breath.

"Can I tell you a secret?"

"Anything."

"Even when I was mad at you, I still knew it would be okay with us. I can't explain it other than to say it felt...safe. I think I've always known we'd end up together." I meet his eyes. "Does that make sense?"

He puffs out a ragged breath, running a hand over his mouth. "Does it make sense?" He shakes his head. "I've just been waiting for you to figure it out." I dry his tears with my thumb, and he pulls my hand to his mouth, kissing my palm. "I'm sorry I didn't tell you sooner about everything with Will and Charles. I should have."

"Yes," I agree. "But I understand why you didn't."

"You do?" He swallows.

"You were protecting me. Like you always have been. I know you."

His eyes line with fat tears. "We know each other pretty well, don't we, Little Bit?"

"Better than anyone else." A new question forms in my mind. "I have to ask you something."

"Okay, but I request at least a month off before I'll agree to solving any more mysteries." He strokes my hand, sending chills up my arm at the sensation. I never want him to let me go.

"Deal." My smile fades away. I run my fingers through his, caressing his hand. "So, if I'm remembering correctly, for a while you thought we might be siblings, and that's why you broke up with me?"

He scratches his neck, then nods. "But we aren't."

"Did you already know that we weren't the night of your graduation party? The night out on the deck?"

Scarlet stains his cheeks, and he looks down. "No, I

didn't." The words hit me square in the chest. "And that's pretty sick. Trust me, I know. I tried to stay away from you. I did. But I just…at that moment, I didn't care. I couldn't care. When it comes to you, everything else falls away. I did what I did that night with full knowledge of how wrong it might be, but I wanted you more than I wanted to be right. I don't know if that's a good answer, or if you're going to need some time with it, or if you're totally repulsed by me now, or whatever. Or maybe you hate me because I took that choice away from you. I should've asked permission, I should've told you everything, but I couldn't. I couldn't, and I couldn't stop myself. I didn't want to. That's the truth. I promised you I would tell you the truth about everything if you just woke up again, so there it is. I would never have stopped wanting you, no matter what that test said. You are it for me, Tessa Becker. You're inside me. A part of me." He touches his chest. "As much a part of me as the blood in my veins and the air in my lungs. I don't know that I could exist without you. I'm just really hoping I never have to find out."

I release a breath, letting the truth sink in. I don't need to think for long to know it doesn't change anything for me. I can't say I would've done anything differently if I'd been in his shoes. Knowing what Garrett was going through that night puts so much into perspective. I'll never forget the strained look in his eyes—his mind clearly warring with itself—as he tried to maintain restraint, then the look of relief when he finally gave in. For better or worse, this man is mine. And I am his. No one has ever held me so completely as he does. "You didn't take my choice away from me." I stroke his face again. "There was never any choice."

He squeezes his eyes shut with such palpable relief it kills me.

"I love you too, you know," I whisper.

"No," he says, the word carrying so much weight as his eyes go glassy. "I didn't." He leans forward and presses his lips to mine. His kiss isn't everything I'm used to from him—it's gentle and sweet and still utterly perfect. I'm realizing the lackluster kisses in my past were not about technique. They simply weren't enough because they weren't him. He's a hard act to follow. "I love you."

"Can you do me a favor?"

"Anything." The response comes in an instant.

"Can you text Will and ask him to give Mom another message for me?"

He pulls his phone out. "Sure. What is it?"

"Could you ask him to tell her I'm staying?"

He starts to type the message but freezes when he realizes what I've said. "You're staying?"

"Turns out we were no good at the whole long-distance thing."

"Are you sure? I'll move to you," he blurts, his words rushed. "I know your mom and Will would love to have you here, but please don't do this because of me. I will go wherever you go. Wherever your life is, I will be there. Whatever makes you happy."

I lift his hand to my mouth and press a kiss to his palm. "*You* make me happy. You are my home and my safe place and my very best friend. You're all I need, and I love you. This—you and me—wherever we are will always be *more than enough*."

I say those three words slowly, dragging them out to remind him of that night. Everything he told me I deserved is exactly what he's given me. Despite all the heartache and the confusion, the years we spent apart and the things we still need to figure it out, we know what matters now.

Truth.

Love.

Happiness.

He kisses me again, this time with a bit more of the fire that I'm used to. He's coming back to me. We always manage to find our way back. He bites my lip gently, and the butterflies in my stomach scatter.

"I hope you know you're mine, Tessa Becker," he whispers, and I know what he'll say next. I close my eyes, thinking back on the moment that started it all as I hear the words I hope to hear every day for the rest of my life. "Because I sure as hell have *always* been yours."

I guess Pastor Charles made at least one good point. What's in our veins does matter, and at this moment, I know without a doubt Garrett Campbell will forever be in mine.

WOULD YOU RECOMMEND WHERE THE DARKNESS GOES?

If you enjoyed this story, please consider leaving me a quick review. It doesn't have to be long—just a few words will do. Who knows? Your review might be the thing that encourages a future reader to take a chance on my work!

To leave a review, please visit your favorite retailer from the link on my website: kierstenmodglinauthor.com/wherethedarknessgoes

Let everyone know how much you loved *Where the Darkness Goes* on Goodreads: https://bit.ly/wherethedarknessgoes

STAY UP TO DATE ON EVERYTHING KMOD!

Thank you so much for reading this story. I'd love to invite you to sign up for my mailing list and text alerts so we can be sure you don't miss my next release.

Sign up for my mailing list here:
kierstenmodglinauthor.com/nlsignup

Sign up for my text alerts here:
kierstenmodglinauthor.com/textalerts

ACKNOWLEDGMENTS

In the acknowledgments of my last book, THE HIDDEN, I wrote: "Sometimes, in the darkest times, we have to be our own source of light." When I wrote that line, I had no idea it would hold so much meaning for this book. At the time, I was still in the early editing stages of what would become WHERE THE DARKNESS GOES (at the time it was called VEIN), and I knew this was a story about life and love, about coming home, about finding your family, about building a family even if it isn't the one you're born with (as was the case with Garrett and the Beckers), and also being willing to stand up in the face of darkness, even when that face is one you know and trust. So I guess in a way, when I wrote those acknowledgments, my heart already knew what my head hadn't figured out.

This book, like so many of my stories, is about the dark and the light. It's about how the world is filled with both, but we get to make the choice every day as to which side we want to stand on.

This story is a deeply personal one for me. One about growing up and figuring out who you are. One about spending your childhood and early years in a small town you love, but leaving it to build a bigger life somewhere new. One about friendship and love. Finding your way home. One about power, and the ones who wield it. One about what it means to be a woman in this world. And one about what it means to be brave.

I love this story. I love these characters. Tessa challenged me. She made me laugh, made me cry, frustrated me, and inspired me. She was imperfect and real and raw with all her teenage angst and adult insecurities. The friendships, love, and community in this story were so special to me and it was such a healing, important journey to go on. I think, at the end of the day, this is one of the books I'm most proud of and it will go down in my mind as one of the most important adventures I've had the complete honor of creating.

This is a story about darkness and light, those who bring the light to our darkness, and the ones willing to sit with us in the shadows until we see the light again.

For me, this part of the book is always about those people. They are the reason I do this, the reason I keep going, the reason I can smile through the hard days when the negative voices get too loud, and the ones who celebrate me on the lightest days of all.

To my husband and daughter—thank you so much for being part of this wild, unpredictable, and beautiful journey. For making the silly promo videos without complaint, for keeping tabs on all the milestones, and for being the first to brag about me every chance you get. I hit the jackpot with you two, and I love you so much more than I could ever put into words.

To my editor, Sarah West—thank you so much for believing in my stories from the messy, chaotic first drafts, until the end. I'm so grateful to have your questions, insight, and advice helping to navigate and shape each story.

To the proofreading team at My Brother's Editor—thank you for being my final set of eyes on each story and helping them to shine!

To my loyal readers (AKA the #KMod Squad)—an entire novel of thanks could never be enough. You guys have given me everything I ever dreamed of and more. The stuff that I thought was impossible? Or that I thought would take me a lifetime to achieve? You guys came in with a red pen, crossed out all my fears and worry, and changed my entire life. Thank you for everything you've done and continue to do for me. For every email, every social media post, every recommendation to your friends and family, every review. Thank you for showing up to my signings, for cheering me on, and for making the KMod Squad a community where everyone is welcome and celebrated. I dreamed of you, I wished for you, and I'm forever grateful and pinching myself that you're here and you're real. Thank you for making little Kiersten's wildest dreams come true. She would absolutely die to see what we've built together.

To my book club/gang/besties—Sara, both Erins, Heather, Dee, and June—thank you for being so much to me. My friends, my biggest cheerleaders, my confidants, the ones I vent to, the ones I cry to, the ones I ask for advice, the ones I laugh with, the ones with all the inside jokes and GIFs. Thank you for Tarantino and murder mystery parties and game shows and bathing and CHEERIO and midnight margaritas and epitome and June's murder sprees and our late night talks and the little boy and his spiders. Thank you for being such a big part of my life over these past few years. I love you ladies more than pizza.

To my bestie, Emerald O'Brien—thank you for all you do for me. This journey has been long, filled with ups and downs and wild curveballs, but it's been better because you're by my side. I love you to pieces, friend. Same moon.

Last but certainly not least, to you, dear reader—thank you for taking a chance on this story and supporting my art. As I write each book, I spend a lot of time thinking about the moment it will leave my hands and no longer be just mine, the moment you will crack it open and it will become ours. I think about which parts will shock you, which ones will make you laugh or make you angry, I wonder if my twists will keep you guessing, and which characters you might love, hate, or relate to. Thank you for seeing this book and taking a chance on it, however that happened. Thanks for seeing it online or in your local bookstore or library, thanks for listening to that social media recommendation, or finally giving in when your friend said you had to check it out. Or, if you've been with me for a while, thank you for coming back like you always do. It will forever mean the world. However you ended up here, thank you for coming on this journey with me. I like to think we were meant to find each other here in these pages. Whether this is your first Kiersten Modglin book or your 48th, I hope it was everything you hoped for and nothing like you expected.

ABOUT THE AUTHOR

KIERSTEN MODGLIN is a #1 bestselling author of psychological thrillers. Her books have sold over 1.5 million copies and been translated into multiple languages. Kiersten is a member of International Thriller Writers, Novelists, Inc., and the Alliance of Independent Authors. She is a KDP Select All-Star and a recipient of *ThrillerFix*'s Best Psychological Thriller Award, *Suspense Magazine*'s Best Book of 2021 Award, a 2022 Silver Falchion for Best Suspense, and a 2022 Silver Falchion for Best Overall Book of 2021. Kiersten grew up in rural western Kentucky and later relocated to Nashville, Tennessee, where she now lives with her family. Kiersten's readers across the world lovingly refer to her as "KMod." A binge-watching expert, psychology fanatic, and *indoor* enthusiast, Kiersten enjoys rainy days spent with her favorite people and evenings with her nose in a book.

Sign up for Kiersten's newsletter here:
kierstenmodglinauthor.com/nlsignup

Sign up for text alerts from Kiersten here:
kierstenmodglinauthor.com/textalerts

kierstenmodglinauthor.com
www.facebook.com/kierstenmodglinauthor
www.facebook.com/groups/kmodsquad
www.threads.net/kierstenmodglinauthor
www.instagram.com/kierstenmodglinauthor
www.tiktok.com/@kierstenmodglinauthor
www.goodreads.com/kierstenmodglinauthor
www.bookbub.com/authors/kiersten-modglin

ALSO BY KIERSTEN MODGLIN

<u>STANDALONE NOVELS</u>

Becoming Mrs. Abbott

The List

The Missing Piece

Playing Jenna

The Beginning After

The Better Choice

The Good Neighbors

The Lucky Ones

I Said Yes

The Mother-in-Law

The Dream Job

The Nanny's Secret

The Liar's Wife

My Husband's Secret

The Perfect Getaway

The Roommate

The Missing

Just Married

Our Little Secret

ARRANGEMENT TRILOGY

THE MESSES SERIES

The Cleaner (Book 1)

The Healer (Book 2)

The Liar (Book 3)

The Prisoner (Book 4)

NOVELLAS

The Long Route: A Lover's Landing Novella

The Stranger in the Woods: A Crimson Falls Novella

Made in the USA
Middletown, DE
11 January 2025

69249780R00223